The Man Who Knew Hammett

Also by Vincent McConnor
published by Tor Books

I Am Vidocq

The Man Who Knew Hammett

Vincent McConnor

TOR

A TOM DOHERTY ASSOCIATES BOOK
NEW YORK

This is a work of fiction. All the characters and events portrayed in this book are fictitious, and any resemblance to real people or events is purely coincidental.

THE MAN WHO KNEW HAMMETT

Copyright © 1988 by Vincent McConnor
All rights reserved, including the right to reproduce this book or portions thereof in any form.

A TOR BOOK
Published by Tom Doherty Associates, Inc.
49 West 24 Street
New York, NY 10010

Library of Congress Cataloging-in-Publication Data

McConnor, Vincent.
    The man who knew Hammett / Vincent McConnor.—1st ed.
    p. cm.
"A TOR book."
ISBN 0-312-93109-3 : $17.95
I. Title.
PS3525.A1653M3 1988
813'.52—dc19
                                    88-20130
                                        CIP

First edition: December 1988
0 9 8 7 6 5 4 3 2 1

for
George H. Madison
with respect and affection

Book One

Allegro con brio

Chapter 1

The world's oldest eye was feeling his years, every goddamn eighty-one of them.

This had been his longest and toughest day in some time. The unexpected slide he'd taken, tittuping down that arroyo, had bruised and shaken him. Stupid to suppose he could do such a foolish thing any more. He might've broken a leg if a dead tree trunk hadn't stopped his fall. Broken bones, at his age, were mighty serious.

Zeke leaned back, hands steady on the wheel, as his Chevy followed the curves east on Sunset. Ever since the boulevard was resurfaced, just before the Olympics, driving through Beverly Hills had become a pleasure again.

His gut murmured softly, not really complaining, reminding him that he hadn't eaten since mid-afternoon when he stopped by Joseph's Cafe in Hollywood for a bowl of vegetable soup.

Better make a sandwich when he got home. Should be

something in the refrigerator, although he seemed to remember finishing the last of that fruit. Maybe fix a cheese sandwich, eat it out on the balcony with a bottle of Perrier before he stretched out in his antique brass bed and, hopefully, sank into instant oblivion.

The beeper sounded again but he didn't bother to reach for the phone.

When he reached his apartment he would call in—as he always did when a job ended—and tell Nettie he wasn't taking messages for the next twenty-four hours.

Tomorrow he planned to sleep late. Been doing that more often, lately, mornings after he wrapped up an investigation.

He squinted at the distant hills, black against the night sky, the Chamber of Commerce called them the Santa Monica Mountains but they were only a low range of foothills separating Beverly Hills from the Valley. They had seemed higher, years ago, when he first arrived. Real estate developments along Sunset had diminished them and put them in perspective.

Three teenagers died up there last week. Bodies sprawled beside a shiny red Mercedes. Golden kids with rich parents and secure futures.

Passing the Beverly Hills Hotel, he slowed the Chevy, remembering how the old hotel looked when he saw it for the first time. Not so different, actually. More awnings then, more trees and shrubbery now. He wondered if the tall palm trees were the same ones he'd seen back then. World's silliest trees! Palm trees . . .

Would it have been any easier for the Burketts if they hadn't hired him to find their son's murderer? They might never have learned the truth. Beverly Hills Division had been convinced the killer was another kook, probably on parole, who picked victims at random. Driving a stolen car.

He'd begun to suspect something was wrong with the setup when he talked to the parents—two couples and one divorced father—none of whom were able to answer his questions because they had, obviously, never been close to their sons.

The Chevy was approaching the western end of the Strip where high-rise buildings framed a blaze of neon signs flashing their garish welcome to the rock joints, motels and bars.

As he turned down the Strip he always glanced at a familiar low building, once occupied by the original Scandia. For years that was one of his favorite drinking spots. The comfortable bar of the old Scandia. Long gone . . .

When hippies took over, in the sixties, the Strip had become impossible. There had been demonstrations and riots.

Tonight's traffic kept moving and the sidewalks were empty.

His beeper sounded again, but he didn't respond.

He was tired of calls from frantic parents begging him to find their missing daughters and runaway sons. Those jobs made him feel like a private eye in a Raymond Chandler or Ross Macdonald novel.

His work had been more interesting when rich broads hired him to locate their straying lovers and young husbands wanted their even younger wives brought back. No drugs involved and he never found the missing person a suicide in some cheap hotel or behind bars, downtown, facing a morals charge.

He would accept no more jobs to look for teenagers. Never again! Let them stay lost. That was final.

He'd stashed enough in the bank, along with his monthly Social Security check, to survive for the rest of his life in comfort.

However long that might be.

A week, two years, ten years?

His father had lived to be ninety-three . . .

Did he want to last that long? Absolutely! Long as he kept his health.

He rarely considered the possibility of his own death. Too many other people's sudden deaths required his attention.

There had been a brief period, in the late fifties, when he was shocked to realize for the first time that, like all other human beings, he was mortal. Could, in fact, kick off at any moment. He was a Senior Inspector, attached to Hollywood Division, and there was always a possibility of getting killed each time he cornered a dangerous suspect.

He saw that he'd reached Sunset and La Brea. Driving automatically through familiar streets. When the lights changed he turned up La Brea.

For the moment—this happened several times a year—the vice squad had swept the pimps and whores off La Brea, but they would return any night. They always did.

Reaching Lanewood he saw the dark entrance to the dimly lighted street, a single block in length, just as it looked when he came to California.

There'd been gates at both ends to keep intruders out, in those days, with guards on duty. A famous silent director lived in a mansion at the other end of the street—rumor claimed it was D. W. Griffith—and there were big parties with canopies stretching down the center, an orchestra playing foxtrots and waiters serving champagne.

Today there were no guarded gates or private estates. Only small apartments with high rents.

He slowed along Lanewood between rows of tall pine trees—the damn ravens silent in their nests at this hour—and turned down a ramp into the underground garage.

His stomach growled again.

"We're home, kid. Quiet down. I'll feed you in a minute."

He aimed the Chevy across the brightly lighted garage where rows of parked cars silently observed their arrival. Eased into his reserved space, headlights glaring on the white wall where GAHAGAN was painted.

Got out and locked the car. Hesitated, eyes darting, looking for the casual prowler who appeared after you parked. One had surprised him, several years ago, but he'd pulled his gun and fired a single shot, creasing the guy in his arm. The kid had fled, scattering drops of blood.

He seldom carried a gun any more.

His rubber-soled summer shoes made no sound on the concrete as he headed toward the elevator. He always wore them, when he was working, for comfort and quiet.

Jabbed the button and heard the elevator respond, like an old friend, then come whispering down for him. He'd lived here more than twenty years and didn't plan to move until he retired.

Wouldn't stop on the ground floor tonight to check his mailbox. Never got anything these days but junk mail and monthly bills. Nobody wrote him letters since his last relative died in Maryland.

Everybody was dying or, after retiring, moving away.

Would he ever retire and stretch out in the sun for the rest of his life? He doubted that, although he'd talked about Palm Springs for years. More likely it would be a small place such as Ojai.

He was born in a small town and would prefer to die in one.

The elevator door opened.

He stepped inside. Pressed the top button.

A faint humming was the only indication that he was rising.

Retire? One morning he would be too weary, body and mind, to face another day of following vague clues given by stupid people and he would never leave his apartment again. He had, recently, considered such a possibility and planned how he would live. Sit on his balcony, enjoying the books he'd always wanted to read or reread. Mark Twain, Poe, Conrad, Robert Louis Stevenson and Hammett. Water his roses and watch his neighbors. He would order everything he needed on the phone. Have to learn how to cook, before he could do that. Although Joseph's Cafe on Ivar was within easy walking distance down Hollywood Boulevard.

The elevator door slid open and he headed up the long

acoustical-tiled passage. A wall of opaque glass on his right filtered eternal sunshine, day and night. Like a mortuary window. But you never had to look at that hideous new condominium they'd put up next door. Like a fancy Hollywood prison.

This barren passage held only a scattering of tall green plants in white plastic pots. Even their leaves were plastic. He'd complained to the manager about that but they remained. Somebody had set fire to one of them, recently, and its charred skeleton was an eyesore.

He pulled out a ring of keys as he reached his apartment. There was a metallic 36 in the center of the door, a small bronze frame underneath holding a card in a Plexiglas rectangle.

An artist friend designed the card for him and he'd ordered several hundred from a printer in Hollywood.

In the middle of the card was a large staring eye. The artist had amused herself by drawing jagged veins around the pupil, like small bolts of lightning, so the eye looked bloodshot. Arched above the eye, instead of an eyebrow, were the words WORLD'S OLDEST EYE and underneath was his name—GAHAGAN—in smaller type over the phone number for his answering service.

The open eye was very like the old Pinkerton trademark, that nobody remembered any more.

He unlocked the door, pushed it open and snapped a wall switch. One large shaded lamp blazed in his living room.

Closing the door he snapped both locks, automatically, before crossing a narrow foyer, lined with bookshelves, and continuing on through the small living room to his even smaller bedroom. Fingered another wall switch, lighting a white gooseneck reading lamp on the bedside table. Dropped his key ring on the chest of drawers and emptied every pocket before hanging his summer jacket and slacks in the shallow cupboard.

The phone rang in both rooms but he didn't bother to pick up the extension beside his reading lamp.

Whoever had been anxious to reach him, as he drove down

Sunset, was still trying. If they kept it up he would have to silence both phones for the night.

They didn't ring again as he removed his contact lenses, cleaned his teeth—his own, not false—showered and prepared for bed.

After drying his weary body with a thick towel he slid his feet into soft leather slippers and put on an old dark blue shantung robe. Secured it around the waist, patting his flat belly affectionately, then went into the compact kitchen and turned on the lights.

Opening the refrigerator he saw, at once, there was no cheese left. Must've eaten it when he came home last night. No point in opening a bottle of Perrier. He was too tired to bother.

Remember to shop tomorrow morning. Fresh fruit, hopefully some early pears, and several packages of Monterey Jack. Cheese was his one indulgence, though he didn't eat too much any more. Only two thin slices on two Ak Mok crackers.

Checking the electric wall clock—past midnight—before he turned off the kitchen lights and crossed the living room to the record player.

He'd left a record on the spindle this morning.

Touching the lever he heard the machine hum as the record dropped into place.

Unlocked the big window, pushed it back and stepped out into his garden. The air always seemed a little cooler out here.

He could hear Glenn Gould inside, turned low, playing Bach.

Except for a padded chaise and a low glass-topped table the narrow balcony was filled with potted plants of every size and variety.

He saw, at once, that his roses needed watering. Do some work out here tomorrow. Spend the day gardening after he returned from the supermarket.

Stars overhead, above that obscene pink glare rising, as usual, from Hollywood Boulevard.

Leaning against the wrought iron balustrade, he looked down at the big pool where two sharks were gliding through the green-lighted water. He watched as they moved together and embraced. A girl in a flesh-colored bathing suit with a young man in barely visible trunks. Sharks . . .

The performances he'd witnessed in that pool, when he couldn't sleep and came outside for a breath of air! During the summer he slept out here most nights.

He had swum in the pool every morning, back and forth twenty times, until his doctor warned him it was too much for his heart. He'd never had any problems with his ticker and didn't want any.

Zeke backed away from the balustrade and returned inside. Leaving the sharks to enjoy, in private, whatever they had planned.

Left the sliding window open and crossed the living room through a cascade of Bach, each note of the bass carrying the music toward its logical conclusion.

He identified with those bass notes. They were the detective in pursuit of a solution. Never distracted by the false clues in the shimmering treble.

Turned the sound down a few decibels and switched off the living room lamp but the piano followed him into his bedroom.

Bach always helped him relax.

Emma had taught him that. Dear Emma . . .

Been weeks since he had phoned La Jolla. Maybe give her a call tomorrow, around noon, when she was between pupils and having lunch.

Most nights he liked to read a new paperback detective novel—at least thirty or so pages—before he slept. But he wouldn't be able to keep his eyes open tonight.

His stomach complained again. "Sorry, kid. You'll have to wait for breakfast. I'll bake you some nice sausages."

He slipped into the king-sized brass bed he hadn't bothered to make this morning, stretched out his aching legs as he pulled up the sheet and snapped off the gooseneck.

A glow of light from the pool sent a greenish haze through the open windows facing the courtyard.

He'd forgotten to close the damn blinds! No matter. Nothing could prevent his sleeping tonight.

He turned over, face to the wall, and shut his eyes.

Harrison W. Burkett's face, tanned and smug, was waiting for him. Complaining about his fee. "That's rather high, isn't it?"

Living in a fancy Beverly Hills mansion and he hadn't wanted to part with two hundred bucks a day and expenses, to locate his son's murderer . . .

That was three days ago.

Burkett had gotten his phone number from a business acquaintance who'd used his services for a complicated industrial investigation. The friend had paid him a big fee, but the case had been boring. Uncovering a pair of stupid junior executives who'd been stealing and selling blueprints for a new type of computer before it went into mass production. He loathed all computers. They would never be able to solve a murder.

Harrison W. Burkett and his cold fish of a wife had shown not a scintilla of grief for their murdered son.

"This psychopath with a gun could kill all of us," she had said. "The police have done absolutely nothing."

The Burketts acted as though their own lives were in jeopardy so long as the murderer remained at large.

A brief story in the L. A. *Times* had reported only that three unidentified Beverly Hills teenagers had been murdered by an unknown gunman in a remote section of Mulholland Drive.

There were two follow-up pieces—he read all local crime news—and they hadn't told much more about the three killings. The first said the victims had not been identified. The next gave their names, but little more. Which, usually, meant important people were involved and information was being withheld from the press.

First thing he'd done, after accepting the job, was visit some friends at Beverly Hills Division to find out what direction their investigation was taking.

He learned from the Inspector in charge—a pal from his years with the L.A.P.D.—that all three youths had wealthy parents. No trace of drugs when autopsies were performed and none found in the red Mercedes. Two were shot in the back of the head, like victims in an old-fashioned Mafia slaying; the third, Harrison W. Burkett's son, had, surprisingly, been shot in the face. As though he had foolishly turned to look at the gunman. His body was found at the edge of a dry arroyo, the other two sprawled near the Burkett boy's car. They had been drinking beer—two cans each—the empty cans were recovered from the high grass. The Mercedes had not been parked on Mulholland but out of sight on a private estate. Young Burkett had turned off Mulholland, down a sloping drive to a terrace at the rear and parked facing the San Fernando Valley.

His detective friends, assigned to the case, thought the teenagers must have surprised a professional who had come to rob the Mediterranean-style mansion that had been built by some long-forgotten movie star. Its present owners, wealthy Iranians, were in France. The killer had, very likely, been on drugs and lost his head when he saw three husky kids and a parked Mercedes. The wonder was he didn't take the expensive car, except that one of the victims had splashed blood across the hood as he died.

There was nothing to indicate anyone had gotten inside the mansion. No windows broken or unlocked. Police were checking on known burglars who specialized in robbing stars' homes and were known to carry firearms.

The autopsy showed all three teenagers had been shot with a

.32 automatic and the bullets, fired at close range, came from the same gun. So there was only one killer.

He'd driven up to the scene of the slaughter but found no sign of what had happened. From the official police photographs he'd been shown he knew where the Mercedes was parked and each victim had fallen. The murders were last week and the terrace had been washed down since then. No trace of blood left. He did see trampled grass at the edge of the terrace which could've been the police or inquisitive neighbors.

He had looked up at the impressive old mansion, high on the hill, with its curtained windows . . .

Alarm bell ringing somewhere.

The dead youths had been found by a private security guard patrolling the neighborhood . . .

His phone?

Zeke roused slowly from his dream . . .

Damn! He'd forgotten to silence the phone.

He reached out and picked it up.

Hesitating, furious with himself, he opened his eyes and checked the glowing clock.

Only five past one?

He couldn't have slept more than twenty minutes.

A woman's voice was rasping in his hand.

Nettie, from the answering service, always kept calling if there was something urgent.

He held the phone to his ear. "Nettie? This better be important."

"That you, Zeke?"

It wasn't Nettie. "You have reached a disconnected number, Madam."

"Don't be like that." She laughed. "I've been trying to locate you all evening. Got this unlisted number and another for your answering service from a friend."

"Who is this?"

"Nettie said you, also, have a phone in your car. She tried to reach you but when I called back she informed me there was no response from the car. This is Faye. I've been calling this number since . . ."

"I don't know any Faye, ma'am. Alice or Dunaway."

"Don't you remember me, Zeke? Faye Manning . . ."

"Manning?" Suddenly the voice matched a face. Only it wasn't the right voice.

"Remember that time, before my first marriage, you took me waltzing at the Coconut Grove?"

"Of course I remember." He pushed himself up in bed, staring at the green reflection from the pool coming through the open windows but seeing only her lovely face. "Faye Manning? Been one helluva long time."

"Did I wake you, love? Sounds as though I did."

"Only got home an hour ago. Been asleep, maybe twenty minutes."

"I am sorry. But, honey, I do need you. Need your help. Most desperately . . ."

"My help?"

"Thought of everybody I know in this miserable burg and there's absolutely no one I could call. Including my attorney. Then I remembered you. Spite of all these years we haven't seen each other. I've read about you—the famous private eye—watched you being interviewed on talk shows. Always looking so uncomfortable."

"And I've read about you."

"Not lately, you haven't. Been years since I made a feature and the last one was so lousy it finished my already fading career. But I'm not and never will be a charity case. Thanks to three generous husbands, each of whom left me a fortune. So I can afford your enormous fee, whatever it is. I need you, Zeke, and I want to pay for your professional services. You and your entire staff."

"I am a staff of one. Me. Is this murder?" he asked hopefully.

"Not yet, but I've a feeling it could be. At any moment."

At least it wasn't a missing teenager. "You want me to prevent a murder? Is that it?"

"I want you to find somebody."

His hopes ebbed. "One of your grandchildren? I read, somewhere, you have several."

"Seven. Last count. None of them in California, unfortunately. This has nothing to do with family. It's an old friend. He's disappeared. I must see you, love. Talk to you and explain."

"We could meet somewhere tomorrow. Maybe lunch?"

"I mean tonight. Right now. This minute."

He sighed. "I'm pretty tired. No time for dinner and when I got home I didn't have enough energy to pour myself a glass of Perrier. Showered and went to bed."

"Can't you come up to the house? I'm on Montcalm Drive. That's off Woodrow Wilson and . . ."

"I know Montcalm."

"Couldn't you do that? For old time's sake."

"Who's this friend who disappeared?"

"Laurence Knight. You remember him."

"The actor?"

"Somebody fired several shots into his garage doors last night or early this morning. He's not sure when. And now he's vanished."

Zeke's interest revived. "Somebody trying to kill him?"

"That's what worries me. He was to call me back this evening. When he didn't, I phoned him. He hadn't been home for dinner or called to say where he was. His housekeeper says he didn't take any luggage and none of his wardrobe seems to be missing."

"He has a family?"

"His wife died years ago and their only child, a daughter, lives in London where her husband's a big man with some oil company. Their son, Lars, lives with Larry. He's in Hollywood trying to be an actor. Like his grandfather."

"Did the grandson report his disappearance to the police?"

"No, and neither did I. In fact, I warned Lars it might cause nasty publicity if the police were called. The newspapers are always eager to spread this sort of thing over their front pages. Hollywood star missing!"

"I've been involved with a few of them."

"I need you, Zeke."

"O.K., my friend. What's that address on Montcalm?"

She gave him the street number. "I'll turn on my outside floodlights and open the electric gates. Be waiting for you, honey . . ."

Zeke put the phone down and snapped the gooseneck. Its light revealed a single framed photograph hanging on the wall beyond the foot of his brass bed.

An enlarged photograph of two skinny young men lounging in an open doorway. He didn't remember any more who snapped the picture. Only that it was San Francisco—the summer of 1921—and they were both working for the Pinkerton Agency.

The tall kid with the pale brown hair was Ezekiel Gahagan. The other young man, shoulders slouched, was his closest friend. Several inches shorter and ten years older. Their solemn faces had faded into the past, but he could still make out every feature of that other face. Especially the eyes, those piercing dark brown eyes that missed nothing. Detective's eyes.

"O.K., Dash." He tossed the sheet back and, muscles protesting, pushed himself out of bed. "Here goes Zeke again. Abyssinia, kid!"

Chapter 2

Outpost Drive was a ghostly blur behind the heavy fog crowding in from Santa Monica and filling the canyons like gray smoke.

No traffic but Zeke held the Chevy to a crawl as he followed the twisting road higher and higher.

Those three boys died near another canyon—Beverly Glen—several miles west of here. Beverly Hills Division had been looking for a killer in an old green Thunderbird. Somebody reported seeing this suspicious type driving erratically on Mulholland, the night the teenagers were shot.

He hadn't bought that from the first.

His hunch, after he inspected the spot where the bodies were found, was that something was wrong with the theory of a single gunman. The murders seemed too neat.

He'd spent two days locating and questioning the boys' parents—two couples, including Burkett who had hired him, and one divorced husband whose wife had remarried and was living in Honolulu—without learning much about their sons, but a great deal about the five parents.

They were young, in their early forties, and looked even younger. The two wives appeared to be Beverly Hills icebergs. All three husbands were business executives, deeply involved in their careers and, apparently, successful at them. Burkett headed an electronics firm, another was a plastic surgeon and the divorced father was a talent agent, with an office in Century City, who handled television actors.

Mrs. Burkett, sleek and elegant, owned an art gallery on Melrose and the surgeon's wife was a gourmet cook who attended classes given by famous chefs in the kitchens of expensive restaurants.

None of them, husbands or wives, had ever bothered to meet the others.

The Burkett boy, according to his mother, wasn't interested in art, but spent his spare time at a riding school in the Valley where he stabled a horse his parents gave him on his sixteenth birthday. The other mother complained that her son wouldn't eat gourmet cooking but lived on junk food, spending his weekends on a friend's yacht, berthed at Balboa, working as a member of the crew. The agent's son, according to his father, was a genius who had a laboratory in the basement of their Brentwood home and planned to become a scientist. All three youths had been active in sports at Beverly Hills High.

None of the parents could tell him anything of importance about their sons. They knew little about their habits or what they did when they were away from home. Each had his own car, but they preferred to ride around in the Burkett boy's new Mercedes. They went to movies and rock concerts together. Each had a generous allowance. Too damn generous for kids that age.

The parents had no idea where their sons had been earlier, the night they were killed, or why the Mercedes was parked in the drive behind that empty mansion. They had never heard of the Iranians who owned the property.

All five parents appeared to be shocked by the murders and were visibly relieved that the autopsies had found no evidence of drugs. They never discussed narcotics with their sons. Or, so far as he could tell, much of anything else . . .

The fathers talked to him in their offices but the two wives had been more difficult to locate.

He, finally, caught up with Mrs. Burkett at her gallery, the other one during a wine-tasting at the Beverly Hills Hotel.

They appeared to be reluctant to discuss the dead teenagers but he had realized they were not being antagonistic. They simply knew nothing about their sons.

The actors' agent had suggested he contact some of their teachers at Beverly Hills High.

He'd talked, first, to the principal who hadn't known the dead boys personally but gave him the names of several teachers he should question. They assured him that all three students had been well-liked and made better than average grades. Each of them had a girlfriend.

He interviewed the three young women who proved to be more serious than he remembered girls at that age in recent years. Each told him much the same story. They liked their boyfriends but there wasn't a chance their parents would approve of marriage until after they finished college.

The Burkett boy's girl seemed brighter than the other two.

He kept her talking because he had a feeling there must be something important she could tell him. A sweet-faced girl with soft brown eyes and a gentle smile.

There had, finally, been a moment of hesitation before she said: "I don't understand why Billy Harper wasn't killed with the others."

"And who, young lady, is Billy Harper?"

"Their best friend. Billy was always with them. Tagging along . . ."

"Was he?"

"I wonder why he wasn't there that night. Why he, too, wasn't killed. He's more than a year younger and smaller, but he was always with them. Whenever you saw them in that Mercedes . . ."

"Billy Harper's a student here?"

"Oh, yes. He's very bright. Skipped a grade last year. Everybody likes Billy, although he's kind of a loner. Too shy to have a girlfriend yet. Keeps to himself, except when he's with Dave and the others."

"Where can I find him?"

"Billy didn't come to school for several days, after the others were killed, but he's here today . . ."

Zeke realized that the fog was heavier as he turned left from Outpost onto Mulholland. Impossible to make out the lights of Hollywood, usually visible, glittering below the foothills.

Instead of looking for Billy Harper he had returned to his Chevy—parked on Whittier, facing Wilshire—and waited behind the wheel, his eyes on the students. Some were loitering near a recreation area—where skinny boys practiced basketball and small children were squealing in an adjoining playground—as older students came up Whittier to get their cars. He was aware that several had recognized him. They must've seen him going from the principal's office to the classrooms and word had spread that he was here. Pairs of students walking past the Chevy—suntanned youths and pretty girls—stared at him, their conversations silenced.

As he waited he had been conscious of heavy traffic on Wilshire and the aromatic scent coming from a row of eucalyptus trees along Whittier.

He'd noticed the blond boy in a sweater, shorter than the

others, hurrying up from Wilshire. Walking with purpose and frowning. Knew he would stop beside the open window of the Chevy.

"Excuse me, sir . . ."

"Yup?"

"You're a cop . . ."

"Oldest private eye in the whole world, kid. That's how I know you're Billy Harper."

The eyes widened in the troubled young face. "You know my name?"

"Been waiting to talk to you." He reached over and opened the door.

The boy got in. "You going to arrest me?"

"Certainly not. I'm looking for information. You've got something to tell me, haven't you?"

"Yes, sir." He sighed. "Guess I do . . ."

He had waited, letting the youngster take his time, not looking at him . . .

Zeke slowed the Chevy to a stop, as an animal was revealed, frozen in the glare of his headlights. A coyote. Old and lean. Staring into the dazzling light before continuing across the road.

He drove on, even more cautiously, through the swirling fog.

Billy had, finally, started to talk. "I was supposed to be with them when they shot themselves. Dave and the others . . ."

"Shot themselves, did they?"

"It was to be the four of us. I backed out. They were upset but they, finally, agreed I didn't have to go through with it. Wasn't, really, because I was afraid. Just didn't think I was old enough to understand what I was doing. Never did want to take my life, not as much as they did. Knew it would upset my family, if I killed myself. They would never be able to understand why I would do such a thing . . ."

"You're a very smart young man."

"It was part of our agreement, from the first, that if one of us didn't want to go through with it—for any reason—he was free to pull out. Long as he swore not to warn anybody about their plan."

"It was a suicide pact?"

"I guess so . . ."

"Is there a lot of talk about suicide among kids your age?"

"All the time. Whenever things get rough at home."

"Where'd they find their gun?"

"Bought it somewhere. It's easy to buy a gun if you want one."

"Too damn easy."

"They planned, from the start, it would look like somebody killed them. They would shoot each other in the back of the head and the last one alive was to shoot himself. Throw the gun into the canyon, so the cops wouldn't find it. They were to draw lots. Who would be last . . ."

"Whose idea was this?"

"I wasn't there when they worked out the final plan. Could've been any one of 'em, but Dave was always the leader."

"David Burkett?"

"He even wrote a note for me to give the cops."

"You did that?"

"No. Dave told me to keep it a coupla days, after their bodies were found. So everybody would think they'd been murdered. Guess they kinda wanted revenge . . ."

"For what?"

"Well . . . They felt their parents didn't love them any more. Didn't care whether they lived or not. I guess that's why I didn't go ahead with it. I love both my parents and I know they love me. Dave and the others didn't even like their parents. And they were frightened."

"Of their parents?"

"Of everything. Mostly of what's happening in the world. What the future will be like when we grow up. The chance of atomic war. Star wars for real . . ."

"And you weren't?"

"Sure, I'm afraid. All of us are. But I love my folks. My little sister . . . If there's an atomic war, I want to be with them."

"You have this letter?"

He reached inside his sweater and pulled out a plain white envelope. "I didn't know how to give this to the police. Was afraid they'd arrest me if I took it to them. Then, a few minutes ago, I heard you were sitting here in this old Chevy Malibu . . ."

Zeke held out his hand.

Billy gave him the envelope.

He tore it open and pulled out a folded sheet of white note paper. Read the neatly typed words as the boy, beside him, remained silent. Saw that all three youths had signed it, but David Burkett's signature was the first.

Their brief note was addressed "To Whom It May Concern" and contained no personal messages to their parents. They had no desire to live any longer because of the hopeless state of the world. Explained their suicide pact and gave the location of the private estate they had found where the house had been empty for several months. The gun would be dropped into the canyon. That was all.

He had folded the note and thrust it back into the envelope as he studied the silent boy. "I'll have to give this to the police."

"I know."

"You didn't read it?"

"No, sir. It was sealed."

"I won't say I got it from you. Your name isn't mentioned in the note. No reason to involve you. I'll tell the police I found the envelope in that arroyo below where they died. The wind could've blown it down there. And I'll look for the gun." Zeke held out his hand. "We have a secret, kid. You and I."

"Yes, sir." He nodded, solemnly, as they shook hands.

"My name's Zeke Gahagan. You won't forget?"

"No, sir."

"If you ever need me, for any reason, I'm in the phone book.

The number of my answering service. Call and leave your name and phone number with the girl. I'll call you back. That's a promise."

"Yes, sir. Thanks."

He had watched Billy Harper hurry back toward Wilshire, his small figure soon lost among the taller students.

He'd gone back up Beverly Drive to Mulholland and down that private drive to the spot where the three bodies were found beside the Mercedes.

No one saw him lose his footing on the steep slope of the sunbaked arroyo, watched him slip and slide—clutching, grasping, falling—until he came to a stop against that dead tree.

He'd stayed there several minutes, gasping for breath in the hot sun and checking his bones, before starting a slow and painful return to the top. Going back, hand over hand, he had found the missing gun—a .32 caliber automatic—caught in a manzanita. Wrapped it in his handkerchief and stuck it into a pocket before scrambling back to his car . . .

Zeke turned the Chevy up Palo Vista, unable to glimpse the big house Ann Harding had built—the front of the property faced Montcalm—and slowed up the incline toward Woodrow Wilson.

He had spent the rest of the afternoon at Beverly Hills Division, explaining to his friends what had happened, after turning the suicide note and the gun over to them. They could call it simple suicide and close the case.

His friends had agreed and were delighted their investigation was finished. Produced half a bottle of whiskey and polished it off—he accepted a glass of water—as they enumerated all their current problems and gripes. He, finally, drove back up to Mulholland and showed them how he had slipped down the arroyo—they could see the deep marks his feet had made—where he found the gun and the suicide note.

He called Burkett's office from a public phone on Sunset and was informed that Mr. Burkett had left for the day. A maid, at the

Burkett residence, said Mr. and Mrs. Burkett wouldn't return until late evening. They were dining out and she didn't know where.

Zeke hadn't felt like eating—his stomach was queasy—so he drove down to the Coast Highway and parked on a bluff overlooking the beach. One of his favorite spots when he had important thinking to do.

Sat there, watching the sunset, considering the growing problem of teenage suicide. A recent national survey claimed the number of such deaths was increasing. Many young people simply didn't want to live.

Life had been different when he was a teenager. No atomic bombs waiting to explode over your head. His only problem at that age had been to escape from his family in Maryland and head west. He wanted to see those mountains he'd read about in books. Wanted to stare across the Pacific Ocean. This same ocean . . .

He'd fallen asleep, watching the hypnotic motion of the waves, and when he wakened it was night. Checking his dashboard clock he found that he'd slept for several hours. He never used to do that . . .

When he drove up to the Burkett house it was after nine o'clock.

The maid said they hadn't come home.

He sat in the Chevy, windows closed against the damp fog, and waited for them.

They didn't show up until after ten, driving separate cars.

He'd let them go inside and gave them a few minutes before ringing the bell.

"Our son a suicide?"

"Yes, ma'am. I found the gun."

"Ridiculous! I refuse to believe that."

It had taken a lot of talking to convince them—they had obviously been drinking all evening—that their son could be a suicide. They would prefer him to be murdered.

He told them he had turned the suicide note and the gun over to Beverly Hills Division but said nothing about his meeting with Billy Harper. Or told them their son had, very likely, murdered at least one of his friends. They would never find out about that. Didn't care enough to be suspicious about how the three suicides were carried out.

Burkett had, finally, made out a check and paid him . . .

Zeke turned off Woodrow Wilson, into another heavy pocket of fog, down Montcalm. Impossible to see the estates on either side but there was a pale glow straight ahead, toward his left, which would be the floodlights Faye had turned on for him.

He glimpsed a high wall with elaborate wrought-iron gates standing open.

Eased the Chevy down the private drive, peering from side to side, but saw no parked cars. Garages must be in the rear.

The heavy gates were closing behind him, controlled from within the invisible mansion.

Faye had heard his car.

Chapter 3

"That you, Zeke?"

"Guilty, as charged." He got out and closed the door. "Heard your car coming down Montcalm."

Zeke went toward her voice. "Fog got heavier as I drove up Outpost."

"It's always worse up here. I feel guilty bringing you out in such weather. Waking you . . ."

"Happens all the time." He saw her now, standing against a halo of light from an open door. Her figure looked as slim as ever. "I can't see the ground. Any steps?"

"None. This is an old house. Lots of rooms but everything on one floor."

"How long have you lived here?" He was beginning to make out her face as he came closer.

"My first husband bought this property in the thirties and I'll never live anywhere else. Too many lovely memories . . ."

Her face came toward him, as though a camera was zooming in for a tight close shot. "Now I can see you. My God! Pretty as ever . . ."

She laughed. "That's not true, as you'll see when you come inside." Holding her arms out in welcome. "Dear Zeke! It's been so long . . ." She lifted her head, in that same graceful gesture he recalled from all her films, anticipating a kiss.

He embraced her, kissing her firmly on the lips. Conscious of her tiny body and expensive perfume. She smelled like a star.

"Come in, love. Out of this dampness."

He followed her across a spacious foyer. Noticing that the wide floor boards were polished and the furniture was antique, heavily carved, Spanish-looking.

"I've a fire in the living room. Been sitting here all evening, reading when I wasn't trying to reach you."

"I was wrapping up an investigation." He saw she was leading him into a high-ceilinged room with a beamed ceiling where logs blazed in a copper-hooded fireplace. Large shaded lamps made pools of light on Oriental rugs. She was heading for a sofa placed at an angle to the fire, facing a low table holding a clutter of objects. Yellow mums in white pots, piles of new books, white telephone, bottle of Perrier in a miniature silver wine bucket.

"You didn't have dinner." Sinking onto the sofa. "So, after we talked, I fixed you a sandwich."

"Needn't have done that." He sat beside her, studying the remembered face in the soft light.

"Cook's asleep, but I still know how to make a decent sandwich. Hope you like cold turkey."

"Sure do." He inspected the sandwich, dark bread cut into neat wedges arranged on a handsome plate, damask napkin and crystal wineglass. "Looks mighty good."

"You haven't changed, Zeke. Same eyes. I've never forgotten those eyes. Steel gray . . ."

He faced her again and realized she had been studying him as they talked.

She smiled. "Same curly hair."

He grunted. "Not the same color."

"Nor mine."

He saw that her hair was gray, instead of blonde. Silver curls framing her delicately boned face.

"You're as lean as ever, twice as handsome. Didn't you, in the old days, work as a stand-in for Coop?"

"And a few others. That's before I joined the L.A.P.D. and became a cop. I'd been a security officer at the studios, by day, bodyguard for some of the stars at night."

"When was the last time we saw each other?"

"I've no idea."

"Neither do I . . . Or, for that matter, the first time. I do remember one night at the Derby. I was with my second husband and you were in a booth with another man."

"No dames?"

"Not that night. We'd met, long before that, so I waved. You were the two handsomest men in the room. Except for my dear husband. You with curly blond hair and your friend with silver hair and a dark mustache."

"I remember the night. It was 1930. That was Hammett I was with. He'd come from New York to work at Warner Brothers."

"Was he an actor? I've often wondered."

"He was a writer. Wrote detective stories . . ."

"I never read mysteries. Keep me awake."

"He wrote *The Maltese Falcon*."

"I saw the movie. Still see it on television. My dear friend, Walter Huston, had a walk-on near the end. His son directed, and Mary Astor was so beautiful . . ."

"That was the third movie version. The first one starred Bebe Daniels and Ricardo Cortez."

"Did it? I knew both of them."

"Dash and I drank more than our quota of booze that night."

"Is your writer friend still working in California?"

"Hammett's dead. Long time . . ."

"You and I survive."

"Yup."

She sighed. "I wonder why . . ."

"We must be needed here for something."

"I've been feeling pretty useless lately. Nobody seems to need me any more."

"Maybe you ought to find yourself another husband."

"Three's quite enough, thanks. I loved 'em all. I'll never find another man to marry. Unless you're available." She smiled, eyes dancing. "Why didn't you every marry, Zeke?"

"You kidding! I've been married four times. Four divorces. They're dead now, all but one." Must remember to call Emma next week.

"I had no idea. Never read, anywhere, that you'd been married—or divorced."

"I'm a cop, not a movie star. The press, thank God, was never interested in my private life."

"But I'm constantly reading about you in the *Times*. Seeing you on the evening news shows. 'World's Oldest Eye' . . ."

"That's only these last few years. Clete Roberts interviewed me on the radio. My seventy-fifth birthday. He said: 'Zeke, you must be the world's oldest private eye.' Somehow that stuck and, since then, I've had all the work I can handle. So I'm not complaining."

"Aren't you going to eat that sandwich?"

"Sure am." He reached for one of the wedges.

Faye lifted the bottle from the ice, wrapped a napkin around it and filled the wineglass.

"How'd you know I drink Perrier these days?"

"You mentioned it on the phone."

"That's all I've been drinking for years." He began to eat as he talked. "A little vermouth and white wine, but no more hard stuff."

"Guess we've both drunk our share for one lifetime. When I think of all those parties! From bathtub gin to vodka martinis. I don't go to parties any more. Two or three charity affairs every year. Cesar Romero's my escort, usually. Such a dear friend! And I give a few small dinner parties. Lunch at the Bistro Garden and tea at the Century Plaza. But I'm getting tired of all those Beverly Hills widows. The same bored faces . . ."

"This sandwich was just what I needed."

"I'm glad."

"Homemade bread, isn't it?"

"My cook makes delicious breads." She watched him finishing the sandwich, pleased to see his obvious enjoyment. "Heard, on the eleven o'clock news, the police haven't found the killer of those teenagers who were murdered on Mulholland last week."

"They never will."

"You think not?"

"I promise you they won't."

"Makes me terribly uneasy. Some crazy with a gun speeding up and down Mulholland, looking for someone to kill. He may have tried my gates! Unless I'm expecting somebody, like tonight, they're kept locked. My cook and her husband live in, he's the houseman, and my gardener has an apartment over the garages. Didn't used to be like this. So much crime."

"Keeps me in business."

"Yes. I suppose it does."

He wiped his fingers on the napkin as he noticed a grand piano, in deep shadow, near a row of curtained windows. "You do any singing these days?"

"Sunny mornings, when I'm in the mood. Mostly Jerome Kern, Rodgers and Hart . . . Oh! It is good to see you. Dear Zeke! Wakened by an old girlfriend in distress . . ."

He set the empty wineglass aside and looked at her again. "You said Laurence Knight appears to be missing."

"Since yesterday."

"Tell me about it . . ."

She faced him, pressing her back against the arm of the sofa and sitting erect. "Well . . ."

As Faye hesitated, he saw that she was wearing no makeup, her face without a wrinkle or blemish. One of the most beautiful dames he'd ever known, and he'd known a good many. She was wearing an attractive caftan, made of some soft violet material, embroidered with silver. Simple string of pearls around her lovely throat, no rings. Expensive-looking silver slippers. Neat ankles, small feet. Somehow she seemed even more beautiful than in the past. Faye had always been more attractive in person than on the screen. Makeup had masked her delicate features and enlarged her sensitive mouth.

He realized as she began to talk that his muscles still ached from sliding down that arroyo this afternoon.

"First of all, I should tell you—Larry Knight is, I suppose, my oldest and dearest friend. All three of my husbands adored him. Larry and his wife were always invited to our parties. I'd known them in New York. Thelma wasn't a professional—her family was wealthy—but Larry and I were starred, together, in two Broadway musicals. Sang the leads. He was one of those stars, like Walter Pidgeon and Cary Grant, who began as singers but after they became famous in films the public forgot they could sing. Larry was signed for Hollywood first. I didn't come out here until the following year. To a different studio. That's when talkies were starting and every major studio planned to make big musicals. I'm going way back, like this, to show you how long we've known each other."

"You liked his wife?"

"Thelma was a love. She died shortly after I lost my last

husband. Larry and I became even closer then. We still see each other every week. He drops in here or I drive down to his place. He turned up yesterday, after lunch. We sat on the terrace, as usual, and talked. Larry hadn't had a drink in years but, as we talked—nothing of any importance—I sensed he had a hangover. Which surprised me. He, finally, asked if he could have a drink. So we came inside, to the bar in the study, and he poured himself a straight whiskey and drank it down. Then another. Told me he'd been to a dinner party the night before—Monday night—and fallen off the wagon."

"Where was this?"

"Paul Victor's house."

"The director?"

"He has a charming home, up behind the Beverly Hills Hotel. I've dined there, many times in the past. Paul is, usually, surrounded by beautiful women—although, as everyone knows, he's never married—but this, for some reason, was an all-masculine party. Four guests, in addition to Larry. Five had been invited but one didn't show up."

"For what reason?"

"Larry never said, and I didn't ask him. Those who did were old friends. They'd worked together, many times, at various studios."

"Did he say who they were?"

"He never mentioned any names, which I thought odd, only that all of them were well known in the industry. There was, apparently, some reason for these particular people to be there but he never explained what it was. Only that they had talked, most of the evening, about their early days in Hollywood. They were served an excellent dinner with many wines. Paul's a gourmet and has a magnificent chef. Somebody made jokes about Larry's not drinking and, finally, he did have one glass of white wine. Then, after dinner, he drank a cognac. That's when he said something which either shocked or surprised the other guests."

"What was it he said?"

"He refused to tell me. Only that he had revealed something about an old Hollywood scandal."

"Lots of them. Which scandal?"

"Larry didn't say. He was genuinely disturbed, that he'd done such a thing."

"Have you any idea what it was he'd revealed? Didn't he give you a hint?"

"Only that it was something, apparently, about a top star that had been told to him years ago, in confidence, by another person."

"If this scandal happened so long ago why's he worrying?"

"He said he's afraid somebody might try to kill him."

Zeke straightened on the sofa. "You mean to silence him?"

"Apparently. Yes . . . When he went downstairs to get his car, late yesterday morning, he saw that someone had fired several shots into his garage doors. There was a line of bullet holes."

"He reported this to the police?"

"Said he didn't dare. I can tell you, Zeke, he's really frightened. Like a scared kid."

"Kid? Laurence Knight's at least . . . Seventy-five?"

"Larry must be eighty—more or less—but he looks younger. He's always been terribly conscious of his health. Dieting and exercising, even when I first knew him on Broadway."

"I've never met him, but I used to enjoy his pictures. Especially the westerns."

"Before he left here, yesterday, I made him promise to call me last evening."

"Where was he going?"

"I'm not sure he knew . . . When he hadn't phoned, by nine, I called him. His housekeeper, Mrs. Svendsen, told me he didn't come home for dinner and hadn't phoned all day. I asked to speak to his grandson—Lars Lyndon—but Lars didn't eat dinner at home either. I finally reached Lars around ten. He'd just gotten in.

Said he dined with friends and went to acting class with them. Had no idea where his grandfather might be. I called him again, this morning, but he still hadn't heard from Larry. Now Lars is worried. Because of those bullet holes in their garage doors."

"Didn't he report them?"

"Lars wants no part of the police. He's such a baby! His mother's fault, not his grandfather's."

"Why is everyone afraid of the police? It's their job to protect you. Doesn't this boy realize his grandfather may be in trouble of some sort? Where'd he get a name like Lars?"

"He was named for his grandfather. Larry's real name is Lars Costigan. That's the name he used on Broadway. The studio changed it when they brought him out here. Wanted him to sound British, so they named him Laurence Knight. But he was born Lars Costigan. His father was Irish, his mother Swedish."

"Born in Europe?"

"Oh, no! Somewhere in Pennsylvania, I think. Or Delaware . . ."

"I was born in Maryland."

"Were you? I always thought you were a westerner."

"Haven't been back East since 1921. Sixty-four years . . ." He looked into her troubled eyes. "Your friend Knight appears to be in some kind of difficulty. Is he wealthy?"

"Larry was one of the first stars to buy real estate. He invested in orange groves, while I invested in husbands. Fortunately, both paid off." She smiled. "You will try and find him for me?"

"Yup. I'll do my damnedest. Better tell you, my usual fee is . . ."

"I'm not interested in what this may cost." She reached out and lifted a copy of *Daily Variety* from the table. "Left this here earlier."

He watched her take a white envelope from under the trade paper.

"My check for two thousand." Handing the envelope to him. "Tell me when this is gone. There's plenty more."

He slipped the envelope into an inside breast pocket. "You love this guy?"

"Love Larry? Not the way I loved my husbands. But, yes, I do love him. There are many kinds of love, you know."

"I've found that out."

"If anything happened to him . . ." She shook her head, considering the possibility. "There would be one more big black hole in my life. Not many of the old stars left. Every year I lose a few more friends. And each loss gets worse. You ever think about marriage again, Zeke?"

"Hasn't crossed my mind in years."

"Give me a call, if it ever should."

"I'll do that."

"Meanwhile, you might give me a ring every day, if you would? Keep me in the picture, what you find out about Larry."

"Right. I'll phone in the evening. After eight."

"Where will you start to look for him?"

"First of all, I should have a talk with his grandson. Then I'd better see Paul Victor. Find out what happened at that dinner."

"I'll write their addresses down for you." She picked up a small leather-bound address book and a gold pen from the table. "Also their unlisted phone numbers."

"Won't get started on this until tomorrow. Right now I'm heading back to bed. This time I'll turn my phone off. Forgot to do that earlier."

"Thank God you did."

Book Two

Adagio

Chapter 4

Zeke slept until after ten o'clock and wakened with no memory of having dreamed.

Sat, for a moment, on the side of his bed. Staring into space. Moving his muscles tentatively.

Yesterday's aches did not respond.

He always made his own breakfast wearing an old robe and comfortable sandals. On a warm morning, such as this, he liked to eat it on the balcony. Seated on the chaise, his breakfast tray on the glass-topped table.

Weekday breakfasts were always the same. One egg baked or two small links of Jones sausage, also baked. A granola muffin split and toasted, with a little sweet butter and orange or apricot marmalade. Half a cup of drip coffee, black, no sugar. Followed by half an unsweetened grapefruit. Sundays he, usually, made a two-egg omelette. His second wife—the French one—had taught him how to make omelettes.

This morning he ate with appetite, darting glances at his neighbors' balconies, checking the condition of their potted plants as he hummed the Offenbach melodies floating out from the record player.

After breakfast he watered his roses.

Then—shaved, showered and dressed—he set out on personal errands.

First his bank, on Sunset, where he deposited the two checks he'd been given yesterday. Harrison Burkett's reluctant fee for three days' work—he hadn't even charged the guy for expenses—and Faye's advance payment that covered his services, mind and body, for twenty days. Cashed a check for three hundred to take care of his personal needs for next week. Didn't withdraw a gun from his safe-deposit box because the search for Laurence Knight shouldn't require one. In spite of the bullet holes in those garage doors.

Second stop was the supermarket, also on Sunset, where he bought fresh fruit, a can of coffee, muffins, butter and two packages of cheese.

As he waited at the checkout counter, he became aware of a growing disturbance behind him. Voices raised and thudding feet.

The Japanese checker, an old acquaintance, looked up as she slid his purchases through the checking machine. "It's those Russian refugees from the Fairfax district, always fighting. Manager had to call the police yesterday. They're on relief, but one of them drives a new Rolls."

Zeke looked around as a woman screamed. Saw a bottle of pickles fly through the air, smash into a display of canned goods and send them crashing to the floor. "They're living in a democracy now."

The checker giggled. "You suppose they acted like this in Moscow?"

"They'd have faced a firing squad." He heard their shouts and smelled the spilled pickles as he carried his bag of groceries out to the Chevy.

Back at the apartment he distributed his purchases, filling a Mexican bowl with ripe Bartlett pears, everything else in the refrigerator. Went into his bedroom to get the slip of paper with the two addresses Faye had given him last night.

As he drove up the ramp to the street, he heard the ravens' harsh cawing in the pine trees.

First stop would be Laurence Knight's residence on Curson Avenue.

He aimed the Chevy west on Hollywood Boulevard to Curson where he turned north past the community gardens facing a row of fine mansions on the opposite side of the street.

This was old Hollywood, where many of the early silent stars had built their first homes.

The address he sought was higher up, facing an impressive view of the new downtown skyscrapers and distant mountains.

He checked the first address, written by Faye, and saw it repeated in gleaming bronze numerals on a pair of wrought-iron gates across the street. Laurence Knight's property was surrounded by a high wall and he was unable to glimpse the house as he parked his Chevy. A drive, on the right, extended up a steep slope from the sidewalk.

Better have a look at those bullet holes before he went to the front door.

The length of the drive, rising along the side wall, indicated the property was sizable. When he reached the top he faced a row of four garages, all their doors closed. The first two had the bullet holes. A neat row of six, three to each door.

He moved closer to inspect them.

Somebody had used a submachine gun. The bullets penetrated the wood and must've buried themselves in the cars, if any were parked inside.

"What you doin' down there, mister?"

Zeke turned and faced the rear of Knight's residence. It had been a woman's voice. Not young.

"Get outta here. Whoever you are. I'll call the cops."

He raised his eyes, past the barred windows of what must be a basement, and saw a featureless face at an open window, barely visible through the mesh of a metal screen. "I'm looking for Mr. Lars Lyndon."

"Won't find him down there. Not at this hour."

"Didn't suppose I would. Wanted to see these bullet holes in your garage doors."

"How'd you know 'bout them?"

"Miss Manning told me."

"You a friend of Miss Faye's?"

"She's hired me to find Mr. Knight. I'm a private detective."

"A cop? You better come inside. Up these steps to my kitchen."

He crossed the drive to a concrete flight of steps rising past a tall cypress tree and went up to an immaculate service porch at the top.

A plump woman, white hair braided around her head, stood at an open door, wearing a white apron and blue uniform. Her friendly face, pink and plump, was scowling. "You must be Mrs. Svendsen."

"How you know my name, mister?"

"Miss Manning said she talked to you yesterday."

"She call me and ask 'bout the boss. Mr. Knight's disappeared."

"I've come to see his grandson."

"Mr. Lars only just finish breakfast and gone back upstairs."

"Suppose he could spare me a few minutes? My name's Gahagan."

"Come in, mister." Moving back from the door. "If you're a friend of Miss Faye's . . ."

He followed her through a large modern kitchen where she had been making a salad. "Fixing lunch this early?"

"Always make salad this hour. So when Mr. Lars gets hungry, it's ready. He eats at all hours."

"You still haven't heard from Mr. Knight?"

"Not a word. Come through here . . ." She opened a door onto a dim hall. "Mr. Larry never done this before. All the years I work for him."

"How long would that be?"

"Nearly thirty years now. His missus hired me. Four years before she passed on. The dear lady! I been here ever since. Anything happen to Mr. Larry I never work for nobody else. Especially his grandson." She went ahead, through the long hall, without glancing back. "I've got enough money saved."

"You plan to retire?"

"I go back Solvang, where I was born."

"That's above Santa Barbara, isn't it?"

"You never been Solvang?"

"I avoid tourist spots when I take a vacation. Which hasn't been in some time."

"Solvang's much more than tourist spot. It was founded by Danes from Nebraska and Iowa. One of 'em was my grandfather."

"I was told Mr. Knight's part Swedish."

"Yes but we're both American citizens, born United States. And we're both of us, also, Scandinavian. Mr. Larry likes my Danish cooking. When I return to Solvang I will live with my sister. She owns restaurant and I help her in kitchen. You wait here, in library." Motioning toward a pair of tall mahogany doors standing open. "I see if Mr. Lars is dressed yet or gone back to bed. Sometimes he sleeps all day."

"Did you hear those shots fired into your garage doors?"

"Nobody heard 'em. I sleep top floor, front, and I'm a sound sleeper. Didn' know 'bout 'em 'til Mister Lars tell me this morning."

"Where do the others sleep? Mr. Knight and his grandson . . ."

"Second floor. They got front rooms, like me. Mr. Larry in master bedroom, the young man in what used t' be his grandmother's room under mine. I tell Mr. Lars you like t' see him, but I won't say you're a cop. He's very nervous young man."

"Is he?" Zeke went into the library where sunlight spilled through open windows. A high-ceilinged room overflowing with books. They were on shelves, tables and piled upon chairs. Larry Knight must be a great reader.

Most actors were, especially the good ones. Always reading a book between jobs, which was most of their lives. Even a big star only worked a few months most years.

Thank the Lord, he'd never wanted to act. The few small parts he'd done when he was young gave him firsthand knowledge of what it was like to be an actor.

A detective's work never stopped and he expected his bank account was healthier than those of most members of the Screen Actors Guild, his living expenses much less. No fine house, fancy cars or expensive habits.

"Wanted to see me, did you?"

Zeke turned to face one of the tallest and handsomest young men he'd ever encountered away from a shooting stage. He was wearing a robe over his pajamas and held a chain leash, restraining an enormous black and white sheepdog that was lunging but not barking. "Lars Lyndon?"

"Who the devil are you?"

He pulled out his wallet and opened it to show the photostat of his license. "My name's Gahagan. I'm a private investigator."

"Detective?" He scowled as he said the threatening word.

"At the moment working for Miss Faye Manning."

"Faye sent you here?" Moving forward now, the dog pulling on his leash. "Why would she do that? What possible reason . . ."

"She's a personal friend. Asked me to find your grandfather."

"I thought private eyes only looked for cheating husbands." He collapsed, as though exhausted, onto a giant-sized sofa, tucking his bare feet under the pale yellow silk robe. "Sit down, sir. I'll be happy to answer your questions. Isn't that what I'm supposed to say?"

"Only if it's what you intend to do." Zeke sat on the edge of a red leather armchair facing him. The young man wasn't, actually, as tall as he'd appeared to be at first glance. He looked taller because he was so thin. Shoulders were narrower than average and his torso didn't seem to be muscular. His long straight hair was blond, eyes pale blue. He looked remarkably like a young Laurence Knight. "I've never met your grandfather but I've seen many of his pictures, back to the silents."

"Then you've seen more than I. Since I came over from London I've caught the ones they show at the film festivals and revival houses, but there must be dozens I haven't located yet. Grandpa doesn't remember how many he made. I wrote down a list of the ones in the files of the Academy but even they don't have a complete record of his early pictures."

"How long have you lived here with your grandfather?"

"Three years, I think . . ."

"Has he ever disappeared before?"

"Not to my knowledge."

"You have a British accent."

"I was born in New York, but my parents took me to England when I was a kid. I'm trying to lose this damn accent, in order to get jobs in Hollywood. They only call me for stupid British parts."

"You've worked since you came here?"

"Why not! I'm an American citizen. Actually, I've only done two bits. One in a bloody awful feature, the other a lousy television series. I'm beginning to suspect I should've stayed in London where I was getting rather good parts in the West End playing Americans . . ."

"That's a fine dog."

"He's a bit nuts. Spooks all the time. Typical of his breed. A mouse sneezes in the attic and he spooks. He's grandpa's dog, not mine. But he won't leave me, day or night, now the old boy's missing."

"Any idea where your grandfather could've gone?"

"Not the foggiest. We never tell each other where we're going. Larry doesn't snoop into my private life, and I'm not interested in his, if he has one . . ."

"Did the dog hear those shots fired into your garage doors?"

"I doubt it. That's the only other thing he does. Sleep. He's never awake more than two hours any given day. Look at him . . ."

Zeke glanced down and saw the dog's head resting on his enormous paws, eyes hidden behind a fringe of hair. He could be asleep or, more likely, watching the intruder.

"Grandpa named him Rip Van Winkle when he was a puppy. Everybody calls him Rip."

Rip's tail moved slightly, hearing his name, but he didn't bother to raise his head.

"Did you hear the shots? Monday night or, more likely, early Tuesday morning?"

"Neither of us did. Grandpa or I. Our bedrooms face the street."

"Who was the first to notice those bullet holes?"

"He was. When he went down, late Tuesday morning, to get his car."

"What did he do?"

"Came back up here and poured himself a drink. I'd never seen him do that before. I was eating breakfast and he sat at the table with me, as he drank it. Told me the bullet holes were a warning."

"Warning?"

"He thought somebody wanted to kill him."

"Those were his exact words?"

"Far's I remember . . . Didn't tell Faye when she phoned, because Grandpa said I mustn't tell anyone."

"Why didn't you call the police?"

"Larry said they wouldn't do anything."

"It's their job to do something. Did your grandfather say who it was wanted to kill him?"

"No . . ." Lars frowned. "He didn't mention a name."

Zeke was aware of the hesitation, the evasive look in his pale eyes. "You should've phoned the police. Told them your grandfather's missing."

"Grandpa would be furious if I did. He's got one hell of a temper."

"But he could be in danger. May even be dead."

"Dead? You're trying to scare me." He clutched the leash without realizing it and the dog pushed himself to a sitting position. "I think Grandpa's gone off somewhere, maybe with friends, and forgotten to call Mrs. Svendsen. He'll phone today."

"What if he doesn't?" He saw that the youth's face was, briefly, troubled. It was a weak face, not really handsome, a blurred version of Laurence Knight's rugged features. "Do you wear glasses?"

"Forgot to put my contacts on when I came downstairs. How could you know?"

"The way you squint. I wear contacts, myself. And, frequently, forget them. You're not telling me the truth, are you?"

"Why do you say that?"

"Your grandfather did tell you something about this person—or persons—he was afraid might kill him."

"I've already said he didn't mention any names."

"But he gave you some hint as to what it was all about. Why somebody put six slugs into those garage doors."

"No. He didn't." He twisted Rip's leash and the dog stood on his hind legs, trying to lick his face. "Stop that!" He shoved him away. "Sit, you sloppy beast. Sit! And stay."

The big dog sank to the floor and stretched out, head between his paws again.

"I've got a hunch something happened at that dinner party, when your grandfather fell off the wagon."

"Know about that, do you?"

"I'm going to see Paul Victor when I leave here. Find out who was there and what happened."

"Paul's a creep. Piss-elegant, but a creep."

"You know him?"

"He's been here to dinner. Grandpa finds him rather amusing. His stories about the early days of Hollywood . . . Okay, Mr. Gahagan. That was your name?"

"Zeke Gahagan."

"Since you've guessed this much, I will tell you exactly what Grandpa said."

"I would appreciate that."

"He called Paul Victor a malicious old woman. Said he'd invited everybody to dinner in order to get them tight and make them talk."

"About what?"

"They were all involved, apparently, with something that happened many years ago. This dinner was to celebrate some anniversary."

"Whose anniversary?"

"He didn't elaborate. Could've been his, for all I know."

"Did he say who else was there?"

"Didn't mention any names, only that all of them were old friends. For some reason, which he didn't explain, only men were invited. Four others, in addition to Larry, but one of them didn't show up. I gathered they'd all been in the picture business."

"Your grandfather had a couple of drinks, it seems, and talked too much. Said something that let the cat out of Pandora's box."

"Mixing our metaphors, aren't we? Yes. He apparently, did say something that upset the others."

"Gave you no hint what it was?"

"Only that he had to warn somebody about what he'd said. Grandpa shouldn't have had those two drinks. He'd stopped drinking while Grandma was alive."

"Did he say who it was he had to warn?"

"He mentioned a name but I don't remember what it was. I'd never heard it before. I suspect it might be somebody from his past. You don't think this person has killed him, do you?"

"I certainly hope not."

"I only came to California because of Larry. My mother thought, from his letters, that he was lonely in his old age. He's eighty, you know . . ."

"I'm a year older."

"Are you?" The blue eyes narrowed. "You look, maybe, sixty . . . I thought Larry would help me get started in Hollywood but he hasn't done a damn thing. Only jobs I've had came through friends in my acting class."

"Maybe he doesn't have contacts any more."

"I'm beginning to believe that. When I mention names to him—young producers and directors—he's never heard of them."

"When you get to our age, son, you loose touch with people. Even old friends. And, through no fault of yours, some of them die." Zeke got to his feet, aware that the dog's head had lifted, eyes watching from behind their fringe of hair. "Did you find any bullets inside those garages?"

"Didn't look. They were aimed so high they missed my MG and didn't hit Grandpa's Cadillac or the end garage where his old Rolls is kept."

"Whose doors did they hit?"

"Mine and our housekeeper's. Mrs. Svendsen has a Toyota. They missed both of them."

"So the gunman didn't know which garage your grandfather uses. The police'll want those bullets."

"Police?"

"If anything's happened to your grandfather, Hollywood Division will swarm all over this place." He started across the library toward the open doors. "I may want to see you again."

"I was afraid of that."

Glancing back, Zeke saw that the lanky figure in the pale yellow silk robe had slumped lower on the sofa, a picture of dejection. He had, curiously, shown no real anxiety about his missing grandfather. Probably disappointed about what would happen to his career now.

The poor bastard, obviously, had no talent. For anything . . .

Chapter 5

Zeke eased the Chevy up San Ysidro Drive, behind the pink stucco Beverly Hills Hotel, until he found the second address Faye had given him.

A large tree-shaded house, cream-colored with yellow awnings and a small front garden bright with flowers, behind a low brick wall. Everything so neat it looked freshly painted and recently dusted.

He slowed past the gate and parked.

This was a familiar area. If he continued on, he could turn off into Pickfair Way which led to the big estate where Mary Pickford and Douglas Fairbanks had lived and entertained.

Sat for a moment, only his eyes moving, studying the quiet residential street with its endless green lawns. No sign of life, except for a green Sparkletts truck parked farther up the hill.

These immaculate lawns in Beverly Hills always had the color of freshly printed money.

He didn't look forward to the next half hour. Questioning Paul Victor would be much tougher than getting information from Laurence Knight's grandson.

Victor was one of the film colony's oldest and most respected figures. Famous for his sharp tongue and the successful films he'd made with top women stars. He had checked Victor's credits in one of his reference books before leaving the apartment and was surprised by the number of features he'd directed. His career dated back to silent films and had survived into the television era. Made his last feature, another box office boffo, four years ago in England.

The World Almanac listed Paul Victor's birth as New York City, 1902, which would make him eighty-three this year.

Zeke left the Chevy, reluctantly, and walked back toward Victor's residence. Followed an immaculate cement walk, between neat flower beds—beautiful white and yellow roses—and went up spotless white marble steps to the front door. Pressed the bell button and heard chimes play a discreet melody inside. The tune was familiar. Probably from one of Victor's films.

The door was painted a curious pale jade color.

It was opened by a dignified black man with close-cropped white hair, wearing a dark gray suit, white shirt and black tie. "Yes, sir?"

"I'd like to see Mr. Victor."

"He never sees nobody without an appointment."

Zeke brought out his wallet and held up the photostat.

The man leaned forward to peer at it. "Poh-lice?"

"If Mr. Victor could spare me a few moments."

"Of course, sir. Come in, please . . ."

He entered the most beautiful house he'd ever seen. Mirrored walls, multiplying open windows, brought the flower garden into the entrance hall. There were more white and yellow roses, in crystal bowls and ceramic pots, on tables and pedestals. A pair of small antique sofas, upholstered in yellow silk, against opposite walls.

"If you'll wait here, sir. I'll inform Mr. Victor of your presence."

"You do that." He watched the dark gray suit disappear down a sunny central hall. Noticed his own image repeated in the mirrors, looking out of place in a rumpled summer jacket. Must remember to buy himself a new suit. Clothes had never been of much interest, although he did like nice ties. He straightened his tie as he saw a dark gray suit reflected in several mirrors and turned to face the smiling houseman.

"He'll see you, sir. If you'll permit me to guide you . . ."

"Guide away!" Zeke followed him, through the hall—windows on both sides, open onto more flower gardens—to a side wing of the house where the houseman indicated a pair of open doors.

Entering the room was like stepping onto a studio set. He found himself facing an elegant man seated behind a small antique desk. Approaching him he was aware of a large framed painting above a white marble fireplace. A portrait of the man seated at the desk.

The real man sat in a reflected glow of light from tall windows open onto a terrace with a sweep of green lawn beyond where sprinklers were spraying small rainbows.

Victor was observing him, suspiciously, through gold-rimmed spectacles. His face was that of an ancient eagle, arched beak of a nose and hooded eyes. Narrow lips. Sparse white hair, flat as feathers against his suntanned skull. Paul Victor was wearing the most elegant jacket he'd ever seen. Pale gray tweed threaded with white. He'd been reading a letter which he put aside. "You are a policeman?" The eyes gleamed with intelligence.

"Private investigator. My name's Gahagan and I . . ."

"Gahagan? Not the 'world's oldest' . . .!"

"You've heard of me?"

"Who hasn't, in this provincial hamlet?" Rising and extending his hand. "This is, indeed, a pleasure, sir. I've a thick file in my office that I began to keep, long before somebody dubbed you the 'World's Oldest Eye' . . ."

Zeke shook the brown hand, aware of its soft flesh, and quickly relaxed the pressure of his own firm grasp.

"Started a file, years ago, when the press began to give you publicity. With the idea that, one day, I might make a film about a middle-aged private eye in Los Angeles. You were in your late fifties at the time. I visualized Burt Lancaster playing you on the screen . . ."

"Burt Lancaster!"

"You don't like Burt Lancaster?"

"I do. Very much."

"I had many such projects in those days. For years I hoped to film Willie Maugham's *Cakes and Ale* with Claude Rains and Elsa Lanchester. What a film that would've made! Nothing came of most of them because the studio moguls had no imagination. They have even less today!" Motioning toward a chair. "Sit down, Mr. Gahagan . . ."

Zeke sank, carefully, into a fragile-looking antique armchair that creaked delicately under his light weight.

"And here we are, finally, face to face. In my own home! May I offer you a glass of champagne?"

"Thanks. No."

"Coffee? Cigarette?"

"Nothing."

"Then, for God's sake, tell me—precisely—what brings you here? What do you wish from me?"

"Information."

"About what?"

"A dinner party you gave the other evening. You invited five guests. One didn't show up."

"And I detest an empty place at the dinner table. In this case, however, it was unavoidable. My dear friend phoned, late that afternoon, to say his health wouldn't permit him to join us. I do think he might've called earlier, but he's an arrogant bastard. Does exactly as he pleases, at all times. And so do I . . ."

"Your guests were male, I believe."

"The dinner had no sexual overtones—or undertones—if that's what you're suggesting. I was the only one at the table who was not, at least to my knowledge, heterosexual. All these gentlemen had one thing in common. They'd worked with a certain famous woman star. My dinner was planned to commemorate the anniversary of her death. September sixteenth, 1935 . . ."

"That's a long time."

"All of us, in spite of our advanced years, remembered the date as though it were last week. Is it that dark and unhappy event—half a century ago—which brings you here this sunny morning?"

"I'm here because one of your guests seems to have disappeared."

"What?" Victor's jaw dropped, the hooded eyes opening.

"His friend—Faye Manning, the actress—has hired me to find him."

"Such a love! Faye worked with me on several films. Tell me, for God's sake, which of my guests is missing. Faye, probably, knows all of them."

"Laurence Knight."

"Ah! I've expected something like this. Ever since Monday night."

"Have you?" Zeke realized that the director had been, unconsciously, picking up small objects from his desk, as they talked, moving them about like pieces on a chessboard. A seashell, a silver box and a glossy brown horse chestnut. "I'm told he said something, during dinner, that shocked your other guests."

"I suppose I must tell you what anniversary we were—not celebrating—observing. It was the night Kara Kolvang was murdered."

"Kara Kolvang?" He vaguely remembered the newspaper headlines.

"Her murder has never been solved."

"I know. In fact, I knew one of the detectives who worked on the case. Jack Casey. Met him when I joined the L.A.P.D. in the late thirties. Jack's been dead for years."

"I would imagine the official files of the Kolvang case repose on a dusty shelf, somewhere in the depths of Parker Center, where all such unsolved murders must be immured."

"Hundreds, every year. Most murders never get solved."

"So I've been told. Which should warm the hearts of all those good citizens planning to commit one."

He wouldn't tell Victor that the files on unsolved murders were destroyed after ten years. "Why did you give a dinner to mark the anniversary of the Kolvang murder?"

"I had, perhaps maliciously, hoped it would remind my guests of some morsel of ancient gossip or recall a long-forgotten fact which, after all these years, might reveal the murderer's identity. You see, each of us—after his fashion—had been in love with Kara."

"Including Laurence Knight?"

"Larry was her leading man in three films. One of which—*Night After Night*—I directed. All her leading men fell in love with her."

"And the other guests at your dinner? Faye didn't know who they were."

"And Larry didn't tell her? That's curious. Four others had been invited. Clem Dalby, who didn't join us, directed four films with Kara and was planning two more at the time of her unfortunate death. Then there was Erik Wulff who composed all the songs she sang—words, as well as music—even before Kara came to this country. Such enchanting songs! Kevin Mallon wrote the screenplays for two of her best pictures and Henri Neri who was Kara's favorite art director. Always designed her costumes. They were invited to dinner because they are, possibly, the five people—still alive—who knew her best. I'd adored her, long before her arrival in California.

"It was a fascinating evening. We drank many toasts to Kara's memory. Told endless personal stories about her. She was a genuine original. One of the first authentic international stars. A great actress and singer . . .

"Champagne flowed, Monday night, like the fountains of the Place de la Concorde. Larry was the only one who got drunk but he didn't touch the champagne. Actually, he drank less than any of us—one glass of Vouvray and a single cognac—but he'd been on the wagon for years. The cognac must've hit him because, suddenly, he began to talk. And what he said was completely unexpected . . ."

"Yes?"

"He told us he had talked to someone, years ago, who claimed to know who killed Kara Kolvang."

"He named this person?"

"A man known as Tim Kerrigan."

"Did you question Mr. Knight about him?"

"Didn't have to. I listened to the others. Kevin Mallon was the most persistent. Writers always have to know motives for everything. Kevin kept at him until Larry rose from the table, knocked his chair over and, after graciously thanking me for dinner—ever the gentleman—stumbled out into the garden and headed for his car. I sent my houseman in pursuit to see that he could start the motor and, presently, we heard his Cadillac take off down the hill. I rang his residence yesterday morning and was informed he was sleeping late. Which didn't surprise me."

"He, apparently, remembered when he woke up what he'd told you and your guests. I suppose they've each told several others."

Victor shrugged and smiled, sardonically. "I, too, am guilty. Phoned half a dozen friends, Monday night, before I retired. Told them what Larry said."

"Somebody must've contacted this Kerrigan person who then got in touch with somebody else—perhaps the killer—because later that night or, more likely, early next morning, someone gave Laurence Knight a warning to keep quiet."

"What sort of warning?"

"Six bullets."

"Six . . . My God!"

"Fired into his garage doors. Knight found the bullet holes when he went down to get his car. No one, including his housekeeper, heard the shots."

"So my little dinner party was a success!" He smiled again. "Did Larry notify the police about those bullets?"

"No, he didn't. I suspect he's much too frightened. He went to see Faye Manning and told her he'd been threatened."

"Did he tell Faye who he thought might do such a thing?"

"He told her very little. Promised to call her next day, yesterday, but never did. She phoned his home and nobody—his grandson or their housekeeper—had heard from him. Faye contacted me last night. Informed me about this dinner of yours."

"And, starting with me, you will question everyone who dined here."

"Perhaps you'll be good enough to tell me how to reach your other three guests."

"Delighted to do so." He picked up an address book bound in silver and green brocade. Opened it, as he talked, reaching for pad and pen. "So you think it was this Kerrigan person or his murderous friend who warned Larry to keep quiet with a fusillade of bullets?"

"Something like that . . ."

"Which would suggest that Larry is, indeed, in real danger. He may have fled to Mexico and gone undercover. When you have money you can buy a new identity. Although a famous actor isn't apt to do that because of his ego. Much more likely to change his appearance." He was writing as he talked. "Every actor knows how to do that."

"Or he may be dead."

"You don't think . . ."

"I must anticipate every possibility."

"Of course." Victor ripped a page from his pad and handed it across the desk. "Here we are. Addresses and unlisted phone numbers for my other three guests, as well as the one who stayed away. You may wish to talk to him—Clement Dalby—because he directed four of Kara's films. Clem hasn't made a feature in years. His health's much too precarious. Those wild days and glorious nights of his youth seem to have caught up with him. All those little starlets, his many accidents—mostly with horses—and the heavy drinking. Clem rarely leaves his ranch any more . . ."

"I will, certainly, contact Mr. Dalby." He folded the small page and slipped it into a pocket. "And I would be grateful if you could tell me of any other intimates of Kara Kolvang who might be helpful . . ."

"I don't recall anyone at the moment, but there must be others. Still alive . . . She had a younger sister but I've not the slightest idea what happened to her."

"Her name?"

"I don't recall. She'd married, so it was a different name. I suppose you should read everything you can find on Kara's murder. This is really incredible! I've only just realized . . ."

"Yes?"

"To find Larry Knight you may have to locate this Kerrigan person who claims to know the identity of Kara's murderer . . ."

"That's possible."

"You may even find out who killed Kara Kolvang!"

"Well, I don't plan . . ."

"All because I gave a little dinner party." He clasped his hands together. "I've kept a file on Kara since her early days in Europe."

"For what reason?"

"I found her utterly fascinating. The publicity and the films, long before she came to Hollywood, had intrigued me. Her fantastic beauty. The blazing talent. She'd had a spectacular career in Paris. Cabaret, stage and films. There were some important properties I hoped to film with Kara in the leading roles."

"I would like to see this file of yours."

"Would you? There must be several rather fat folders. I'd be honored to let you borrow them. But you must swear to return them intact. Every photograph and clipping."

"Of course."

"Hold on." He snatched up a white phone and jabbed a button, his eyes on Zeke. "Aggie? I want everything we have in our files on Kara Kolvang. There's a gentleman with me, in the study, who wishes to borrow all that material for several days. Put it in one large envelope. Hop to it, love. We shall be waiting." He put the phone down. "Aggie's my secretary, curator, and guardian of the files. Complete records of everything I've ever done, as well as the projects I planned, those brilliant ideas that never came to fruition. One day it will all go to some university but, at the moment, it occupies an entire wing of this house. The artifacts of a peculiar civilization called Hollywood—from 1922, the year I arrived, bursting with talent, from New York—until I die." He stopped short. "Dear me! I suppose all my dinner guests will be under suspicion. Involved with the Kolvang murder. Even I!"

"That investigation will not be reopened. I assure you."

Victor smiled, benignly. "I wonder . . ."

"Fifty years is a long time. The L.A.P.D. would have no interest in such an old case. Clues will have evaporated, evidence lost or misplaced."

"And you, sir . . ."

"I only want to find one missing person. Laurence Knight. That's all I'm being paid to do."

Victor's eyes became crafty. "What if I were to offer you the job of tracking down Kara's murderer? Ferret out his identity. Even if he's long dead . . ."

"That would take months of plodding. Endless false leads and dead ends. No certainty I'd ever turn up a damn thing. No, thank you."

"To find Larry Knight you have to locate Tim Kerrigan . . . That might open a whole can of butterflies!"

"Why do you say that?"

"Larry has, I should think, tried to reach Kerrigan about what was said here. That he told several people that he—Kerrigan—knew the identity of Kara's murderer."

"And who is Tim Kerrigan?"

"He was a minor, rather curious member of the film colony, back in the early thirties. An Irish youth with startling red hair and the most extraordinary musculature. Even for this overstated town."

"An actor?"

"Not really. He'd been an amateur boxer, with some success, and was hired to play a pugilist in a Broadway show. That's when I first noticed him. This was in the late twenties. After the show closed, like many others in those days, Tim caught a train to Hollywood. Unfortunately, he had no talent and his speech was vintage Brooklyn. To survive, I suppose, he became a masseur and bodyguard. Worked for many of the big stars—male and female—as well as producers and directors. I barely knew him but many of my friends took advantage of his special services . . .

"I encountered him, frequently, at their swimming pools and less exclusive parties. He was always ingratiating. Extremely shrewd! That's how he survived for so many years. Long after his curly hair turned gray and the muscles flabbed. People confided in him as he kneaded their imperfect flesh. Louella was one of them! Always overweight. He gave her many items. Tim knew everybody's secrets including, it would seem, who murdered Kara Kolvang . . ."

"What became of him?"

"I've no idea. Until Monday night I hadn't heard Tim Kerrigan's name mentioned in years. People constantly vanish in Hollywoodland and nobody asks questions. Some of the biggest stars." He'd been moving objects around on his desk again as he talked but now he was staring at his graceful hands, resting on the desk in front of him.

Zeke smiled and waited. What a vain man! Admiring his own hands.

"I've just thought of something. Two things . . ."

"Yes?" He saw that the hands were moving, picking up other objects and fondling them.

"First, about Larry Knight . . ."

As he waited for Victor to continue he recalled what Hammett had said, long ago, about Kara Kolvang's murder. "They'll never find the guy. Never . . ." Dash was, probably, right.

"The police, at first, suspected Larry had killed her . . ." Victor's voice was low, as he put his thoughts in order. "He was drinking heavily in those days. They learned that he and Kara had quarreled the afternoon before she was killed. They'd been doing some dubbing—this was the last feature Kara made—*Park Avenue Girl*—and they suddenly started shouting at each other. She accused him of being drunk and causing production delays. Which was, I suppose, true . . .

"The police found out about this when they questioned people at the studio after her murder. Newspapers carried hints that Larry was being questioned. There was some delay because he had an enormous hangover and when he came out of it had no memory of the previous night. He and his wife had hosted a dinner party and their guests gave him an alibi. He'd been there all evening, getting loaded.

"This was after he'd been drinking that afternoon and spoiled the dubbing session, causing Kara to explode. She was a perfectionist in every phase of her work. Always the first person on the shooting stage. The police had to issue an official statement that Laurence Knight was not a suspect. Actually he was the first and only one. They never came up with another."

"You think he killed her?"

"No way. Larry wouldn't kill anybody. Which brings me to my other thought. The only person close to Kara who might've murdered her—many of their friends made nasty jokes about this—was Kurt von Zemmering."

"Who the hell's that?"

"Kurt was the manager who discovered Kara in a Copenhagen cabaret and put her under contract for a stage show he was producing in Paris. He was Kara's agent and manager until she died. Produced all her films in France and Hollywood. Everyone of them was a Kurt von Zemmering production. He came to America with Kara. Some of the French papers called him her Svengali. Garbo had Stiller, Dietrich had von Sternberg and Kolvang had von Zemmering . . ."

Zeke was aware that Victor's busy fingers continued to rearrange the objects on his desk. "What happened to this man?"

"He returned to Europe—supposedly to Vienna—soon after Kara's death and, far's I know, didn't make another film. I never heard of him again. Except for rumor and gossip. He'd claimed to be an Austrian, but some of us suspected he was German. Although there was one report he had died in a concentration camp. Nobody ever learned the truth. His entire life appears to have been made up of myths. A true man of mystery. Yet he could always come up with enormous sums of money to produce a spectacular opérette in Paris or a major film in Hollywood. Every feature that starred Kara—in France and America—made Kurt another fortune."

"And you think this man—von Zemmering—might have killed her?"

Victor shrugged. "The papers said he was in New York the night she died in California. Several people saw him there. At the theater and afterward, dining at the Plaza, with an unidentified woman."

"Were they lovers? He and Kara Kolvang?"

"They were loving and affectionate, certainly, but I doubt they were ever lovers. Too much of an age difference. Kara was only twenty-one when she died and Kurt must've been in his late fifties. Possibly older. A tremendously tall man. Perhaps six feet four. I've only known two men who looked truly elegant in top hat and tails. Kurt and Fred Astaire. I'd seen pictures of Kurt, in foreign magazines, long before he came to Hollywood. At the opera or some famous restaurant. Always with a beautiful woman. Frequently opera stars like Mary Garden or Jeritza. I've heard Europeans call him Count von Zemmering . . ."

"Was he a Count?"

"Who can say? In those years—the early thirties—film royalty liked to entertain European royalty. From the Prince of Wales to the Queen of Rumania. Many of them dined up the road from here at Pickfair. Some were fakes. If Kurt was a phony, he was a splendid phony." He reached across his desk to pick up a small rectangular box. "This belonged to Kara."

Zeke saw that it was made of some kind of milky stone, the lid edged with shiny metal.

"Kurt gave it to her. A cigarette box made of chalcedony, the lid rimmed in gold. I bought it when her possessions were sold at auction." He raised the lid with a forefinger.

The box was empty.

"My only physical memento of an exquisite lady." He closed

the lid and set the box down, gently, as he glanced toward the door. "Here's Aggie! Come in, love . . ."

Zeke looked around to see a squat woman with short gray hair wearing a tailored white jacket over yellow slacks.

"Here's your Kolvang file." Striding across the room with a large manila envelope. "Everything we have about her. One folder covers the European career and four contain the Hollywood years."

"Thanks, Aggie." Victor took the envelope and set it on the desk. "I'm sure Mr. Gahagan will return it intact."

"I noticed in the television schedules that PBS is showing a Kara Kolvang film this week. The last one she made?"

"Which night?" Zeke asked.

She faced him. "Friday, I think. It's the only Kolvang film that's been shown in years. I shall certainly catch it." Turning to Victor again. "Curious your wanting her file today."

"Not at all, my sweet." Victor smiled smugly. "Monday night was the anniversary of her death."

"Was it? I'd forgotten. Of course, I wasn't born when the lady was killed."

"Mr. Gahagan is a detective who, I hope, may turn up the identity of her murderer."

"Gahagan?" She whirled to stare at him. "The 'world's oldest' . . . ?"

"So they say, ma'am."

"We have a file on you." She stuck out her hand. "A great honor, Inspector Gahagan."

Zeke got to his feet and shook the muscular brown paw. "My pleasure, ma'am."

"Detective novels are my favorite reading. One day, I plan to write one myself. Knock off a few people I don't like. Thinly disguised, of course." Glancing at Victor. "Not you, love. Mustn't interrupt any longer." She nodded toward Zeke as she left them.

He faced the desk, his eyes on the bulky envelope.

"You do make people confess things, don't you?" Victor's tone was serious. "I'd no idea Aggie planned to write a detective novel. And, knowing Aggie, she just may do it." He picked up the heavy envelope with both hands and held it out. "Hope this may be helpful."

"Thank you, sir." Zeke took the envelope.

"Will you keep me informed? What you find out about Larry Knight . . ."

"I'll call you."

"Let me give you my private number."

"I already have it."

"You would." Victor chuckled as he rose from the desk. "Been delightful, sir. Talking to you. I suppose you'll locate Tim Kerrigan?"

"I'll certainly make every effort."

"I hope you can persuade him to talk. Tell you who killed Kara . . ."

"Old murders should remain buried. I'm looking for one person—Laurence Knight." He turned away, envelope in hand, and went toward the door.

"What if Kerrigan names one of my guests as the murderer?"

"You needn't worry, sir. I don't think you're the type would murder anyone."

"I rather resent that. I've considered murdering several people, in my time . . ."

Zeke smiled as he went through the door.

Chapter 6

He turned off San Vicente, down Fifteenth Street, checking the numbers of each private residence. The one he wanted was painted on a wooden gate in a low adobe wall and the house, beyond a shallow garden, was imitation early-California roofed with apricot tiles.

No drive leading to a garage, so if Erik Wulff was home he must be parked in the street. There were several crumpled foreign cars, bumper to bumper, along the curb.

He found an empty space for his Chevy and walked back.

These were one-story houses, old and comfortable-looking.

He pushed the creaking gate open and went up a pebbled walk, between overgrown flower beds in which yellow mini-mums bloomed. The windows, including a large arched one, were curtained. As he approached the entrance he heard a woman singing. The words were German and the melody was unmistakably Schubert. A trained voice, sweet and pleasant.

When he rang the bell the song was silenced and a dog began to bark.

Small dog, from the sound.

The barking came close to the door.

Zeke stepped back as the door opened.

A Yorkie shot out, dancing and yipping.

"Don't be afraid of Wolfie! He has no teeth."

He saw that she was an extremely beautiful woman, tall with auburn hair. Slightly overweight, in her fifties or older, wearing some kind of flowered muumuu with too much jewelry. "I'd like to see Mr. Erik Wulff, if he's free."

"Does he know you?"

Even her speaking voice was musical. "No. He doesn't." He pulled out his wallet and showed her the photostat.

"Lieber Gott! Another traffic ticket?"

"Nothing like that, ma'am. This concerns a dinner, Monday night, given by Mr. Paul Victor."

"I told Erik he shouldn't go! He hadn't heard from Paul in years, then this sudden invitation. And no ladies invited. Very suspicious . . ." Pushing the door back. "Erik's in his studio and I am Madame Krauss. I must tell you, Erik doesn't mean to break your American laws. He is good citizen, but lousy driver." She closed the door and went ahead through a dim and narrow hall, past several closed doors.

Zeke followed, passing rows of framed photographs which covered the walls. All of them, men and women, were smiling professionally.

"You are first American policeman ever to come here. Erik will be amused."

The dog darted ahead, barking again.

"No, Wolfie! No noise. Erik is working."

"Is your dog named for Mr. Wulff?"

"Certainly not. Wolfie's named after a genius—Wolfgang Mozart—who, also, loved dogs." She grasped the knob of a door and flung it back. "Liebchen! Here's a gentleman from the police to see you."

"Not the police, ma'am. I'm a private investigator." He followed her into a high-ceilinged white-walled room where a pink-faced little man sat at a large table covered with music scores, a small upright piano beside him.

The chubby composer, pencil in hand, looked up and smiled. "It's Inspector Gahagan! I am, already, expecting you."

"Expecting him?" Madame Krauss seemed surprised.

Wulff rose, dropping his pencil onto the table, holding out a plump hand. "Welcome, sir. I had a phone call from Paul Victor. He tells me you are on your way, and what you want from me."

"Did he?" Shaking Wulff's hand. "That was kind of him."

"Will somebody please tell me what's happening?" Madame Krauss asked.

Wulff chuckled. "It seems, Lottie, one of my fellow guests at that dinner party, Monday night, has disappeared."

"Thank God it wasn't you! Which one is it?"

"Larry Knight."

"That sweet man. Ach! So handsome. Such a voice . . ."

"Could you bring us some coffee, liebchen?"

"Right away." She hurried toward the door, the Yorkie scampering at her heels.

"Please . . ." Wulff motioned to a chair.

Zeke glanced around, quickly, as he sank into the armchair. Saw another piano, a baby grand, near windows open onto a sunny garden, many pictures on the walls—more portraits, photographs and paintings. An elaborate record player with stacked albums and piles of music scores.

"So Larry Knight really is missing?" Wulff asked.

He faced the composer across his worktable. "Since Tuesday. Day before yesterday."

"And Faye Manning has asked you to find him . . ."

"Mr. Victor told you everything."

"I never knew Larry away from the studio. Wrote the music for those three films he made with Kolvang, but I hadn't seen him in years—thirty, at least—until we met at Paul's for dinner. For that matter, I hadn't seen Paul since we did a picture together back in the sixties. Except to run into him at Farmers Market or some restaurant. Lottie's such a good cook I prefer dining at home. We give intimate dinners. Dear friends, mostly musicians. European artists in Los Angeles for a concert, along with a few composers and their wives . . ."

As Wulff talked, Zeke studied him. A roly-poly chipmunk of a man. Round head covered with tight white curls which he fingered as he talked, pulling them apart then pushing them into place again. Intelligent blue eyes, florid complextion. Constantly smiling.

". . . and, of course, all of us were shocked when Larry, out of the blue, announced he knew someone who claimed to have known who murdered Kara. He had seemed completely sober to me. A glass of wine during dinner but then he tossed off a cognac. That's when he began to talk. Such a flood of words! And, suddenly, realizing he'd said too much, he jumped up from the table and fled . . ."

"I'm not interested in who killed this Kolvang woman. I've been hired to find Laurence Knight. Nothing more."

"I've always hoped that, one day, the mystery of Kara's death might be solved, the killer revealed. She was such an exquisite creature. Everybody loved her."

"Did you?"

"Of course! We had a charming affair in Paris when we were young. Before either of us came to California, where our relationship was resumed, briefly. Karen was one of those Continental stars the studios brought to Hollywood. Garbo talked and laughed but Kara Kolvang could, also, sing and dance. Her real name was Karen Jensen. That's the name she used in her

European films, as well as the revues and opérette she did on the Paris stage. The Folies-Bergère and the Mogador . . ."

"Why did she change her name?"

"The American studio heads insisted when she signed their contracts. She agreed but nobody—even her personal press agent—came up with a name she liked. Karen wanted to keep her first name but was willing to change the Jensen if they would suggest something better. This went on for many months. Until one summer night in Solvang . . ."

"Solvang?"

"This is a Danish village, north of Santa Barbara . . ."

"I know where it is. Although I've never been there. What did Solvang have to do with her name?"

"We used to drive up there, in the early thirties, for a weekend away from Los Angeles. Many of the European colony, but especially the Scandinavians. At that time Solvang was only two cross streets with a few shops and restaurants. We could have a glorious weekend in complete privacy without anyone prying or bothering us with questions. Excellent food and good local wines. The public hadn't discovered Solvang and we could do as we pleased. Most of us rented cottages outside the village. Which was even more private.

"There must've been a dozen of us, this night, dancing in the moonlight. Karen was with several friends at a long table, eating dinner, under an arbor hung with lighted lanterns. Somebody, *comme toujours*, asked her when she was going to change her name and Karen said she would when the studio came up with a better one. Somebody, finally, said, 'Why not Karen Solvang?' And somebody else called out 'Kara Kolvang!' Nobody could remember, next morning, who it was. Karen liked the name and, when she returned to Hollywood, informed the studio heads that, in the future, she would be Kara Kolvang. And that's the name she used in all her American films."

"Am I interrupting?"

"You are, liebchen. But we can use that coffee."

Zeke watched Madame Krauss balance a painted tray holding a large pottery coffeepot, two mugs and a plate of sliced coffee cake.

"I baked kuchen this morning." Resting her tray in front of Wulff. "Little thinking it would be eaten by the police."

"Looks good, ma'am, but I'm afraid I can only have coffee. Don't even take sugar in my coffee."

"What a pity!"

"That coffee, however, smells like the real thing."

"Lottie makes the best coffee in Santa Monica." Wulff was filling the mugs as he talked. "Where's the little monster?"

"In the kitchen. Eating a very small slice of kuchen."

"Which is why he has no teeth."

"Enjoy your coffee, Herr Inspektor."

"Thank you, ma'am." His eyes followed her plump figure toward the door.

Wulff handed him a mug across the table. "Black for the law."

Zeke took the mug, savoring the aroma of the coffee. "Your wife's a mighty handsome woman, Mr. Wulff."

"Yes. My wife's a real beauty, but she's in Vienna. Gott sei dank! She won't come to America. Lottie's been my mistress for many years. I could not survive twenty-four hours without her. She was a famous lyric soprano in Europe but, after fifty, the voice diminishes." Splashing cream into his coffee as he talked, adding three heaping spoons of sugar. "When my wife dies, I marry Lottie. Meanwhile . . ." He shrugged. "We have good life. All three of us."

Zeke sipped the coffee and relaxed for a moment.

Wulff was carefully stirring the sugar in his cup. "To get back to Kara . . . You probably know—I wrote all the songs she sang. Every one of them! First in Paris, then Hollywood. We arrived when talkies had taken over and big musicals were popular. Every

Kolvang film was a tremendous success. Especially those with Larry Knight . . ."

"Do you have any idea, Mr. Wulff, where he might be?"

"None."

"Or where I could locate this man he mentioned—Tim Kerrigan—who, it seems, knows who killed Kara Kolvang?"

"I hadn't heard of Tim in years, until Monday night. He used to come here, twice a week, to give me massage. He fought a losing battle with Lottie, trying to keep my weight down. Lottie won."

"What can you tell me about him?"

Wulff shrugged. "Everyone liked the guy. Women because he told them the latest studio gossip, who was sleeping where. The men because he knew about sports, the horse racing and the prize fights . . ."

"Any idea where I could locate him?"

"I'm afraid not. I looked through an old address book yesterday, thinking I still had his phone number but I must've thrown it away many years ago. I don't remember where he lived, if I ever knew . . ."

"Where do you suppose Larry Knight could be hiding?"

"You think he's hiding, do you? Because of what he told us?"

"That's a strong possibility. Something caused him to disappear. He may have gone to look for Kerrigan. Warn him about what was said."

"Did Paul tell you the reason for his giving that dinner party?"

"He said it was to commemorate the anniversary of Kara Kolvang's death."

"That's what he told us early in the evening but later, at dinner, he announced that he planned to make a new film and wanted all of us to work on it with him. I was to compose a score from the hit songs I wrote for Kara. I've been sorting through them this morning. Such memories . . ." He gestured toward the scores spread out in front of him. "Henri Neri would design the production and, of course, Kevin Mallon will write the script. We discussed this through dinner with tremendous enthusiasm. Paul wants to make one last big feature before he dies—as do we all—a musical about the life, career, and death of Kara Kolvang."

"He didn't mention any of this to me."

"I suppose Paul doesn't want his idea to get around. Somebody else could grab the material. Except nobody knows as much about Kara as our little group seated at that dinner table. Which is why Paul wanted Clem Dalby there. Clem directed Kara in four films—more than any other director—but, unfortunately, he wasn't able to join us. Paul felt Clem could contribute many ideas to such a project. You must talk to Clem . . ."

"I intend to."

"If he'll see you. I'm told he never invites anyone to his ranch in Mandeville Canyon any more. How our lives change as we get older! Clem used to be very social when his wife was alive. They gave big parties every weekend. Polo followed by an enormous barbecue. I was surprised when Paul told me, on the phone, that Clem had accepted his dinner invitation but then, of course, he never showed up. Paul was furious . . ."

As Wulff ate a slice of coffee cake, Zeke wondered why Paul Victor hadn't mentioned that he was going to make a film about Kara Kolvang?

Could the disappearance of Laurence Knight have been staged? Part of a plan to get publicity for Victor's proposed picture?

"Was Larry Knight to be involved in this film?" Zeke asked.

"Oh, yes! Paul wanted Larry's advice, of course, and arranged for him to have long talks with Kevin. Larry agreed to spend several days with him to reminisce about Kara. Put it on tape. Larry was like a brother to Kara. I've always thought she was in love with him but Larry was happily married. Wouldn't it be curious if Larry was the only man Kara really loved?"

"I suppose you, also, knew Kurt von Zemmering?"

"Nobody ever knew Kurt. He was a man of mystery. I worked

with him in Paris when he produced revues and opérette for the theater and, later on, Kurt brought me to Hollywood . . ."

"There seems to be some question about what happened to this man."

"I've heard every kind of rumor. The most persistent seems to be that he wasn't Austrian. I'd always suspected he was German. I heard he went to Berlin and became a powerful figure in the Third Reich. I doubt Kurt is alive. He would be a very old man. I had a letter, years ago, from a friend—a concert pianist—who claimed he'd seen Kurt in Rio where he was managing some ballet company and using another name. That certainly sounds like Kurt. Who knows? He was a mystery man to the end."

"Do you think it's possible this Kerrigan man does know the identity of Kara Kolvang's murderer?"

"Tim knew everything about everybody. All the inside gossip. Paul Victor could tell you more about Tim than I."

"Why do you say that?"

"In the old days—as well as today—Paul lived on gossip and Tim Kerrigan was one of his chief sources. I suspect Paul paid him a weekly retainer. Not only as his masseur but as a waiter, whenever he gave a large dinner, or lifeguard when there was an afternoon party around the pool. Tim was always his chauffeur, in a smart uniform, whenever Paul took some lovely actress to a premiere . . ."

"They were friends? Paul Victor and Tim Kerrigan?"

"More like Hollywood prince and his court jester. They used to say Paul Victor didn't have a friend."

"Thank you for the coffee." Zeke was frowning, puzzled, as he got to his feet.

Paul Victor had said he barely knew Tim Kerrigan.

Chapter 7

Zeke continued to frown as he drove up the Coast Highway.

He had learned nothing of importance, as yet, about Laurence Knight. Not a clue as to where he might've gone.

But he was learning a great deal about Kara Kolvang. More than he wanted to know.

Interesting but confusing information about Kurt von Zemmering . . .

Driving toward Malibu he glanced up at Thelma Todd's old cafe and wondered if the flight of steep steps was still there, leading to the top of the palisade. Another early star whose death was never fully explained. In the bright afternoon sunlight the complex of low buildings looked freshly painted. He'd heard that some priest was making films there for television. Religious films . . .

Next on his list was Kevin Mallon. The scriptwriter . . .

He realized, after a moment, that he was whistling.

What was the tune?

Whistling it again.

"They Didn't Believe Me . . ." He said the words aloud.

Why would he be whistling that?

Faye! She said, last night, she still sang Jerome Kern's songs.

He and Hammett used to sing them in San Francisco, standing around Nell Martin's piano. That pretty music teacher Dash was seeing . . .

Hammett had moved into an apartment, away from his wife and two daughters, because of his tuberculosis.

Then, when his health got better, he took off for New York with Nell.

She was a bright and classy dame, but so was Jose, his wife.

Hammett had told him, that night Faye saw them at the Derby, that Nell only lasted a couple of years.

He never understood Hammett's fickle attitude toward women. There were dozens of others after Nell, Dash had boasted, and he was still married to Jose.

Zeke frowned.

His own marriages had lasted for years, all four of them, and he'd never played around. Each of his wives divorced him because he spent more time on his investigations than he did with them. Their lives had become impossible, they said in court, incompatible. He was a stranger.

Maybe so . . .

Remember to call Emma next week.

He slowed through the center of Malibu, found Mallon's address and made a fast turn off the highway. Parked south of the writer's pseudo-Mediterranean villa, which looked like a flimsy movie set, and walked back toward the entrance.

This was an open stretch of sand, before the film colony discovered it and built their expensive hideaways, in every style of bastard architecture.

The beach was barely visible now, between two properties, in a glare of sunlight. Two girls, wearing string bikinis, tossing a large rubber ball.

He could remember when decent women wouldn't stick their noses out into the sun. They wore floppy straw hats to protect their delicate skins and sat in the shade under large parasols.

Walking past Mallon's open carport—where an old gray Cadillac, a red Toyota station wagon and a yellow Volkswagen were parked—he continued on, along a high redwood fence, to the entrance gate with its painted numbers. No name displayed above the bell button. He pressed it and heard a distant buzzer.

From the position of the sun he judged it must be past one o'clock. He wasn't feeling hungry, but when he finished here he would stop by one of those fish places he liked in Santa Monica and have a bite of lunch.

The sound of padding feet became audible, behind the fence, above the susurrus of passing cars.

One of Hammett's words. Susurrus. He'd learned a lot of first-class words from Dash . . .

"Is that Gahagan, himself?" A rough baritone, from behind the gate.

Zeke grimaced at the fake Irishness. "Himself, in person."

There was the click of a lock and the gate opened.

He saw a heavyset man, deeply tanned, with tremendous shoulders and an unruly mass of white hair. "You must be Mallon . . ."

"I am that."

"And someone—Paul Victor, I suppose—called to inform you I was on my way here."

"It was Erik Wulff."

"I only left him twenty minutes ago."

"So he said."

"Then you know why I've come."

"I do." He shoved the door back. "Come in, my friend . . ."

He was always suspicious of anyone who called him their friend at first meeting.

"Come along in . . . ."

Zeke stepped across the threshold into a narrow open space, edging the whitewashed stucco villa, where tall cacti in beds of sand stretched toward a distant door that had been left open.

Mallon slammed the gate and went ahead toward the open door. "Claim to be the world's oldest eye, do you?"

"I never made such a claim. It was thrust upon me and nobody, as yet, has disproved I am." He saw that the writer was wearing a long sand-colored robe of terrycloth, hanging loose over white bathing trunks. His brown feet were bare.

"Been reading about you, these many years. Always interested in cops—especially private eyes—inasmuch as I've written a number of crime films. Erik said you're looking for two men. Larry Knight and that chap he mentioned at dinner Monday night. Tim Kerrigan." Going inside. "Enter! And welcome."

"I've been hired to find Knight but it seems, to do that, I may have to locate Kerrigan."

"Hired by the beauteous Faye Manning."

"Mr. Wulff told you everything." Glancing around the vast room as he followed Mallon toward a solid oak table-desk holding an electric typewriter. A wall of windows, facing the beach, had been partially covered by sheets of ivory-weathered sailcloth.

"Can I offer you a libation at this hour?" Mallon lowered himself into a collapsible director's chair. "I've got a bottle of Bushmills."

"Don't touch the hard stuff any more, and very little of anything else."

"Such a terrible thing, what age forces upon us. I only do a little social drinking, myself. Like Monday night." Making a broad gesture with a beefy hand. "Sit where you like."

As Zeke sank onto a cushioned rattan chair he saw pages of typing spread across the desk. "I've interrupted your work."

"I enjoy interruptions. Like Joyce, himself! The great man told Gogarty that, at one time, he enjoyed an interruption which lasted six months. He was, I suspect, jesting. Joyce never stopped writing for six months, unless his poor eyes were troubling him. I'll tell you, straight off, I've no glimmer as to what's happened to Larry. And I would suspect you should start your search for Tim Kerrigan in that curious maze of streets, south of Santa Monica pier, where you'll discover rows of rooming houses, hostels for ancient pugs, along with gyms where young muscle punks work out, hoping one day to become ancient pugs. Not too bright, any of them. Poor sods . . ."

"I know the area."

"There's one gym, more decrepit than the rest, called Cantrell's Corner, that was run for many a decade by an ex-trainer named Willie Cantrell—long since defunct—where Tim Kerrigan used to hang out. They always took messages for him. I phoned Cantrell's, yesterday, but the Mexican kid who answered had never heard of Kerrigan."

"You knew Kerrigan?"

"Not really . . . Years ago I had a terrible weight problem. Tim pummeled and pounded my unwilling body twice a week. With little success but, like his other customers, I enjoyed hearing him spin his Decamerotic tales about the famous movie stars. You realized he was making most of them up, on the spot, but his yarns were more plausible than the truth, in most cases. Never malicious, but if you knew the people involved—and I frequently did—there was always a wee kernel of veracity to what he was saying . . ."

"Why did you call him yesterday?"

"I thought it might be an act of kindness to warn him about what Larry said at dinner. In case there was more than a kernel of fact to his knowing Kara's murderer. If the killer's alive, and finds out, Tim's life could be in jeopardy. As well as Larry's."

"How long since you've had any contact with Kerrigan?"

"Ten or more years, I should think. He used to drop past here, from time to time, walk down the Coast Highway or hitch a ride. Unexpected, but not unwelcome. I would invite him in and give him a wee belt of the best. Listen to his yarns about the old days. Always slipped him a few bucks as he left."

"How much would you call a few?"

"Usually a twenty. More, if Tim looked hungry. He would promise to come back and give me a Kerrigan massage, but I knew that was only talk. He'd gotten much too frail and he knew it."

As Mallon talked, Zeke was aware of women's voices in the distance. Chattering and laughing. His eyes, without moving, noticed the comfortable furniture, the paintings and books, the pleasant disarray of a happy household.

". . . been thinking about Tim Kerrigan this morning. Wishing I could talk to him about Kara . . ."

"He knew her?"

"In some ways, I wager, better than most of us. She was a mite chubby when she arrived from Europe and the studio hired Tim to take the chub off her exquisite young body. Which he did. Kara was a great little talker and she must've told him things about herself she never told anybody else. Perhaps something that gave him an idea who might've killed her. He must've charmed Kara the same way he did the rest of us."

"Are you suggesting they had an affair?"

"I'm suggesting nothing. I won't say it wasn't possible but I'm not implying they did. In those days I suspected Tim was a virgin. There was something innocent about him, in spite of the corrupt world of the studios to which he was exposed. I had a feeling, most of the time, he didn't understand most of the scandalous gossip he repeated. Later on, of course, he wasn't quite so naive. . . ."

Zeke turned as a corner of the sailcloth curtain was raised, hot sunlight slashing across the black linoleum-tiled floor, and a young girl stepped through an open window from a terrace overlooking the beach.

"Sorry." She appeared to be startled. "Didn't know you had a guest."

"That's all right, luv," Mallon responded. "No harm done."

As Zeke watched her go toward a distant door he decided that when he left here he would postpone seeing Henri Neri—the third name on Paul Victor's list—drive back to Santa Monica, instead, and try to locate Tim Kerrigan. He saw that this young woman was strikingly beautiful. Auburn hair streaked with gold from the sun, firm brown body in a brief bathing garment, rubber cap dangling from her hand. He watched until she went through the door and heard the others greeting her as he turned back to Mallon. He, too, had been observing her, smiling, waiting until she left before resuming their conversation.

Mallon sighed. "Oh, to be young again . . ."

"You have a beautiful wife."

"Wife? That's my grandchild. Eldest of three. She's visiting us from Boston. My wife's in the kitchen, murdering several lobsters for dinner."

"You were born in Ireland?"

"Dublin. But, at an early age, I had a rather scandalous novel published in London and, immediately, moved there."

"You said you wanted to talk to Kerrigan about Kara Kolvang?"

"I do, indeed. I've started a rough treatment for a screenplay." He indicated the pages of typing scattered across his work table. "The life of Kara Kolvang. Her life and her death . . ."

"For this film Paul Victor plans to direct?"

"Direct and produce. Paul's even raising the money for this one. He's a wildly talented man. I've done scripts for him, in the past, so I know. A man of taste, which is mighty scarce in the film business. One of the last of the great directors. I had no idea, when I went to dinner, that he was going to get us involved in a film about Kara. I'd forgotten it was the anniversary of her death. There hadn't been anything in the papers. Kara was a top star but even the brightest of them don't shine for fifty years. Today nobody remembers Marguerite Clark, Agnes Ayers or Lilyan Tashman. Stars, all of them, fifty years ago . . ."

Zeke smiled. "I remember them. I knew Lilyan Tashman."

"Did you? Paul's convinced that a film about Kara—made honestly, not camped—with everything true to the period, could be a box-office smash. He's paying me to work out the story line and write a preliminary script. Henri Neri will be designing the sets and costumes and Erik Wulff's in charge of the music. Paul told us about his project during dinner. Naturally, all of us were surprised. But delighted."

"Would there be a part in this film for Laurence Knight? Perhaps play himself?"

"Too many years have passed for Larry to carry that off. Paul wanted him to help with the screenplay. Give me his ideas. Larry knew Kara intimately, from her first days in Hollywood. Was her leading man in three films, including the last. He was cautious at first but, finally, agreed to drive down here and talk about Kara. Answer all my questions regarding incidents in her life where he was involved. Paul offered to pay him but he wouldn't accept a dime. Said he would do anything he could to help us tell the truth about Kara."

"I suppose you knew Kurt von Zemmering . . ."

"That arrogant bastard! I worked for him but never liked him. And he was aware of it. He will, unfortunately, play a major role in the film. God knows who Paul will find to play him! Pity Basil Rathbone isn't alive. Nobody ever knew where Kurt came from. Kara told me no one knew who he really was. He had one thing going for him in California. An endless supply of money. Gave him instant stature. Opened all doors. It was rumored his wealth—remember, this was the early thirties—came from German munitions manufacturers . . ."

"Why didn't you like him?"

"He was a fake. Under all that arrogance—the elegant gloss and glitter—Kurt was a genuine phony. Even his accent wasn't for real. Sometimes he'd forget it and then he sounded British. Cockney British . . ."

"You think he could've murdered Kara Kolvang?"

"He could have, but I don't believe he did."

"Why not?"

"He didn't impress me as having the guts for violence. He was a soft man. I could've put my fist through him. And, frequently, had the urge."

"Any idea what happened to him?"

"The police questioned him, naturally, regarding the murder but he claimed he was in New York that night. Witnesses confirmed that fact. He stayed in Hollywood for a few months after Kara died then, suddenly, he simply wasn't here any more. No one knew when he left the country or where he'd gone. Nobody, far's I know, ever heard from him again.

"I suspect the bastard went back to wherever he came from, originally, and spent the remainder of his days looking at Kara. He must've had prints of every film she made. He'd always been photographed with beautiful women, opera and film stars, but I never heard anyone—even Tim Kerrigan—say he had affairs with them. I've a hunch the guy might've been impotent. All he could do was look at a woman . . ."

"Who will play Kara Kolvang in this film you're writing?"

"Paul claims he's found an incredible girl. A new star, in Paris, who's a double for Kara. We're going over to look at her in December when she opens in some stage show. Paul and I and, perhaps, Erik Wulff. We've seen pictures of her and the likeness to Kara is startling. She's not Danish, however, but Dutch. We heard tapes of her singing, Monday night at Paul's, and her voice is glorious. Even better than Kara's . . ."

"You think Paul Victor will make this film?"

"Who knows . . ." Mallon shrugged. "Meanwhile it gives all of us something to do and talk about. Keeps us from being bored in our old age. Including Paul. I think he may have come up with this idea for a film about Kara to provide himself with a reason for living. He's a rich man—has more money than any of us—so he can afford to pay everyone for their work on the project. Guarantees us a year's full salary. We make him a splendid tax deduction!"

"Was Mr. Dalby to be a part of this project?"

"I asked Paul about that, Monday night, and he said he would've liked Clem to be present when he told us his idea. As an old friend he wanted Clem's advice and suggestions. Paul was, genuinely, disappointed when he didn't join us. I haven't seen Clem Dalby in years but Paul keeps in touch with him. Paul manages to keep in touch with everybody! Of course, he has nothing else to do. Afraid I've not been much help, have I?"

"Quite the contrary. I'm particularly grateful for your tip about Cantrell's Corner. I'll check the place this afternoon. Someone there may know where I can find Kerrigan."

"If you find him tell him I'd like to see him."

"I'll do that."

"Will you be talking to Clem Dalby?"

"Eventually."

"He wasn't at Paul's dinner. So he doesn't know what Larry blurted out about Tim Kerrigan. And I doubt if he'd give a damn. Clem doesn't have much interest in the past. I've never heard him mention Kara, and he directed one of her best films. He's much more interested in those big westerns he made in the late thirties and early forties. Those were Clem's golden years. All the films he directed before that are forgotten. And he did some classics, even in the silent days. I guess all of us are more interested in the things we did in our golden years. The other years, before and since, tend to blur. My screenplays were nominated for Oscars twice and those were my great years. Even though I never won the silly statue. Human nature is perverse and inexplicable . . ."

"I mustn't keep you from your work any longer." Zeke got to his feet.

"Let me walk you to the door." Pushing his heavy body up from the chair. "Have you seen Henri Neri?"

"He's next on my list."

"Henri was the art director on all of Kara's films." Placing an arm around Zeke's shoulder, like a clumsy bear. "In recent years he's worked with Paul Victor several times. Henri was an extremely handsome young man. I've always suspected he had an affair with Kara. God knows, I didn't. Never got a chance to touch her. Though I had plenty of ideas. You know actresses seldom glance at the guy who puts all those words in their beautiful mouths. They prefer a handsome face—even an electrician—to a writer. And, except for Gene O'Neill, there've been damn few handsome writers . . ."

As they walked toward the entrance, Mallon still talking, Zeke's stomach growled softly. Better get some food before he visited Cantrell's Corner.

All this talk about Kara Kolvang wasn't getting him on the trail of Laurence Knight.

That's all Faye wanted him to do. Find Larry Knight, not the murderer of Kara Kolvang.

Chapter 8

Zeke drove south on Appian Way, between Seaside Park and the ocean, looking for Cantrell's Corner and gulping fresh air.

He had enjoyed a quiet lunch at a small restaurant below the approach to the Santa Monica pier—fresh piece of broiled halibut with a baked potato—aware of a distant clatter of mechanical music from the old carousel.

Appian Way was nothing like the ancient Roman road for which it had, apparently, been named, but was an ugly street of low buildings facing the beach. Small shops with dirty windows. Diving equipment for rent, fortune teller, souvenirs. A skinny black kid in bathing trunks was whirling a skateboard on the sidewalk.

Ahead, at the corner, he glimpsed a sign—CANTRELL'S CORNER—projecting from the roof of a squat stucco building.

Parked the Chevy across the street and walked toward the gym.

As he came closer he saw a crude picture of a prize ring painted under the establishment's name on the sign above the entrance. He hadn't realized, from the car, what it was supposed to represent because the paint had, long ago, lost its battle with sun and rain.

Double doors stood open into chilly darkness.

Zeke went in, immediately aware of a familiar stench of sweat and liniment, like the smell of a caged animal. Walked toward the open area ahead, eyes adjusting to the dark, where a Mexican bantamweight was working on a punching bag in a circle of light from a single overhead bulb. He was dancing alone and unwatched.

"Lookin foh somebody, Mistah?" The voice was deep and pugnacious.

He turned to see a black man, facing him from behind an open box office window under a faded TICKETS sign. The man must be sitting on a high stool. He was thin, with white hair rimming his bald skull, a squashed nose sniffing the air like a hunting dog.

"Cop, aincha?"

"Private detective." He brought out his wallet and held up the photostat toward the window. "How'd you know?"

"The way you stopped walkin suddenly an started lookin around. We got no problems heah. 'Cep' mosta us is starvin . . ."

He realized the old man's eyes hadn't checked the license and slipped it back into his pocket. "Blind, aren't you?"

"Smart fella. Most folks talk t' me without nevah findin out I can't see their physiognomy. What's brung you heah?"

"Looking for a man."

"This guy got hisself a handle?"

"Tim Kerrigan."

"Tim's been mighty popular lately."

"That so . . ."

"Nobody mentioned his name in six months—an I ain't heard

his voice in weeks—then all of a sudden, this week, folks been askin after him."

"Who's been asking?"

"Strangers. Three of 'em . . ."

"You couldn't see them, but you heard them talk. What did they sound like?"

"If you is a private eye, a little information oughta be worth something . . ." He rested a large hand, palm up, on the window ledge.

"Ten bucks?"

"Worth more than that, man."

"How's twenty?"

"I could be persuaded t' tell you everything I know an suspect foh twenty."

As Zeke pulled out his wallet again and found a twenty, he noticed that the young fighter had stopped punching leather and was watching them. Laid the twenty, lightly, against the dusky pink palm and returned the wallet to his pocket.

The fingers closed over the bill. "Sure feels like a twenty." Folding it into a pocket of his sweater. "Twenty feels a whole lot softer than a ten spot."

"Did these three guys give you their names?"

"Only the second. Young fella . . ." Hesitating. "I disremember the last part but his first name was . . . Somethin like—Yars!"

"Lars?"

"That's it! I was close."

"When was he here?"

"Yestaday. Round noon."

"And the other two?"

"The first guy showed up the day before. Late afternoon."

"What did he sound like?"

"Friendly sort. Deep voice, like you. Big fella. Not young, mebbe in his seventies. Tall guy . . ."

"How could you know that?"

"I can tell, tall or short, from the direction the voice comes. How tall might you be?"

"Six feet two."

"That's 'bout what he was."

"And the third fellow?"

"He come last night. Short guy. Pushed the bell after I'd locked the joint. Kept punching the bell an bangin on the door, 'til I opened it. This last guy had some sorta furrin accent."

"What sort?"

"Maybe Eyetalian or Mex . . ."

"And you told all three of them where they could find Kerrigan?"

"Tol em where they could look foh him."

"Where would that be?"

"Round the corner. Tim's got hisself a room in a house on Seaside. That's a cross street, northa here."

"What's the number of this rooming house?"

"Don't recall no numbah, if I ever knowed it. Gotta front porch an a sign says rooms to let. Can't miss it. Least that's how it used t' look when I had my sight."

"Thanks for the information, friend." Zeke headed for the street.

"Hope this keeps up," the deep voice called after him. "More guys lookin foh Tim Kerrigan. I, sure's hell do . . ."

He stepped out into a hot glare of sunlight and walked back, up Appian Way, his mind occupied with what he'd learned.

Three men asking for Tim Kerrigan. The first, obviously, had to be Laurence Knight. Come to warn Kerrigan about what he'd said at Paul Victor's dinner. The second was Lars Lyndon, looking for his grandfather. Which meant that Knight had told him about Kerrigan. But who was the short man with a foreign accent?

The sun was fading and he looked up at a low band of clouds moving in from the ocean. This could mean heavy fog again tonight.

Zeke saw the sign—ROOMS FOR RENT—when he turned the corner and started up Seaside Terrace. This had always been a neighborhood where you could find a cheap room. Mostly people who worked nearby, or old people looking for a place to die.

The neat clapboard house was painted gray with white trim. There was a narrow porch around the front with three empty rocking chairs, cushions faded by the sun.

He went up the steps to a front door that held a small sign.

OPEN—WALK IN

Zeke entered a long hall with a narrow staircase leading upstairs. No furniture, only a healthy looking Boston fern in a large pot. A door to the right of the entrance had a bell button under a small sign—MANAGER—with smudges on the wall left by fingers fumbling for the button.

He touched it with a forefinger and glanced along the hall toward the other two closed doors in the same wall.

The only sound was a distant murmur of voices from two television sets and he wondered if Kerrigan spent his days watching old movies.

He would never come to that. When he got too old to function at his job he would spend his time reading. Starting with everything Hammett had written. His five novels and all the short stories. He looked forward to reading them again. Would be like listening to Dash talking . . .

"Who is it?" Woman's voice, high-pitched and querulous, behind the door.

"I'm looking for Mr. Kerrigan. Tim Kerrigan . . ."

"Just a second."

He stepped back as two locks snapped and the door slowly opened. Saw that she was in her sixties with purple-black dyed hair. Pleasant face, but shrewish. Plump body in a plain house-dress.

"I was eating my lunch."

"You the manager?"

"I own this damn building. I'm Mrs. Mawkins and you're the fourth person in three days who's come askin for Tim."

"Was one of them a man with a foreign accent?"

"How could you know that! He was the third. Late last night."

"What kind of an accent was it?"

"How should I know? Could've been Mexican. He looked Mexican. Oily black hair and a mustache."

"Could you describe him?"

"Ordinary lookin. But piercin black eyes. Never looked away while he was talkin."

"Did all three of these men see Mr. Kerrigan?"

"Couldn say. They didn come back t' me, if they didn. Why you askin so many questions?"

Better not say he was a detective. "Thought I might know them. Where will I find Mr. Kerrigan?"

"Upstairs. Number Six. Ain't seen him t'day. Never lissen when my roomers go in an out. Unless they owe money. Tim always pays on time, after he cashes his Social Security check. Unless he forgets. Which he's been doin, more and more, lately . . ."

"How long has he lived here?"

"Maybe ten years. He's my oldest guest."

"Does he have many visitors?"

"These three were the first in a long time. I worry 'bout Tim. He's been failin a lot lately. Used t' be a big man but he's shrank t' skin an bone. Drinks too much an don't eat enough, you ask me."

"I'll go up and see if he's in."

"He's, usually, home at this hour. Comes back from his walk on the pier. Number's on the door. Number six . . ."

"Thank you, ma'am." Zeke heard the door close as he went upstairs.

Another narrow hall with a row of four closed doors. Number six was at the top of the steps.

Those television voices were coming from rooms toward the front.

A window in the rear stood open and he glimpsed people on the pier a block away.

He knocked on Kerrigan's door and waited. Knocked again and pressed his ear against the wood but heard no sound of movement inside the room. Knocked once more then went downstairs and rang the owner's bell again.

The door opened at once, as though she'd been waiting for him to return. "You're back, are you?"

"Mr. Kerrigan doesn't answer. I wonder if you'd be kind enough to unlock his door. I'm worried, he might be ill."

"I'll open it an you can look inside, but I won't let you go in."

"That's fair enough."

"Let me find my spare key." She turned back into her apartment and lifted a key from a wall rack. Snatched up another one as she passed a table. "Leave my own key handy, so's I can get back in here." She closed the door and checked that it had locked before going ahead up the steps. "Does Mr. Kerrigan have any relatives?"

"I couldn't say, ma'am."

"He rarely gets mail. I worry 'bout my guests. Most of 'em have lost track of their folks. Everyone in California seems to be from someplace else."

"Everyone—everywhere—is from someplace else."

"I came from Baltimore, myself, after my husband got himself killed in the Second World War."

"Did you? I was born on the Eastern Shore."

"Now ain't that a coincidence! Been years since I met anybody from Maryland." She knocked, sharply, on Kerrigan's door and waited for a response. "He's out." Inserting her key into the lock and pushing the door open. "Oh, my God!"

Zeke moved past her toward the tiny figure crumpled on the small bed. The thin body was in faded blue pajamas. His puffed white face was ghastly, pale blue eyes protruding, tongue hanging from the open mouth. Zeke touched the cold flesh as he saw dark bruises on the throat. Rigor was complete. Kerrigan had been dead for hours.

Mrs. Mawkins, behind him, was moaning softly.

"He's dead, ma'am."

"Oh, no . . ."

He turned and saw her, near the door, wringing her hands. "Looks as though he's been murdered. Strangled."

"Murdered!"

"Better call the police, ma'am."

"Couldn't you do that for me?"

"You're the owner of the building."

"I've never had a murder in my house before. The poor old man . . ."

"Just dial 911. They'll connect you with the police."

"Yes, sir. I'll do that." Heading for the hall. "Right away."

"Tell them it's an emergency."

"You wait right there." She hurried toward the stairs.

Zeke leaned closer to examine the dead man's throat.

Bruises on the neck. A faint one made by a thumb. Three barely visible shadows from the fingers.

Moving quickly he went to a small chest of drawers and, using his handkerchief, pulled each drawer out, one by one. Finding nothing of interest. No letters or scraps of paper with scribbled notations. Only a worn leather wallet.

Took a pen from his pocket and used it to flip the wallet open. It contained a faded Social Security card, a bank book—with a balance of thirty-seven dollars—fifteen more in folding money. Loose change in a plastic saucer, next to some handkerchiefs. Shirts and underwear in the lower drawers were worn and shabby. He closed each drawer again.

Went into the bath and opened the medicine cabinet. Checked the small bottles.

Returning to the body he noticed, for the first time, faded photos of boxers thumbtacked to the walls around the bed.

He wondered if any of them were young Tim Kerrigan . . .

Zeke lifted an edge of the pajama jacket with his pen and saw the white emaciated body of an old man. Not the body of a prizefighter. His skin was unusually wrinkled because of the weight he'd lost. Hair, what remained of it, was white.

Someone had found Kerrigan. Last night . . .

Zeke returned the pen to his pocket as he left the room and went down the steps, careful not to make a sound.

Mrs. Mawkins was explaining that one of her tenants had been murdered. Her voice was hysterical.

As Zeke passed the open door he saw her, phone in hand and facing an open window, her back turned to the hall.

He escaped from the house and headed back toward Appian Way.

By the time she returned upstairs he would be in the Chevy and several blocks away.

Fortunately, he hadn't told her his name or his profession, so he wouldn't have to explain his presence to the local police. There was nothing, at the moment, he could tell them and he didn't want to involve them in his search for Laurence Knight.

The sun was bright again, as he turned the corner and headed for his car, but more clouds were moving in, casting dark shadows across the beach.

He inhaled deep breaths of the ocean air to clear his lungs.

The animal stink of that gym and the sweet smell of death in Tim Kerrigan's room.

Chapter 9

He found a deserted bar on Ocean Avenue, facing the Santa Monica pier, and ordered a dry vermouth with a twist of lemon, the nearest thing to a drink he permitted himself during working hours.

The bartender was polishing glasses he'd used during the lunch hour, returning each to its place in sparkling rows behind his bar.

As Zeke drank the vermouth he heard a siren pass, speeding toward Mrs. Mawkins.

Maybe, in her excitement, she wouldn't tell them he'd been there.

He tossed off the last of his drink and left some change on the bar.

Continued on his way, chewing a shred of lemon peel.

Next stop would be Henri Neri, also in Santa Monica, and then, last of all, he would try to see Clement Dalby, the man who hadn't shown up for Victor's dinner.

Turned the Chevy off the Coast Highway and followed Sunset until he saw Rustic Canyon. Swerved left, at the next intersection, drove back and turned right up the wooded canyon. Slowed beside the narrow stream running down the center until he saw NERI on a mailbox, ivy almost covering the name, and braked to a stop.

Impossible to see anything of the house because of dense shrubbery.

He climbed curving steps to the top of a hill where, glancing back, he couldn't see his parked car. Even the house was covered by ivy, leaving only a carved wood entrance door exposed.

Pressed a bell button and faint chimes responded. As he waited he was aware of birds singing overhead. The branches of the trees were so heavy with leaves he couldn't glimpse any sky.

The door was opened by a pair of Chinese girls with inviting smiles, wearing tangerine silk cheongsams, their feet in embroidered slippers.

They bowed and spoke in unison. "Welcome, sir." They giggled. "Monsieur Neri expects you."

"Does he?" Zeke stepped from the tree-shaded terrace into a narrow paneled foyer opening out into a big studio filled with sunlight where a tiny old man, wearing a paint-smudged smock over dungarees, was perched upon a pillowed stool, his back to a row of open windows, working on a large canvas. Impossible to see what the artist was painting.

"Come in, Monsieur Inspecteur Gahagan! Welcome . . ." He set his brush and palette on a table and hopped down from the stool. "I am Henri Neri. I was informed you would be arriving and here you are." Holding out his hand. "I have never, before, met an American flic."

Zeke shook the hand, aware of its fragility. "I suppose Paul Victor called you."

"Not Paul. Erik Wulff and Kevin Mallon, they both phoned." Motioning toward a tremendous sofa placed at an angle to the wall of windows standing open onto a green forest of trees. "May I offer you a glass of wine?"

"Nothing. Thanks." As he sat on the sofa, with Neri, he glanced back, but the Chinese girls had vanished.

Neri noticed his interest. "You met my little Oriental beauties? My virgins. When I die they will have enough money to open a charming restaurant in Beverly Hills. At least that's what they say it'll be. I say 'bonne chance!' Whatever it is . . ."

Zeke saw that the studio stretched off into shadow and the sofa faced a living area with a stone fireplace and a dining table that should seat a dozen people. Fresh flowers in pottery bowls. Life-sized portrait of a woman, elaborately framed, over the fireplace. He was unable to see her face in the shadow. "What a comfortable place you have here . . ."

"I'm sure the famous detective—known as the 'World's Oldest Eye'—isn't here to make small talk about my studio. I was told you've been engaged by my dear friend, Faye Manning, to investigate the curious disappearance of our mutual friend, Laurence Knight . . ."

"That about covers it."

"Eh bien! I'm afraid there's nothing I can tell you. I hadn't seen Larry in years, until we were both invited to Paul Victor's for dinner. In fact, I hadn't heard from Paul in a long time. We used to meet at the big premières but they don't have those any more. I don't know the people who are making films today and don't wish to know most of them . . .

"Grace à Dieu! I worked in the industry when giants were making films. The studio heads—men with imagination—the great directors and, above all, the stars. Especially the fascinating women. Today there are no stars left and most of the actresses have no sex. Romance has vanished from American films. No more subtlety. No beauty . . ."

"Do you have any idea," Zeke interrupted, "what could've happened to Laurence Knight? Where he might've gone?"

"I would imagine—if Larry does know this Kerrigan individual, who knows the name of the person who killed Kara—he must fear for his own life. Either Kerrigan or the murderer, if that person is alive, might want to silence Larry before he can divulge anything more."

"That seems very likely." He wouldn't tell anyone, as yet, that Kerrigan had been murdered.

"I've no idea who killed Kara but I could talk for hours about the living woman. I knew her more intimately, I suppose, than any of the others at that dinner. I worked on all her films, in Paris and Hollywood, as well as the stage productions. Saw her every day, for many years. On the set, at her home or here in my studio."

"You lived here when she was alive?"

"Bought this place soon after I came to California. There was a large colony of creative people in this canyon—then and later—and property was cheap. Today this small plot of land is worth a fortune but, as long as I live, I shall never sell." He glanced around. "I glimpse the past in every shadow . . ."

"That's how Faye Manning feels about her home in the hills."

"We both remember those good years. The thirties and forties before television destroyed the public's taste. Those great times will return, one day, and the film industry will be reborn. Man and his arts have been computerized. There's no great painter in the world today. No first-class composer or novelist. I can't watch television and rarely venture out to see a new film. Unless it's from my native France. They, at least, haven't forgotten wit and beauty . . ."

"If you can't tell me anything about Laurence Knight, what do you know about Kara Kolvang?"

Neri sighed. "She was a most elusive human being. That was part of her charm. Always slipping away. Forever escaping. But she was a woman. A real flesh-and-blood woman. Not like these sticks they star in films today. Did you ever see Kara in person, Inspecteur?"

"I never even saw her in a film."

"She was, without doubt, the most beautiful woman I've ever known. And I worked with many of the female stars, year after year, saw them without makeup. Painted their portraits. There was never a face—or a body—like Kara's."

"One of her films is to be shown on television this week."

"Her last picture—*Park Avenue Girl*—with my costumes and sets. Larry Knight was her leading man again. By all means see it. Saturday night, I believe. But I must warn you, Monsieur, you'll be seeing only a shadow of Kara. Her public image. The real Kara was tender, delicate and loving. That was the Kara I knew . . ." He glanced toward the shimmer of leaves beyond the open windows. "There is a secret, Monsieur Inspecteur. I have never confessed to anyone. Even those detectives who questioned me, years ago, about Kara's murder. Such stupid questions . . ."

"You had an affair with her?"

"That is no secret. Everybody knew about that." Neri laughed, facing him again. "We both talked about it, Kara and I, told people of the glorious year we spent together in Paris, before she met Sacha Guitry. That arrogant monster! He only lasted a few weeks and, after Guitry, there was a young Italian composer . . ." He shrugged. "Kara was like a oiseau-mouche—a colibri—what is your American word for this tiny bird that always darts from flower to flower . . ."

"Hummingbird?"

"I was the one gave Kara that name in Paris. Mademoiselle Colibri! Darting from man to man. That was her nature. She was as beautiful as that delicate bird. As bright-colored and as sensuous. One of the films she made in France was called *Mademoiselle Colibri*. I gave the idea to our producer, Kurt von Zemmering. Kara was delighted and, as always, had a tremendous success. Erik Wulff wrote his most beautiful melodies for that one." He sighed, recalling the past. "But I've not yet told you my precious secret. I will show it to you. That should reveal more about Kara than I—or any other living person—can tell you with words. Yours shall be the first eyes, except mine, ever to see this." He leaned forward, producing a ring of keys from a pocket of his smock, selected one and inserted it into the lock of an oblong ebony box on a table beside the sofa. Turned the key and raised the lid. "Kara never knew I painted her portrait. I did it from memory—loving memory—while she was alive. But never showed it to her . . ."

Zeke saw that the box held a row of levers and Neri was reaching down without looking at them. Watched him finger several.

"Observe that painting, Monsieur Inspecteur. Above the fireplace."

He turned as hidden spotlights focused on the portrait. "That's Kara Kolvang?"

"Certainly not. You are about to see the only true portrait of Kara in existence."

Curtains were closing over the windows and the light in the studio was fading.

Zeke heard more levers snapped in the ebony box.

The framed portrait of a strikingly beautiful brunette, above the fireplace, slid aside to reveal black velvet curtains which began to part. The spotlights revealed a much larger painting that seemed to float in moonlight.

"This is Kara," Neri whispered. "My beloved. So delicate! So intangible. Si ravissante . . ."

Zeke leaned forward, studying the painting. The face was that of a child but the nude body, partially hidden under long yellow hair flowing down to her ankles, was that of a mature woman. The hair was like golden silk against her pink flesh. One leg extended toward the lower left corner of the painting and the knee of her other leg rested on a violet-colored cushion. Right arm raised, hand reaching toward the sky, fingers spread as though to grasp a butterfly or a star. Only one breast was visible. Her face was the important thing. One of the most delicate faces he'd ever seen. A face glimpsed in a dream. Although he'd never had such a dream. He studied the features intently. This face of a young woman who had been brutally murdered . . .

"Have you ever seen such a face?"

He turned to the artist whose features were diffused in the muted light reflected from the distant canvas. "Was she really this beautiful?"

"I swear to you, she was the most exquisite woman I've ever known. She made the other so-called beauties—in Paris and Hollywood—appear artificial. Her features were perfection!"

Zeke stared at the portrait again.

"Some film critic called her the golden queen of the silver screen and that phrase was used again and again to describe her. I suspect they got 'movie queen' from all those reviews calling Kara a golden queen . . .

"Compared to her, the others—Harlow and Monroe, who came later—were tawdry. Only three—Garbo, Dietrich and Bergman—were her equals. But Kara was unlike all of them . . . Elusive, even as you held her in your arms. Her body without weight, as you embraced her. The subtle perfume of her flesh. And her eyes! They were green with flecks of amber like the eyes of an exotic bird. Mademoiselle Colibri! There will never be another woman as exciting."

Zeke heard the levers clicking and turned to see the black velvet curtains closing. Kara Kolvang had vanished.

"Now you have seen her, Monsieur Inspecteur."

"And I'm very grateful." He watched the other portrait slide into place, spotlights fading as window curtains opened and sunlight reached across the studio again. He faced Neri who was closing his ebony box.

The artist returned the keys to his pocket. "I have presented you to Kara with the hope that you will find her murderer. That is all I want. To avenge her death, the destruction of this exquisite creature. I am eighty years old and I would like to do this before I die. Help reveal the man who killed such beauty . . ."

"Do you have any idea who that was?"

"None. The police found no clue to his identity."

"I've learned they suspected Laurence Knight at first."

"Only for twenty-four hours. Larry would never have harmed her. He adored Kara. Like all of us . . ."

"But someone killed her."

"She had been raped. Her exquisite neck broken. I've always thought it had to be a complete stranger. Someone she'd never met before. Her body was found on the beach near her car. He could have been someone who followed her to rob her . . ."

"If it happened like that the murderer will never be found."

"But Larry said this Kerrigan person knew the identity of her killer. Perhaps, as you search for Larry, you will come upon a trail that leads to the man who destroyed my golden princess."

"There's not a chance anyone could solve the case after so many years. I'm looking for Laurence Knight. Nobody else."

"I will pay you, Monsieur Inspecteur, if you will—at the same time—seek for the one clue that will reveal Kara's murderer."

"I doubt such a clue exists. The killer is, very likely, long since dead. Any evidence, if it ever existed, has vanished. I'm told that Kurt von Zemmering was also, for a time, under suspicion."

"Which was ridiculous. Kurt was a gentleman. A sophisticate and a person of taste. He, too, adored Kara. I never knew them to quarrel in all the years she was under contract to him. Kurt produced every one of her films, here and in France, and they made him personal fortunes. There was no possible reason for Kurt to kill her."

"All men are jealous. He must've been aware of the affairs she was having with other men."

"They amused him. There was never anything sexual between Kurt and Kara. Much too great a difference in their ages. Kurt was always seen, in public, with older women. I never knew whether he had affairs with them. He was intelligent; therefore he was, also, discreet."

"What happened to him?"

"Nobody knows. He disappeared, shortly after Kara's death, and I never heard from him again. Only rumors . . ."

Zeke rose from the sofa. "Thanks for showing me the portrait. It's as though I've actually seen her."

"That was my purpose." Neri rose and walked beside him toward the entrance. "You should've heard her voice. It, too, was golden. If only she could speak to you. Kara would plead with you to reveal this person who killed her. She would reason with you. Persuade you . . ."

"I am looking for Laurence Knight. Nobody else."

As they reached the entrance door, Zeke heard the two Chinese girls giggling in the distance.

Chapter 10

Zeke was preoccupied as the Chevy sped up Mandeville Canyon.

Was he hoping to find the murderer of Kara Kolvang, as well as searching for Laurence Knight?

A long-dead actress and a missing actor who might be dead . . .

He hoped to find Knight alive, for Faye Manning.

Already one dead man, Tim Kerrigan. That was a problem for the Santa Monica police. For the moment . . .

He wondered if Mandeville Canyon went all the way up to Mulholland?

Which reminded him of that terrace, on the Valley side of Mulholland, where those three rich boys had died beside a shiny red Mercedes.

Three kids whose parents showed no grief for them. Which explained why they were dead.

Two people were, certainly, grieving. A girl with soft brown eyes who loved the Burkett boy. And Billy Harper to whom they had entrusted their suicide note.

Would anyone grieve for Zeke Gahagan when he died?

The way he'd mourned when he finally, months later, learned that Hammett would never turn up out of the blue again.

He couldn't think of anybody, offhand.

Not his four wives. Three were dead. The other one—his last wife—would, probably, be interested in whether or not he left her any money. And he, very likely, would . . .

Must decide about that one day. Who he wanted to get his savings.

He'd never bothered to make a will.

Maybe leave everything to a home for lost dogs. He liked dogs—they were four-legged detectives, always investigating everything. He'd never owned a dog, except when he was a kid in Maryland. His work didn't leave him time for a pet.

That was why his wives had left him. Because he was never home.

He'd loved all of them. Was shocked and surprised when they wanted a divorce, but didn't give them an argument.

He might leave his money to a home for aged private eyes. Only he'd never heard of such an institution. Most private eyes died before fifty. From ulcers, not bullets.

He checked the mailboxes beside the entrance drives to each property he passed. Expensive homes on acres of landscaped land between sprawling ranches with cows in pastures and horses in paddocks. One of his all-time favorite actors, Richard Widmark, used to have a ranch up here but he'd heard somewhere that he'd moved to Santa Barbara.

As he passed a flock of sheep he began to whistle softly.

"Sheep May Safely Graze" . . .

Which reminded him of Emma again. She had played that on the piano, after dinner, sitting in the twilight . . .

He'd wasted a day looking for a clue to the whereabouts of a missing movie star and he'd only found a dead star. Dead for fifty years...

He realized he was tired. He'd been interrogating people for hours. In the old days with Hammett in San Francisco—when they worked for Pinkerton—he could keep going forty-eight hours.

Hammett was the one who tired. He had a health problem. Even then...

Must remember to call Faye tonight. Report he hadn't turned up a damn thing about her missing friend. Not a trace of the guy.

He had a strong feeling, in advance, he wouldn't learn anything from Clement Dalby...

Zeke slowed the Chevy as he approached a mailbox under a fancy wrought-iron silhouette of a cowhand on a bucking mustang.

RANCHO ELDORADO was lettered on the side of the mailbox.

The name of an old Clement Dalby feature that had starred Laurence Knight. One of Hollywood's great films and, probably, Dalby's biggest success which—like John Ford's *Stagecoach*—had become a world classic. He didn't remember whether any of Dalby's pictures won Oscars but then he could never remember who won them this year.

He turned the Chevy up a long drive toward a distant stand of eucalyptus trees shivering in a breeze. Fenced pastures on either side stretched toward a line of low hills topped with more trees. No sign of any ranch house.

Dalby must be loaded to own this big property. All those films must've brought him a sizeable fortune. He'd been in the business since silent pictures. Made comedies at first, then musicals after sound came in but, in later years, directed nothing but westerns.

He saw that the drive curved around the eucalyptus trees, planted to form a windbreak, and led toward another clump of trees. These looked like sycamores. As he turned a final curve they became a backdrop for the most photogenic adobe ranch house he'd ever seen.

Zeke slowed the Chevy past a white picket fence with an open gate and got out. No dogs barking and no sign of life.

He strode up a long gravel path, past recently mowed lawns and neat flower gardens, to a columned veranda. Solid-looking entrance door with wrought-iron hinges. He grasped the bell-pull, gave it a hard yank, and heard a deep-throated bell respond.

Glanced around, as he waited, at the Mexican leather chairs and settees on the veranda.

Somewhere, in the distance, there was the faint clanking of a blacksmith. Birds complaining in nearby trees. Disturbed, no doubt, by his arrival.

"Yes, sir?"

Zeke turned and saw that the door had been opened.

A small compact man in a black and white jogging outfit stood there. Thin, with cropped gray hair. His tanned face was gaunt and perspiring, gray eyes inspecting the intruder.

"I'd like to see Mr. Clement Dalby."

"Mr. Dalby knows you?"

"No. We've never met."

"In that case, sir, I'm afraid . . ."

Zeke produced his wallet, flipped it open and held it up. Watched the gray eyes peer at the photostat without any reaction.

The eyes came up to inspect Zeke's face more carefully. "And why do you wish to see Mr. Dalby?"

"I can only tell that to Mr. Dalby."

"Certainly, sir." Moving out of the way and motioning for him to enter.

Zeke stepped into a flagstoned entry with archways on both sides leading to low-ceilinged corridors. He was facing double doors that stood open onto a sunny central courtyard where pots of red and white geraniums were placed around a circular pool with a fountain.

The houseman had closed the entrance door. "If you'll wait here, sir. I'll tell Mr. Dalby you wish to see him."

"Thanks." He moved toward the open doors as the houseman headed down the corridor on his left. Stood, senses alert, staring at the fountain.

This place reminded him of a hacienda in a big-budget western movie. A Clement Dalby production . . .

The only sound now came from jets of water splashing into the pool and the soft cooing of doves. Wings flashed in the sunlight as they circled overhead while others perched on the rim of the fountain, dipping their beaks into the water. White patio furniture with tables shaded by yellow parasols.

This ranch house, apparently, had two wings, one on either side of the courtyard, behind columned arcades with rows of shuttered windows. The place appeared to be old but he suspected it had looked like this when it was new. Probably built after World War II. That's when many of these canyon properties had been bought by film stars who then had their dream homes made reality by some expensive Beverly Hills architect. Many of their homes were vulgar and ridiculous but Rancho Eldorado appeared to be comfortable and unpretentious. The perfect place for a famous director of westerns to retire and dream of past achievements.

"Mr. Dalby will see you, sir."

He faced the houseman who was smiling now.

"His health hasn't been too good this week, but he's feeling somewhat more comfortable today."

Zeke walked beside him down the long side corridor. "Has he been ill for some time?"

"It's his arthritis, mostly. Comes and goes. He suffers at night when the fog rolls up from the ocean but on a sunny day, like this, the pain isn't too severe. Later, if he's in a good mood, he'll sit outside in the sun for a bit . . ."

Zeke realized that the houseman, if that's what he was, spoke with a slight accent. Sounded British . . .

"He won't take cortisone or gold injections. And refuses to diet . . ." Gesturing toward an open door they were approaching. "Mr. Dalby's in his study . . ."

Zeke hesitated, on the threshold, looking into the room. All the windows were hidden behind heavy curtains and the air was chilly from air conditioning.

Dalby sat hunched down behind a flat-topped desk, a heavily carved Spanish antique, in a circle of light from an overhead spot perched on a ceiling beam. The effect was strikingly theatrical because of the director's thick and unruly white hair above the bright-colored sport shirt he was wearing.

Blue eyes, behind black-rimmed spectacles, were focused on his face as he walked across an American Indian rug toward the desk. "You're a cop?"

"That's right."

"Don't look like any cop I ever saw. Would never have cast you as a cop."

"I'm a private detective. We look different."

"In what way?"

"Less worried. More relaxed . . ." The distance to the desk was farther than he had realized. He saw that Dalby was seated in an enormous black leather armchair and had been looking at some glossy photographs. Copies of *Daily Variety* and *Hollywood Reporter* were on the desk, so he still read the trades. There was a large magnifying glass in his right hand. "I've been called the world's oldest eye . . ."

"Not Gahagan! Ezekiel Gahagan?"

"You've heard of me?"

Dalby chuckled. "I hear about anyone in this damn town who's an original. Very few are, these days." Resting his magnifying glass on the photographs. "World's oldest eye . . . How the hell old are you?"

"Eighty-one."

"And still functioning at your job?"

"Most days."

"I'm two years older. And, for several years now, I've been quite aware of that fact." Raising the spectacles from his nose, onto his forehead and peering across the desk. "Damn it, man! You don't look an hour over—sixty. Don't stand there! Pull up a chair."

Zeke pushed a small black leather armchair closer to the desk. "Didn't anyone phone you this morning to warn you I'd be arriving?"

"Who the hell would do that?" He let the spectacles drop onto his nose again.

"Any one of four persons." He sat, facing Dalby. "Most likely Paul Victor."

"Why would that idiot call me again? I was rude to him, the other day, when he wanted me to drive into the city for dinner. Phoned twice and tried to persuade me. Damn fool! Why would I dine with him in that rococo bird cage he calls home?

"I agreed, reluctantly, the second time he phoned, but thought better of it later. Had my man, Godfrey, call back and say I wasn't feeling fit enough to venture out. Only good thing about this goddamn arthritis is I can use it when I want to get out of doing things. And I had no desire to spend an evening with Paul Victor. The man never stops talking and fiddling with his precious doodads. Has them in every room! Someone said his beautiful hands have a life of their own . . ."

As Dalby talked, Zeke had a chance to observe him. The large head and massive shoulders. Black eyebrows arching over the spectacles. Generous mouth, prominent jaw. His nose had been broken years ago and carelessly repaired. Big-boned body, but not an ounce of excess weight. Face and hands dark from the sun. The folded hands, resting on the desk, were knotted with arthritis. He wondered what those film stills were that Dalby had been studying. He could see, upside down, that one was a picture of horses.

". . . haven't explained why you thought Paul Victor would call to tell me you'd be coming here."

"Mr. Victor knew I was seeing all his dinner guests. Including you—the missing one . . ."

"There were others? I thought Paul and I would be dining alone. If he'd told me others were coming I might've accepted his invitation. Who were they?"

"Erik Wulff, Laurence Knight, Kevin Mallon and Henri Neri . . ."

"Now there's an odd little group. I know them, of course. Worked with all of them. But why the hell would Paul invite them to dinner? Told me he wanted to discuss an idea for a new film. Planned to direct it himself, but would be grateful for my advice."

"That's what he told the others. And they did discuss an idea for a picture . . ." He watched Dalby's eyes as he explained. "It's to be a film about a top woman star of the thirties . . ."

"I worked with most of 'em."

"A film about Kara Kolvang." He saw no change in the eyes and the folded hands remained motionless. "I believe you directed several of her pictures."

"Four of the best she made. Yes . . ." He smiled. "I adored Kara. She was an incredible person, tremendously talented. I proposed marriage to her—when I was between wives—but she turned me down. Kara never did get married. Far's I know. Legend had it that she slept with a different man every night, but I never enjoyed that privilege. Sex was something Kara liked immediately after dinner. As the British enjoy a savory. Casual, with no strings or future demands. Kara was an angel. But she could also be a bitch. I remember one night . . ."

As Dalby talked, Zeke had a feeling he was being watched. He looked around the dim room, without moving his head, and saw they were surrounded by large pre-Columbian stone heads, on tall wooden pedestals. The primitive faces with their blank eyes seemed to be staring. Beyond the ring of heads he could see that the walls were hidden behind crowded bookshelves, except for one section with an elaborate display of guns in softly lighted glass cases. Every make and caliber . . .

". . . wonder what gave Paul Victor the idea to make a film about Kara. Not a bad idea, actually. Those other guests you say he'd invited to dinner were all involved with Kara. Professionally and privately . . ."

"That's why they were there. He wants them to work on the project. One to write a screenplay, another would compose the music, a third to be his art director."

"That would be Henri Neri. What about Larry Knight? He's much too old to play himself in the film. Although, last time I saw him he still looked damn good. But I don't think he could look thirty, or whatever he was in those days, even with makeup."

"Victor wanted his advice. In fact, Knight agreed to help Mr. Mallon with personal material for the script."

"But why the hell would Paul want to make a feature about Kara after all these years? The public's forgotten her. Long ago."

"He explained what had given him the idea for such a film, after they finished dinner. Told them the dinner was to commemorate the anniversary of Kara Kolvang's murder. That's what gave him the idea for the film."

"Anniversary?" Dalby reached across his desk and snatched up a leather-framed calendar. "My God! It was . . . Been fifty years!" Pushing the calendar aside. "Would you care for a whiskey?"

"Haven't touched hard liquor in years."

"And I'm not supposed to. My man, Godfrey, keeps it locked up. When I think of the barrels of booze I've tucked away . . ."

Zeke remembered the director's reputation for drinking and brawling, in public and at private parties. His escapades had been familiar to every policeman in Los Angeles.

"I don't enjoy old age. What about you, Ezekiel?"

"It has its positive side. The simple fact of being alive."

"How the devil did you get the name Ezekiel?"

"My father was a religious man. Liked to read aloud from the Old Testament."

"And you?"

"My only belief is that all of life is a series of unpredictable accidents. Many of which we, ourselves, cause."

"People think I'm Irish—like Jack Ford—but I'm only half Celtic. My beautiful mother was a Jew. I'm proud of my Jewish blood." He smiled suddenly. "Ezekiel's an excellent name for a detective. He was a Hebrew prophet of doom."

"But with hope of restoration, as I remember."

"So you know about the guy?"

"Checked him out, years ago, in the San Francisco public library. When I was working for Pinkerton. Wanted to know whose name I'd been using."

"How do you manage to look so young? What's your secret?"

"Proper diet and plenty of vitamins. My third wife taught me that."

"I've been forced to the same things. Reluctantly and, I suspect, too late. By my doctors and my houseman. Godfrey's a nut on both subjects. Hands out the vitamins every morning and tells cook what to feed me." Peering at Zeke again. "I've a feeling you and I have met somewhere before."

"We never actually met, but I worked in one of your features."

"I knew it! Which one?"

"This was long ago. *The Laredo Kid* . . ."

"What part did you play?"

"Wasn't a part. I was one of the cowhands."

"Dammit, I do remember your face. I remember hundreds of faces I never see any more. You ever work as an actor?"

"Nope. Knew I'd never be able to remember all the lines. In

those days I was trying to get on the force—L.A.P.D.—and while I waited did some extra work and stunts. Took a few stand-in jobs. Mostly for Coop and the Duke."

"Two gentlemen."

"Once I was accepted by the L.A.P.D. I never worked at another studio. That life's not for me."

"You preferred the dangerous life of a cop?"

"I think an actor's life is more dangerous. The jungle wars of the studios are tougher to survive than a cop's war against crime."

Dalby chuckled. "I've got scars that'll never heal. Mental and physical . . ." He scowled, suddenly. "Why the hell would Paul Victor have a dinner to 'commemorate' the anniversary of Kara's murder? Can you tell me?"

"I'm beginning to suspect his purpose was to bring five people together, any one of whom might have a clue to who killed her. The old Agatha Christie gimmick. Dinner party or old house on some remote island . . ."

"The identity of Kara's murderer? All these years after the event! Not likely. Why the hell would Paul want to do that?"

"You'll have to ask him."

"He's too devious to ever give a straight answer. Of course, if he's planning a film about Kara's murder, it would be a tremendous publicity break if he could name her killer. Newspapers would front page the story again. If her murder's ever solved they'll dig up all the forgotten facts, play up the old rumors and lies. Television would have her picture on every news show. Her films would be dug from the vaults and run on all the midget screens. They didn't have television when Kara was alive. Even radio was fairly new then . . ."

"One of her films is to be shown on TV tomorrow night."

"So I've been told. I never watch television." He pushed himself back against the chair, his arthritic hands resting on the edge of the desk. "I can't imagine what Paul thought he would get from those four guests—or, for that matter, from me—which might reveal the identity of Kara's murderer."

"Matter of fact, he did learn something."

"Like what?"

"Didn't anyone phone you, yesterday, and tell you?"

"If you mean those others who were invited to dinner, none of them are close friends. I'm not a guy who permits casual acquaintances. Total waste of time! So what did Paul learn?"

"Laurence Knight, apparently, revealed that there was a man who told him, many years ago, that he knew the identity of the murderer."

"Larry must've been in his cups!"

"He's supposed to have had one glass of wine during dinner, a cognac afterward, nothing more. Seems he'd been on the wagon and the drinks hit him."

"That can happen. Who was this person who claimed to know the killer?"

"A man who worked for many of the stars. Including Kara Kolvang."

"His name?"

"Tim Kerrigan."

"That guy was the highest paid flesh pounder in this town. Heads of studios, directors, stars. They all used him. He worked on their bodies while they listened to the latest gossip he'd collected and gave him a few choice morsels of their own."

"Did you ever employ his services?"

"Never needed a masseur in those days. I played tennis and rode my horses. I've always detested gossip, the rotten stories repeated behind people's backs. Including mine! Careers were ruined, decent lives besmirched. I never listened to gossip, at the studio or when I went to parties. There's one thing about this town that's changed for the better. The gossip market died with Hedda and Louella and I, for one, hope it stays dead." Leaning forward.

"You're opening up an old murder case that was never solved? Looking for Kara's murderer?"

"Certainly not. I'm only looking for Laurence Knight. He seems to have disappeared."

"What, precisely, does that mean?"

"He hasn't been seen since Tuesday. The day after Paul Victor's dinner. I suspect he's gone off somewhere to keep out of sight. Someone learned what he said and has threatened him."

"You mean Tim Kerrigan?"

"I doubt that. Whoever it is, they've scared him enough to send him into hiding." He wouldn't tell Dalby that Kerrigan had been strangled and someone had shot holes in Knight's garage doors. "His grandson and housekeeper have no idea where he's gone. The last person to see him, apparently, was Faye Manning."

"Now there's one helluva fine actress! Worked for me many times. Where'd she see Larry?"

"He drove up to her house, Tuesday afternoon. Said he'd repeated something at Paul Victor's party he shouldn't have told anyone—about an old Hollywood scandal—and he was afraid somebody might try to kill him. Promised to call Faye that evening. Never did."

"How the hell did you get involved?"

"Faye contacted me. Hired me to locate Knight."

"And you hoped I might be able to tell you where he is?"

"Not exactly. I wanted to find out why you didn't go to that dinner. You've explained your reason."

"I've not seen Larry in years. We never were close friends, although he worked in several of my films. Two of them starred Kara Kolvang. One was *Park Avenue Girl*, the one they're showing tomorrow night. I suspected, while we were shooting, that Kara was in love with Larry. Most of his leading ladies were. But he never looked at any woman but his wife. For good reason! She was a raving beauty. I've no idea where Larry could be hiding. If that's what he's doing . . ."

"What can you tell me about Kurt von Zemmering?" He asked the question abruptly but Dalby didn't react.

"That elegant creep." His words were barely a whisper.

"You didn't like him?"

"Very few did. Only the women, older women. He was a figure of mystery from the first day he turned up in Hollywood with Kara. Kurt lived alone in a Beverly Hills mansion, with a staff of servants—all foreign—where he gave endless parties. Those were years of spectacular entertaining but Kurt outdid everybody else. Soon after Kara's death, he returned to Europe. Never made another film."

"You think that was because of her murder?"

Dalby hesitated, dramatically. "I've always thought Kurt killed her. Thought so fifty years ago, and I think so now."

"But he was in New York. A dozen people gave him an alibi."

"Maybe he had a twin brother or he hired some actor to impersonate him. Kurt was devious enough to plan things carefully if he wanted to commit murder."

"Was he?"

"There was talk, when I was shooting that last film with Kara, that she and Kurt had been quarreling. She came to the studio one morning, her eyes red and swollen. Said she had a cold, but I knew otherwise. The makeup girl had to hide it. Under all his charm, I suspected Kurt had a violent temper. It flared once or twice with me, but I managed to avoid a serious argument.

"I realized, from our first meeting, Kurt was in love with Kara but she wanted no part of him. Or, perhaps, they'd had an affair in Europe and she wanted to end their relationship. That frequently happens with a young girl and an older man.

"We'll never know, I'm afraid, who murdered Kara. But until the identity of the murderer is established, I shall always think it was Kurt von Zemmering.

"Did you tell the police?"

"Certainly not! I didn't wish to get involved. And I hoped Kurt would arrange backing for another film I was preparing. One without Kara. Hoped he would produce it for me . . ."

"But you didn't like him."

"I've liked very few of the producers I worked with. Hysteric egomaniacs, most of them."

"Any idea what happened to von Zemmering?"

"There were many rumors. He had died in Vienna during a bombing and he drowned with a shipload of refugees. Sunk by a Nazi sub. Who knows what is the truth?"

"I won't trouble you any longer." Zeke pushed himself up from the armchair.

"Been my pleasure. Meeting the 'world's oldest eye' . . ." Extending his suntanned hand across the desk again. "I hope you find Larry."

Zeke shook the outstretched hand, gently, aware of the arthritic knuckles.

"I'm glad you're not looking for Kara's murderer. No chance of finding him, whoever he is—Kurt von Zemmering or someone else—not after this many years. Evidence of guilt, if it ever existed, would've been eliminated by time. No possible way to get at the truth."

"I agree. When I saw Mr. Victor this morning, he offered to pay my fee if I would take on the Kolvang murder."

"What did you say to that?"

"The offer was intriguing, but I turned him down."

"Paul always was a fool. I hope we meet again. You and I . . ."

"That's not likely, I should think. Good day." Zeke headed for the open door, without glancing at the ominous circle of stone heads, and strode through the corridor toward the entrance where the gray-haired houseman waited. He was wearing a striped sport shirt, gray slacks, leather moccasins.

He sensed Zeke approaching and swung the entrance door open onto the veranda.

"Your name's Godfrey, like in the old movie?"

"That's a rather tiresome joke, I fear." His British accent was even more pronounced. "William Powell was one of Mr. Dalby's favorite actors. Hope you got what you wanted, sir."

"Don't know about that. But then I didn't know what I hoped to learn here."

Zeke was frowning as he crossed the veranda.

What the hell had he expected to find out from Dalby?

Not a damn thing . . .

Chapter 11

Zeke put the large magnifying glass aside and removed his reading glasses. Placed the last clipping face-down on top of the others in the fifth blue-cardboard file folder. Turned the stack over, carefully, then closed the folder. Slipped it under the other four and leaned back from his desk, against the padded leather armchair.

He was puzzled and engrossed.

Now then! What did he remember . . .

The first clipping in the first folder had a photograph of a very young Karen Kolvang, cut from a Copenhagen newspaper in 1929. He couldn't read the Danish caption or the brief story under her picture but each clipping was stapled to a sheet of paper with a typed translation and explanatory notes dictated by Paul Victor. Every page was dated.

That first newspaper caption said Karen Jensen, fifteen, had won a prize for acting and dancing. The story explained that she was a local girl appearing in a school production of *Peer Gynt*. The reporter predicted young Karen would be heard from again because her performance had outshone those of her fellow students.

In the faded picture, blonde Karen Jensen posed awkwardly in a fanciful costume. Her figure was that of a plump teenager. It wasn't the figure that held your eye but her face. Strikingly beautiful and innocent. Except for those eyes, staring at the camera. They were the knowing eyes of a mature woman.

He slid the five folders into the manila envelope which he would return to Paul Victor tomorrow. Leave it at his door. Tell the houseman, or whoever answered, that the envelope was for Mr. Victor's secretary. He didn't want to see Paul Victor again. Not just yet.

His desk clock said it was past nine.

He'd been studying Kara Kolvang's file for more than two hours.

Better call Faye Manning . . .

What could he tell her? Certainly nothing about the murder of Tim Kerrigan. That would only make her more anxious about her missing friend.

He snapped off his desk lamp, swiveled the armchair and lurched to his feet. Crossed the dark living room and collapsed onto the sofa facing the terrace—he'd opened the sliding window when he came home—relaxed for a moment, staring at the apartments on the far side of the building. Some of their windows were open but he didn't see any of his neighbors. Only the flickering lights of their television screens.

Those windows made him feel like Jimmy Stewart in *Rear Window* but he'd never witnessed a murder yet. No sign of Raymond Burr.

Mustn't tell Faye anything he had learned today. Not that he'd turned up that much.

Lars Lyndon had gone down to Santa Monica, after somehow tracing Tim Kerrigan, in an effort to locate his grandfather. Was that before or after Kerrigan was murdered? If before, did Lars talk to Kerrigan?

Had Larry Knight found Kerrigan, Tuesday, after seeing Faye? Told him what he'd said at dinner?

Was Kerrigan alive last night when that man with a Latin accent went up to his room?

Lots of questions but not one goddamn answer.

In spite of a long hot shower he was tired. His back muscles still aching from yesterday's fall.

He hadn't actually walked that much today.

Hammett used to say a private eye spent most of his time asking questions and wearing out shoe leather. These days he still asked questions but he wore out tires.

Better have his tires checked next week . . .

Tomorrow morning he would make a list of every person he'd questioned today. Write down what he'd learned from each.

Hammett had taught him to do that.

At the moment he couldn't remember all their names or what they'd said, but he would recall everything after a good night's rest. Or would he? Was his memory getting worse? That was to be expected, of course, but he resented the thought. Better take a couple of choline tablets before he went to bed.

He reached across the coffee table, switched on a shaded lamp and picked up the phone.

Faye's number? He'd written it down last night. Damn! That slip of paper was in his wallet and he didn't have enough strength to go into the bedroom.

The number surfaced slowly in his mind and, smiling now, he dialed. Heard the phone ring twice before it was picked up.

"Good evening, Zeke!"

"You psychic, or something?"

"Don't get many calls any more. Not at this hour."

"Sorry I'm a mite late."

"You said it would be after eight. I've been sitting here, waiting. Hoping you'd have news."

"Spent all day seeing people. Without finding a trace of Larry Knight."

"Didn't think you would this fast."

"Talked to the other guests at that dinner, Monday night, including their host, Paul Victor, and the guest who didn't make it because of illness. It was the director, Clem Dalby."

"I've heard Clem is ill . . ."

"Arthritis. Hands crippled, and I suspect at his age he has other health problems."

"Poor Clem! I must phone him one day. Worked with Clem, years ago, when he was making comedies. That's before he became involved with westerns. I don't work with horses. Clem was a fine director, but we never became friends. For one thing, I detested his wife. Such a bitch! Shouldn't say that about the dead, I suppose. We belonged to completely different social circles. The Dalbys were into horses. Thoroughbreds, polo games, and race tracks! My husbands were businessmen and, surprisingly, interested in music. All of them on the board of the Philharmonic. There's something I wish you'd do . . ."

"What's that?"

"I phoned Larry's residence this evening, but no one was there. Dialed several times. Lars may have gone out for dinner but Mrs. Svendsen, certainly, ought to be there."

"She may have gone to a movie."

"But she told me Larry asked her to stay near the phone until she heard from him."

"Maybe she did hear from him. She's gone to meet him somewhere."

"Oh? I hadn't thought of that."

"I'll stop by there, first thing in the morning. Right now I'm heading for bed. This has been one helluva long day. Always tires me when I don't accomplish anything."

"Well, keep at it, love. For me."

"I'll do that."

"Good night, Zeke . . ."

"Good night." He put the phone down.

What could have happened to Knight's grandson and that housekeeper?

Much too tired to get dressed and drive over there tonight, although instinct told him he should.

He snapped off the lamp and sank back against the pillowed sofa.

Then, very faintly at first, he heard water splashing in the pool.

Sharks nuzzling?

His hearing, at least, remained pretty damn good.

The air seemed warmer than last night. But damp . . .

More fog sneaking through the canyons again?

He glanced toward his silent record player, set against the wall beyond the open kitchen door. Bach or Scarlatti would've relaxed him after his shower but he hadn't felt like changing records.

His apartment got enough greenish light from the pool without turning on any lamps.

He peered toward the corner of his living room, between the open bedroom door and the big window, the space used for his office. A four-drawer steel file stood against the window beyond the old roll-top desk with the comfortable padded armchair.

This was the first apartment where he owned every piece of furniture. Things he'd wanted all his life, like that desk chair he could swivel to look at his potted roses on the balcony.

A light flashed on in one of the opposite apartments.

Sometimes those rows of identical balconies, on the other side, reminded him of cell tiers in a prison . . .

His gut growled faintly.

"Can't be hungry, kid. I won't accept that. Not after all the Mexican food we ate . . ."

He'd eaten before he came home because he knew he wouldn't go out again.

"Maybe you had too many hot peppers, but you're not hungry."

The phone rang on the coffee table.

He wasn't going to take another call tonight.

Only one ring?

He stared at the ghostly white shape in the dark. Smiled and waited.

It rang again.

He reached out and picked it up. "Emma! Sweetheart . . ."

"That you, honey?"

"Who else? Nobody here when I'm not home."

"Called twice. Earlier . . ."

As she talked he heard a piano playing Chopin, very softly, behind her gentle voice. With Emma there was always music in the background. "Why didn't you phone Nettie and leave a message?"

"Wasn't important . . ."

"Had a busy day but I'm off to bed in ten minutes."

"Solving lots of crimes, as usual?"

"Now and again. How are you, my lady?"

"Surviving. For, at least, another day . . ."

"And Aldo?"

"Weary. He taught two master classes this afternoon at the college. Matter of fact, he's asleep. I can hear him snoring. Out on the terrace. I'll wake him, presently, and take him to bed."

"You doing another concert tour this winter?"

"No more concerts."

"When did that happen?"

"Last month. Our manager offered us a short tour—shortest ever—and we decided we're too old."

"Ridiculous!"

"We can't look at all those tacky little auditoriums again. Same old faces staring at us. They get older each year, and so do we. Aldo standing there with his fiddle ready. While I pose gracefully at the Steinway, in this year's gown. Never again . . ."

"I can't believe this!"

"Be different if Aldo were Isaac Stern and I was Alicia de Larrocha. Each year our tours have gotten shorter. Been months since you called . . ."

"No!"

"Well, not months, I guess. But then you were never there, while we were married, whenever I had to make some sort of decision."

"So you used to say."

"You weren't there the night I decided I wanted a divorce, in order to marry Aldo. You were off on one of your investigations and it was weeks before I could tell you my decision. That I'd already seen an attorney. You never did bother to see him. Moved out that night . . ."

"I was furious. Still in love with you. Couldn't understand what had happened."

"Guess I'm still in love with you, Zeke. After all these years. Always will be. Remember that . . ."

"What? What're you saying?"

"I simply had to get away from you and have a life of my own again. Back to my music. Even if it only meant a lousy tour every year with Aldo."

"You told me you loved that fiddler."

"I lied. I like him, but I've never loved him. Wanted to tell you but you were involved with some murder. I think you were in Hawaii that time . . ."

He sighed. "I don't remember what job I was on."

"Aldo's a dear man but I never loved him. Not the way I loved you. Still do . . ."

"Divorce him! Marry me again."

"Too late for that. Way too late . . ."

"There's never been another woman in my life. Since you left me."

"Did you say that to your other wives?"

"I loved all my wives. Every one of 'em!"

"Your voice sounds so young, Zeke. Like when we first met."

"I still love you, Emma. Think of you every day and always will."

"When you're not thinking about some criminal? Some murderer . . ." She laughed. "Why not drive down here tomorrow for lunch?"

"Well, I—I . . ."

"Aldo would enjoy that. He's always been fond of you. Never could understand why I left you. The famous private eye! I'll fix your favorite Basque omelette in that big copper pan. Remember?"

"Sure do."

"Or what about my barbecued prawns? You used to like them."

"Can't eat prawns any more. No shrimp or lobster. Not since those kidney stones, two years ago. I never go off my diet."

"I'll cook anything you can eat. Just tell me."

"Afraid tomorrow's out of the question."

"I knew it would be. Another murder?"

"I'm looking for a man who disappeared this week. Here in Los Angeles. It's involved with the murder of a famous actress."

"Haven't read anything like that in the paper."

"She was murdered fifty years ago."

"You're standing me up for some actress who's been dead fifty years?"

He recognized the familiar hint of anger in her voice. "Sorry, sweetheart. Maybe I can make it for lunch next week."

"We may all be dead before next week. You used to say there was a bullet waiting for you in somebody's gun. Somebody you didn't even know. Now there's an atomic bomb waiting for all of us. Good night, Zeke . . ."

"Wait a second, honey!"

"Only called to let you know—I still think about you. Still love you . . ."

"But, Emma . . ."

"And I always will! Remember that . . ."

He heard the connection broken and, slowly, returned the phone to its cradle.

Emma hadn't changed. And neither had he. Nobody ever changed . . .

When they were first married their arguments would end with her sitting at the new baby grand and playing something with crashing chords. He never knew what the music was and, usually, left the apartment before she finished.

Hours later, he would return to find her in bed, asleep. Next day their argument was forgotten. At least she would never say anything.

He bought that baby grand for her and she had taken it when she left him. He wondered if she still had the same one. Used it to teach her pupils. That piano he heard tonight, behind her voice, was a recording. Maybe one of her own tapes. She'd made several, playing Chopin. He knew it was Chopin, but didn't recognize the composition.

When he married Emma he'd known damn little about music. Those were the happy times, their first years together, going to summer concerts at the Bowl or listening to Emma play Bach, after dinner, in their apartment on Havenhurst.

Remember to call her next week. Drive down to La Jolla for lunch in their apartment overlooking the ocean. Or take them to dinner. Maybe that French restaurant in Ensenada they both liked. Emma and Aldo . . .

He wondered if their marriage continued to be happy? Would

the end of their concert tours cause friction? Put an end to their marriage?

Emma had sounded remote on the phone. As though she hadn't finished what she intended to say...

Mustn't forget to call her. Soon as he located Laurence Knight.

Instead of lunch he would spend an evening with them. Let Emma cook dinner. Next to music, cooking was her greatest passion. There would be music afterward. The two of them—Emma and Aldo—playing a Mozart violin sonata for an audience of one. He would watch them, study their faces. Find out what was wrong...

Emma had been his favorite wife. Or was that only because she was the last?

He was beginning to forget the others...

Zeke pushed himself up from the sofa, wrapping the striped robe around his body as he went through the open window onto the balcony.

Glanced at his roses before sinking onto the chaise. Kicked off both sandals and wiggled his toes in the cool night air as he relaxed.

He enjoyed stretching out here, aware of the dark city pulsating around him, whenever he had serious problems to consider. Conscious of brakes protesting as cars stopped suddenly for traffic lights on Sunset. Aware of the distinctive sirens. Squad car, fire engine, ambulance. More people in trouble...

Before turning in he wanted to consider the few important facts he'd learned about Kara Kolvang from those file folders. Her public and private lives. Her murder...

Newspaper coverage of the Kolvang murder was far from complete. The police, in those days, kept a much lower profile. Rarely gave a detective's name or released important information on a case until long after it had been closed.

The second clipping in Paul Victor's first file folder—this one from the *New York Times*—reported that several Hollywood studios were interested in a young Danish actress—Karen Jensen—who had starred in Scandinavian and French films and was, currently, performing on the Paris stage.

A color photograph, from some foreign magazine, of a beautiful girl with long blonde hair and delicate features. The face almost childlike. Not a Hollywood face. That picture had been taken before she came to America and it was the face in the painting Henri Neri had shown him.

More clippings reported Metro considering her as a new personality to develop into an international star.

Miss Jensen—her name was still Karen Jensen—had been in European films for several years. She had tremendous talent, singing and dancing, as well as acting. There were enthusiastic quotes from foreign critics about her distinctive qualities, with more photographs.

Paul Victor's attached notations explained that Metro had not followed through with a contract and Miss Jensen was continuing on the Paris stage as star of an operetta, *The Snow Princess*, an adult version of *Snow White*. There was another memo that said this was before the Disney cartoon version.

Victor explained that the show was a musical about a Parisian waif whose home was a cold attic, who dreamed of a princess who dwelt in a castle of ice with her parents who ruled a faraway land where it was always winter. Instead of seven dwarves there were seven tough street urchins from Montmartre who were her protectors. In her dreams she became the snow princess and they were her courtiers. The prince of her dreams carried her off to a sunny land of flowers—the Riviera—where they were married and lived happily ever after. Victor pointed out that the plot made no sense but the musical score by a young Viennese composer, Kurt Wulff, was charming. If the story could be laundered for an American audience, it would make a film that should have an international success.

He added that when he saw the Paris production, while on

vacation, Miss Jensen was a sensation. Brilliant actress, superb soprano—almost operatic—and exceptional talent as a dancer. She was, in fact, a second Marilyn Miller.

A further note said that Victor had suggested to Adolph Zukor, at Paramount, that he should put Karen Jensen under contract.

Other clippings featured Karen Jensen's personal manager, Kurt von Zemmering, who had rejected all Hollywood offers for Miss Jensen and was starring her in a musical film—*The Girl On the Corner*—that was being shot in a French studio.

There were photographs of von Zemmering in each file folder. Arriving on a French liner with Karen Jensen, their first visit to New York. Stepping off a train in Los Angeles. Dozens of photographs of them in the following years.

The producer was odd and mysterious looking, even in photographs. For one thing, his face was never in focus because he always stood slightly behind the actress. She was in bright light, but he stayed in the shadow. An extremely tall man. Thin, almost skeletal. Long black hair. Handsome face dominated by penetrating eyes, always focused on the camera. An unforgettable face. Never smiling in any of the photographs.

Pictures of Kara with her sister, Inga Jensen. Younger and plumper, with the same delicate features, but not as strikingly beautiful. The flesh seemed to blur her features.

Some shots of Kara in Solvang. Standing beside a white Packard Victoria Convertible in front of what appeared to be a farmhouse. Other people around her, their faces unfamiliar.

One of Kara with von Zemmering in what must've been the main street in Solvang. Kara laughing, the producer scowling, as usual, his eyes hidden under the brim of a straw hat. Didn't the man ever smile? The street seemed only a single block in length. A few young trees and small shops.

Another picture of Kara with her sister wearing an elaborate wedding gown, surrounded by a wedding party. Inga Jensen, according to the caption, had married Nels Andersen, a handsome blond giant, who looked uncomfortable in his best dark suit. All the faces smiling, except Kurt von Zemmering. This was the only picture in which his face was revealed. He looked much older than the other members of the party.

A dozen or more pictures of Kara with Laurence Knight. Some were stills from films they had made together. Others showed them arriving at a theater for the opening of a film. Kara always wearing white furs, Knight in a tuxedo. The two of them beside a swimming pool, dining in a fancy restaurant and laughing in front of a shiny Plymouth Sport Phaeton. Kurt von Zemmering was missing from those pictures.

He'd learned very little from the file of clippings covering the murder. Only that the body had been found behind some boulders on a stretch of beach beyond the northern edge of Malibu.

Young couple noticed a bare foot and went closer to investigate. Saw it was the nude body of a young woman. Somebody had called the police.

When they arrived they didn't identify the actress. Her identity wasn't established until someone at the morgue, next morning, recognized her battered face.

That must've caused a sensation and the delay in identification would have resulted in a loss of evidence and clues.

When homicide detectives reached the scene, finally, the sand would have been disturbed by so many feet that the murderer's prints—if any—would've been destroyed.

The dead girl's clothing was never found but her car had been discovered at the edge of the Coast Highway abandoned behind some bushes.

No prints on the car—not even the owner's—so the killer had wiped it clean. The victim's purse was in the glove compartment with a large sum of money and an assortment of personal documents. The car was locked but the keys were never found. The autopsy revealed that Kara Kolvang had been beaten and raped, her neck broken. Probably a complete stranger had followed her along the beach, attacked and killed her.

If that was how it happened, the murderer would never be found.

Hammett had been right.

Impossible to take prints from bruises on her throat that many hours after the attack.

This explained why the police, eventually, gave up and closed the case. Lack of evidence. The killer must've taken her clothes, burned them and disposed of the keys. Far from the murder scene.

Zeke closed his eyes and saw their faces . . .

Kara Kolvang with Kurt von Zemmering.

She was dressed in white with flashing diamonds. He wore tails, looking distinguished and elegantly evil. Holding out his hand as he helped her down from a shiny black Cadillac.

She was smiling.

Long blonde hair. Dazzling blue eyes.

She was dancing with Laurence Knight at some fancy party.

Crowd of people in evening clothes. Dancing and smiling . . .

Kara smiling. Always smiling.

Everybody smiling . . .

Chapter 12

Rock music. Harsh and insistent.
 The air felt chilly on his bare ankles.
Zeke opened his eyes slowly to see daylight.
Goddamn!
He'd fallen asleep and spent the night on his balcony. It was a struggle to get up from the chaise, legs stiff, back and shoulders one solid ache.
He glanced across to the other balconies but nobody was watching him and no sharks were gliding in the pool.
The music was coming from an upstairs apartment on his side of the building. Young punks playing rock at this hour! He would complain to the manager again.
Clear blue sky but the sun hadn't risen from behind the opposite roof. So it couldn't be late.
He secured his robe as he stumbled inside, across the living

room and into his bedroom. Checked the bedside clock on his way into the bath.

Six thirty-seven!

Glanced at his undisturbed bed. At least he wouldn't have to make that today.

Before showering he took his usual vitamins with extra choline and rutin tablets.

Shaved and showered, he fixed breakfast and ate it standing in the kitchen. Left the dishes in the sink for his maid.

Pulled the morning paper in from the corridor and checked the local crime news. Nothing about Tim Kerrigan or Laurence Knight. The aged man strangled in his furnished room wasn't important enough and the police didn't know Knight was missing.

Zeke dropped the paper on a chair and sat at his desk, still in his robe and sandals.

He made out two lists.

First the names of Paul Victor and his four dinner guests, with the name of the guest who didn't join them. Beside each name he wrote down what they had said in answer to his questions. The few facts he had learned. More about Kara Kolvang than the missing actor. Odd how all of them brought up Kurt von Zemmering. Their dislike for him. Dalby was the only one to say he thought von Zemmering was the murderer.

Then a list of what he remembered from those five file folders about the dead actress. Nothing important.

Both lists were brief.

He reread them and put them in a drawer of his desk for future reference.

Found Faye's list of private numbers and called Laurence Knight's residence. Let the phone ring several times before he set his down.

Maybe Knight had returned but wasn't taking calls. Had ordered the housekeeper not to answer.

He wondered if that sheep dog—Rip—barked when the phone rang?

In the bedroom, as he dressed, he planned what he must do this morning.

First—return those file folders to Paul Victor before he checked the Laurence Knight residence.

If Knight returned last night he might be sleeping late. People didn't like to be questioned early in the morning. Put them in a bad mood and you never got much information from them.

The bedside clock said eight forty-five as he left the apartment.

Must remember to get gas.

He pulled into the gas station, at Sunset and Fairfax, and had them fill the tank of his Chevy.

Continued on, out Sunset, through heavy morning traffic.

Preoccupied with thoughts about the missing man and the dead man.

Who was that Mexican who, apparently, was the last person to see Kerrigan alive? Was he the one who fired six shots into those garage doors?

Remember to call Emma later today . . .

She had sounded depressed last night. He could tell from her voice. Emma had always gone through low periods. Especially after she realized she would never have a career as a concert pianist and the best she could hope for were recording jobs with pickup orchestras.

He parked on San Ysidro again and carried the clumsy manila envelope up the freshly watered walk to the entrance. Jabbed the bell button. Heard the chimes play their same corny tune inside.

Glanced at the flower garden, as he waited, and imagined Paul Victor trimming his rosebushes. Not likely! Japanese gardeners would arrive two or three times a week to do that.

"Good morning, Inspector Gahagan."

He turned, startled from his reverie, to see the black houseman. Today he was smiling.

"Mr. Victor said it might be you."

"Did he? Will you give this to Mr. Victor's secretary?" He held out the bulky envelope. "Afraid I don't remember her name."

"Miss Aggie?"

"She's the one. Tell her everything's here."

"I'll be sure to do that, sir. Mr. Victor will be unhappy, if he doesn't talk to you. He's having breakfast on the east terrace. Waiting to find out who rang the bell."

"This morning I'm in a hurry."

"Mr. Victor would be happy to delay you for at least half an hour."

"I'm sure he would, but not today. Give me two minutes to reach my car." He hurried down the walk toward the gate. Avoided a large leaf that had dared to drop on the immaculate cement. Paul Victor wouldn't like that.

Driving back to Hollywood, he wondered if Victor's secretary —Miss Aggie—would ever write her novel. Did people do that? Sit down and write a book . . .

Hammett had talked about writing one for years, before he ever did . . .

He was reminded that he hadn't bought any books in weeks. Should pick up a few paperbacks. He liked new writers and he was always looking for old books by Simenon. He must have fifty Simenons but the man had published hundreds. Some day he wanted to own all of them.

Simenon was Hammett's favorite . . .

He could never understand how Simenon had written so many books and Hammett only wrote five. Of course his health had been bothersome. Tuberculosis, off and on, most of his life. Even so, *The Maltese Falcon* was as good as Simenon or anybody else ever wrote.

Zeke parked the Chevy on Curson and jogged up the sloping drive to the rear. Saw, as he reached the top, that all the garage doors were closed.

His eyes checked the row of bullet holes as he walked closer. Were those six bullets buried in the walls of the two garages?

He grasped the handle of the first door—the housekeeper's garage—and felt the door move. Raised it and peered inside.

The space was empty.

Lars said that Mrs. Svendsen drove a Volkswagen. She was Danish, so it would, very likely, be blue. Danes seemed to like blue. He recalled she was wearing a blue uniform yesterday.

Stepping inside the garage he saw that Lars's car—a white MG—was in the second space. So the grandson must be home.

Beyond the MG was another empty space. Laurence Knight hadn't returned.

At the far end he could make out the unmistakable shape of a black Rolls in the fourth parking space.

He wouldn't look for those bullets. Leave them for Hollywood Division.

Zeke came out from the garage and looked at the steps leading up to the kitchen landing. The kitchen door would be closed and it would be impossible to see through the screened windows. He would have to go around to the front.

Suddenly the morning silence was broken by the howling of a dog. Unmistakably a large dog. The sound was like that of a wild animal in pain.

Moving quickly, he crossed the parking area and bounded up the steps, unaware of the aches in his body.

At the top, breathing heavily, he covered his right hand with a handkerchief and tried the screen door.

It wasn't locked.

Swung it open and grasped the handle of the kitchen door with his covered hand.

Also unlocked.

Didn't people lock their doors in this neighborhood? Very foolish . . .

As he pushed the door open, slowly, the dog howled again.

Laurence Knight's sheepdog.

He stepped inside, cautiously, and paused to listen.

The big mansion was silent.

Through the open door, behind him, he could hear birds singing in the trees.

The dog howled again, at some distance, toward the front.

Zeke closed the kitchen door and glanced around.

Nothing had been changed. Everything seemed to be in place, neat and tidy, as though Mrs. Svendsen had cleaned here this morning.

He crossed the kitchen, his rubber soles silent on the tiled floor, to the open door leading to the rest of the house.

Stepped into the remembered hall where faint light seeped through several pairs of open doors from distant windows.

Moving more quickly, across thick carpet now, he started toward the front hall.

The dog stopped howling, abruptly.

Had he sensed an intruder?

In the silence, for the first time, he was aware of a steady hum from air conditioners.

An immense black and white shape hurtled toward him through the dim light.

Zeke stopped dead and waited.

The dog was coming fast.

"It's all right, boy," he whispered. "Everything's fine, Rip. Good dog. That's a good boy . . ."

The sheepdog slowed to a halt, facing him, sniffing the air.

He could see its muzzle, the open jaw and white teeth. "Remember me? I hope . . ."

The dog moved closer, slowly, and nudged him.

He could feel the hard skull through his jacket, rubbing against his hip. "Such a good boy." Holding his voice down. "Rip's a good dog." The tail was wagging. "Especially when he doesn't bite."

The dog had remembered his voice or his scent. "You alone here?" Patting him on the head. "Everybody left you?"

The dog whimpered then turned and ran back, ears flopping, toward the front.

Zeke followed, still moving cautiously, looking through each pair of open doors into empty rooms. Saw sunlight through the closed windows.

Rip turned right, as he reached the broad staircase, bounded up the carpeted steps and began to howl again.

He quickened his steps and approached the foot of the elaborately carved staircase. Was the dog going upstairs?

In the faint light Zeke saw him crouching beside a body sprawled on the carpeted steps. A man's body.

Laurence Knight?

He hesitated, peering around the shadowy hall. Saw pale light through the stained glass panels in the massive entrance door. More doors standing open toward the front, on both sides, and the daylight coming from distant windows seemed to be getting brighter. Or his eyes could be adjusting to the faint light.

Zeke turned back to the staircase and approached the bottom step.

He had found Laurence Knight . . .

Rip was whimpering softly and looking at him, as though for help.

Knight's body was twisted, one long leg under the other. He had fallen backward against the steps. Head turned at an awkward angle.

Zeke moved farther along the bottom step to get a better view of Knight's face. The face he had seen in those clippings last night. Young Laurence Knight . . .

It was the grandson!

His soft, childlike face was untouched by death but the thirty-three-year-old baby's life was finished.

Zeke looked around for a light switch. Noticed a row of them in a brass wall panel at the side of the staircase near the carved banister. Hurried along the edge of the bottom step and, covering his fingers again, snapped several switches.

Lights blazed overhead in a crystal chandelier he hadn't noticed on his previous visit and in candelabra along the walls and in the upstairs hall.

Zeke blinked in the sudden glare as he turned to the body on the steps.

Lars was wearing pale blue pajamas and his feet were bare again.

The dog continued to whimper, crouched above the dead man's head.

"Quiet, Rip. No barking." He went up several steps and bent to inspect the dead man more closely.

His pajama coat was soaked with blood. That amount couldn't come from a knife wound. It had to be a gun. No powder burns. The shot had been fired, most likely, from the bottom of the steps. Probably a .45 automatic. The blood had dried so Lars had been dead for several hours. The wound was near his heart. Not close enough to cause instant death. The bullet must've severed the aorta. At least, after a few minutes, he would've lost consciousness.

The dog howled again, suddenly, head thrown back.

"Quiet!" Zeke ordered as he looked and saw that the whiskers under his chin were stained with blood that had dried dark brown. He had nudged the body, trying to rouse his friend.

Lars must've heard a noise in the night—maybe the dog had barked—and come downstairs. The intruder saw him on the steps and, in the dark, thought he was Laurence Knight.

For what other reason would he have killed the grandson? This had to be mistaken identity.

Zeke turned from the body and went down the steps.

Stooped to examine the carpet at the bottom but there was no possible way to find prints on the elaborate design.

There had to be some evidence here that would give him a clue to the killer. Or lead him to Laurence Knight.

Could Knight have shot his grandson?

Lars said his grandfather had a hell of a temper . . .

No! It had to be whoever put those shots into the garage doors and strangled Kerrigan.

And murdered Kara Kolvang?

The dog was moaning again.

No point in wasting time here.

Zeke, moving automatically, clicked off all the lights and went to the front of the house where he checked each room, Rip trotting beside him.

First a large sitting room and, directly across the hall, a study or den. Everything in order. Nothing seemed to be out of place.

He had a feeling he was walking through display windows in a big department store. Nothing to indicate that people lived here.

Toward the rear, beyond the staircase, was the dining room. An immense bare table gleamed with polish and every antique chair was set against the paneled walls. Nothing to reveal anything about the murderer.

Zeke crossed the hall and went into the library where he had waited yesterday.

Seemed like a week ago . . .

Books and magazines piled everywhere. One pile of books had fallen from a leather armchair and spilled across an Oriental rug.

Had the killer knocked them down in the dark? He didn't recall seeing them on the floor yesterday.

Crystal ash trays on the tables. All were clean.

Antique desk against one wall, between two windows, with stacks of papers spread out.

Moving closer he saw they were letters and bills. Each pile held by a paperweight. An ivory telephone placed in the center, as though someone had used it.

He stood there, not touching anything, handkerchief still covering his hand.

Rip sat beside him, watching every move he made.

Bending closer to the desk, he squinted at the top letter through the glass paperweight.

A personal note from some actress in London who hoped dear Larry might suggest her for a film job in Hollywood.

His attention was caught by something white protruding from under the phone.

He lifted the ivory telephone with his handkerchief-covered hand and set it to one side.

Leaned down to examine the slip of paper. Saw that it was a page torn from a pad. There were words printed in blue ink.

> Rancho Sanjo
> Santa Ynez

Followed by a phone number under which was written:

> confirm reservation
> Friday morning

Had Lars made a reservation and planned to confirm it this morning? Or was this his grandfather's handwriting?

Santa Ynez was north of Santa Barbara.

He pulled a small pad and a pen from his pockets and copied the notation. Returned them to the same pockets and, after setting the phone on the slip of paper again, left the room.

The sheepdog followed him to the kitchen where two metal bowls sat, in a holder, near the big refrigerator. There was water in one bowl but no food in the other.

Rip sniffed at the empty bowl before taking a drink of water. Then, whiskers dripping, he turned to look up at Zeke.

He saw that the water was stained pink with blood.

The dog whimpered.

"Sorry, boy. Can't feed you. There'll be people here in half an hour. They'll find your food. Tell them a big dog like you needs two cans." He scratched Rip's head, behind one of the floppy ears.

Rip wagged his tail but returned to the empty food bowl again.

Which gave Zeke a chance to escape.

He made it to the outside landing and closed the door before he heard the dog's head bumping against the door.

Folded the handkerchief and returned it to his pocket as he checked the neighbors' houses. No windows visible through the trees. So nobody was watching him.

Rip was howling again inside.

Zeke hurried down the steps to the parking area and on, down the sloping drive, to the street.

Young woman walking a Yorkie, higher up the hill, facing the other direction.

He could no longer hear Rip.

Zeke got into his car and drove down to Sunset where he pulled into the parking lot of the supermarket where he did his shopping.

Went inside to a row of pay phones near the entrance.

Dropped in coins and jabbed buttons to get a familiar number. Better disguise his voice.

"Hollywood Division. Can I help you?"

"Police, Señor?"

"That's right, amigo."

"I call—report somethin. I am gardener for Señor Knight—big movie star—lives on Curson . . ."

"Curson? What number?"

He gave it to him.

"What's the problem?"

"I call from neighbor's house. When I drive up to water trees in back I see bullet holes in garage doors . . ."

"Yeah?"

"Six beeg bullet holes. I go to kitchen door but, when I knock, nobody answer. I hear dog bark but nobody home. It is beeg dog, Señor."

"Is the door unlocked?"

"I didn try it. You better come fast, Señor. Somethin is very wrong. Watch out for dog!"

Zeke hung the phone back in place and moved to another one at the far end of the row. Pulled the pad from his pocket. Inserted several more coins and dialed 1-805 as indicated, then the Santa Ynez number.

A woman's voice answered, after the third ring. "Good morning. Rancho Sanja Motel . . ."

"Good morning, ma'am. You have a reservation for Mr. Lars Lyndon?"

"Been expecting him to call and confirm it. Didn't say what time he'd be arriving, but then he seldom does."

"I'm afraid he won't be able to make it today."

"Oh . . . Well, that's no problem. I told him, when he phoned yesterday, we'll be full this weekend. I'll have no trouble renting his room to someone else."

"But I want you to hold the reservation for me, ma'am. I'll be arriving around noon."

"Be glad to hold it for you, if you're a friend of Lars. Your name?"

"Gahagan. I'm calling from Los Angeles."

"I'll be looking for you, Mr. Gahagan. This is our big weekend of the year. How long do you plan to stay?"

"Two or three nights. Maybe longer."

"That's fine."

"You say this is a busy weekend?"

"It's the annual Danish Days celebration in Solvang. Lasts two days. Tomorrow and Sunday."

"Solvang?"

"Every hotel in Solvang is filled. We get their overflow. I told

Lars he wouldn't have found a room anywhere if I hadn't gotten a cancellation."

"You're near Solvang, are you?"

"Two miles east, on Highway 246."

"Thank you, ma'am. See you later this morning." He set the phone back on its plastic holder and headed for the parking lot.

That woman, she must be the motel manager, obviously knew Lars. He must've stayed at the Rancho Sanjo before. She sounded in her forties. Maybe older. Friendly sort of voice. She might know Laurence Knight and be able to tell him where to find the missing actor.

Solvang?

Kara Kolvang . . .

Was the answer to Laurence Knight's disappearance waiting in Solvang?

Could that be why his grandson planned to go up there today?

As he came out, through the automatic sliding glass door of the supermarket, he heard a distant police siren.

Squad car, moving fast.

He smiled.

Hollywood Division was losing no time.

While they looked for Lars Lyndon's murderer he would spend the weekend in Solvang.

Book Three

Andante

Chapter 13

Late morning traffic on U.S. 101 was sparse, except for a few big diesels puffing greasy smoke into the bright sunlight.

Zeke turned off, onto Highway 154, after passing Santa Barbara which, according to the Automobile Club map, was a scenic route.

Signs said it was the San Marcos Pass.

He had packed an overnight bag, careful to include his bottles of vitamins and an extra pair of contact lenses in a leather case.

Didn't bother to stop at the bank to withdraw a gun from his safe-deposit box. In spite of two murders, Tim Kerrigan and Lars Lyndon, he saw no reason to arm himself.

He'd never liked guns, although he'd won prizes for marksmanship when he was a young cop. He always had a strong feeling that if he didn't carry a gun he wouldn't kill anybody, and nobody would kill him.

Thus far his theory had worked. Shots had been fired in his

direction many times, over the years, but they always missed. Criminals, he had learned early, were lousy shots. If they got you it was an accident.

He noticed several immense oak trees and saw he was approaching what appeared to be a sizable body of water on his right. A clear blue lake sparkling in the sunshine. Signs said it was Lake Cachuma.

He'd had no idea there was a large lake in the Santa Ynez Valley. Probably manmade, from the look of it. There seemed to be a park along its edges. Sailboats gliding on the water but nobody was swimming. No sharks here. Narrow strips of yellow sand edging the shore must've been hauled up from the coast.

Driving higher, between low foothills, he was aware of thick green foliage edging both sides of the highway. Hardly any traffic now. Some tanned kids in pickup trucks raced past, heading for the lake.

He'd never visited Solvang in all the years he'd lived in California. One of his wives—he thought it was the French one—talked about driving up for a weekend but he'd never had the time . . .

Of course he'd had the time!

But he always preferred to stay home for a day of rest on Sunday—particularly summer weekends—then take his wives out to dinner at one of his favorite restaurants. Musso's or the Hollywood Derby.

Hammett liked Musso's . . .

Frequently, to celebrate the finish of a big job, he'd taken his wives to Perino's or one of the upstairs restaurants in Chinatown.

Emma was the one who enjoyed Chinese food.

He couldn't eat it any more because of the damn monosodium glutamate . . .

Must be careful what he ate this weekend in strange restaurants. Not fall off his diet.

Two diets! For arthritis and kidney stones . . .

He realized he was whistling softly. Feeling pretty damn good today. He'd slept well, last night, on that balcony. Thank God it hadn't stirred up his arthritis.

What was he whistling? He tried the melody again and decided it was from one of the Scarlatti sonatas Emma used to play.

Meant to call her back today . . .

Maybe it was better he hadn't because he had no idea what was waiting for him in Solvang. He might not return to L.A. before Monday . . .

Nobody knew he was coming up here. Except Nettie. He'd called her, this morning, and given her the name of his motel and the phone number. Warned her not to contact him unless it was absolutely urgent. Hold all messages. Even Faye Manning. Tell everybody he was out of town on a job.

What did he hope to find in Solvang?

One missing actor—age eighty—named Laurence Knight.

Eighty-year-old men were seldom reported missing. You always knew where they were, at that age. Most of them . . .

He'd heard, somewhere, that Knight owned a property in Solvang.

Ring his doorbell and the actor would open the door . . .

Not likely!

Maybe Knight's housekeeper, Mrs. Svendsen, would be here. She said her sister had a restaurant in Solvang. Check that . . .

There had to be an important reason for the grandson to phone and make a reservation at this motel. The woman who ran it might have some idea why he was planning to stay there this weekend, instead of with his grandfather.

Solvang also meant Kara Kolvang.

Solvang—Kolvang . . .

The young actress had spent many weekends here. According to those clippings.

Had any of the men he interviewed yesterday come up here with her?

Certainly Laurence Knight had. Probably Henri Neri and Eric Wulff. Dalby? Not likely. And he doubted that Kevin Mallon ever made it.

There were several photographs of Kurt von Zemmering in Solvang with the actress.

What about Kerrigan? Had Kara or one of her guests brought him up for some long ago weekend to amuse her friends? Spin his stories for them while he massaged their bodies?

And Kara's sister! Was she alive? Still living in Solvang . . .

Now that he was considering his purpose here—what he must look for—he realized there was, very likely, much to be learned in Solvang. People he should question.

But he mustn't get sidetracked and try to solve that Kolvang murder.

He was here to find Laurence Knight. Nothing more.

Hammett always said you must follow a single trail when you're searching for a missing person. Keep your nose pointed toward that one set of footprints.

Faye was paying him to locate Knight. Not Kara Kolvang's murderer.

He'd turned down two people who were eager to pay him to do that. Paul Victor and Henri Neri . . .

He slowed the Chevy as he saw a sign indicating where Highway 154 crossed Highway 246.

A smaller sign said Solvang with an arrow pointing left.

Zeke swerved onto 246 and was soon passing small ranches where sleek horses ran free in the fields. Must be horse breeding country.

He considered, briefly, what Santa Monica Division would be doing to solve the death of Kerrigan. Those prints on his throat would be of no help. Much too faint. Nothing in his room to tell them anything and his name would mean nothing. An old man strangled in a cheap rooming house.

And what had Hollywood Division done about Lars Lyndon? They would learn from neighbors that he was Laurence Knight's grandson. That should send them looking for Knight and his missing housekeeper.

He hoped, for the moment, no clue would bring them to Solvang.

They would, certainly, find that phone number and name of the motel on Knight's desk. Would call and be told that Lars had made a reservation but never showed up. Nothing suspicious about that . . .

There was nothing to connect the two dead men. Nothing to indicate that Lars was one of the men who had visited Kerrigan . . .

What if Laurence Knight was dead? Shot by the same gun that killed his grandson?

He had a strong feeling that the actor was alive and he would find him in Solvang . . .

Zeke slowed the Chevy as he saw signs pointing right, off the highway, saying that a scattering of houses and small shops was the town of Santa Ynez.

Driving on, past a filling station and a store, he saw more signs. This was East Highway 246 and Solvang was only three miles away.

Straight ahead was a neat motel that looked like a small barn. Swimming pool in the center, cars for rent in front. Was this the one he was seeking?

He slowed to check the sign. Sanja Cota Motor Lodge . . .

Continuing on he passed a large supermarket on the opposite side of the highway—El Rancho Market—its parking lot full of cars. As he crossed Alamo Pintado Road he glimpsed the sign he sought.

RANCHO SANJA MOTEL

These must be Mexican names—Sanja Cota and Rancho Sanja—so there was a Mexican colony here.

The Rancho Sanja was a one-story motel. Imitation Early-California. Stucco painted to resemble adobe. Office on the right, at the front, an arcade beyond with wooden columns supporting a red-tiled roof extending toward the rear of the complex.

Turning into the entrance drive he saw a swimming pool in the middle with patio furniture and parasols. A tall woman in a neat yellow dress was standing under the arcade, talking to a maid whose utility cart stood between the open doors of two rooms.

The woman looked around when she heard the car. Gave some final instruction to the maid and came toward the office.

Zeke got out, glancing at the front office through a large picture window. There was nobody at the small information desk. He went to meet the woman who, as she came closer, looked even more attractive.

She walked along the arcade, in the shade, her body solid under the yellow summer dress. Arms and legs dark from the sun, bare feet in huarches. Tall woman, probably five foot ten. Beautiful face with intelligent brown eyes that were appraising him. He paused as she came closer, and saw that her hair was chestnut with some gray at the sides, brushed back from her forehead. Large mouth with white teeth. She was smiling.

"You must be Mr. Gahagan."

"That's right."

"I'm Hildreth Johnson." Extending her hand.

"Mrs. Johnson . . ." He shook the hand, aware that the flesh was firm from manual labor and her grasp was strong.

"So you're a friend of Lars." Leading him toward the office. "What happened to him?" She pushed the glass door open and went inside. "When did you see him?"

"Matter of fact, I saw him yesterday." Following her inside. "Talked to him."

"He knew, yesterday, he couldn't get up here and didn't call me? That was rather thoughtless of him."

"Something changed his plans. Unexpectedly."

"He's always changing his plans." She slipped behind the information counter to a desk with a miniature switchboard and brought a leather pad holding registration forms to the counter. "Lars has a large problem, I'm afraid. He doesn't like to make decisions. Too indecisive to make plans for anything." Revolving the leather pad to face him and handing him a pen. "If you'll sign this . . ."

Zeke took the pen and signed his name as they talked. Adding Los Angeles and the number of his license plate. "How long have you known Lars?" he asked, before she could ask the same question.

"Almost three years, I believe. That's the first time he stayed here. Soon after he arrived from London."

"I thought his grandfather had a house here."

"He does. But, unfortunately, most weekends there are guests and there's only one extra bedroom. When that happens Lars gives up his room and stays here. He's a darling, Lars—just like Larry—but without Larry's drive or ambition. Larry worries about him. Afraid he'll never get anywhere as an actor. No need to worry! He's to get all his grandfather's money one day."

"Will he?" Zeke handed the pen back and turned the leather pad around.

She thrust the pen into its holder and glanced at his signature. "Ezekiel Gahagan? Now there's a fine, respectable name."

Zeke waited for some sign of recognition but was relieved when it didn't appear.

"You're in number one, Mr. Gahagan. Right here, next to my office. Lars always likes that room because it's quiet. And he can slip in here whenever he wants a fresh cup of coffee or a can of beer." She lifted a key from the small board near a row of mailboxes.

He noticed all of the hooks held keys and the mailboxes were empty. "You said you'd be filled this weekend?"

"Booked solid. Could only give Lars a room because I'd had a cancellation." She came from behind the counter. "I'll show you the room. Then you can move your car." Leading the way, out of the office and along the arcade. "You live in Los Angeles?"

"I have an apartment in Hollywood."

"That miserable place! I've been there and loathed it."

"I've wanted to leave Los Angeles for years, but my business keeps me there. Anyway, I like Los Angeles. Always have."

She motioned toward the first door under the arcade, beyond a large curtained window.

Zeke saw a metal number one in the center of the door.

"My other guests will be arriving all afternoon. Should be filled up before sunset. Everyone coming for the big celebration—tomorrow and Sunday—Danish Days, they call it . . ."

"You are Danish?"

"Not I. My late husband, Carl Johnson, was. I'm Irish, like you." Thrusting her key into the lock and pushing the door open. "Here we are."

Zeke followed her into a large air-conditioned room. Two king-size beds with attractive quilted covers. Large curtained windows, front and rear. The back curtains had been left open, revealing flowers growing in bright sunlight against a tall green hedge. All the furniture looked comfortable. "You run a nice place here, ma'am."

"Don't get too many complaints. Hope you'll enjoy your weekend. There's fresh Danish and coffee every morning in the office. It's on the house." Turning to face him. "Since you're a friend of Lars you're welcome to drop in at any time. It's real coffee. I get a special blend from a gourmet shop in Solvang."

"Thank you. I may do that. Although I'm only permitted a cup and a half each day."

"How, in God's name, can you manage that? A cup in the morning and half a cup for dinner?"

"Tried that. Didn't work. I would forget how much I had for breakfast. So I have half a cup, three times a day."

"There's a practical man."

"Could you tell me . . . Where is Laurence Knight's home? I understand it's outside of Solvang."

"You're going there?"

"I'm hoping to find Mr. Knight there."

"Didn't Lars tell you where it was?"

"He said anyone would be able to tell me."

"That's Lars . . . Larry owns a fine property with a beautiful old house. He's had it for years. On Alamo Pintado Road . . ."

"I crossed Alamo Pintado, just now, seconds before I saw your sign."

"Turn left twice, after you leave here, and drive north toward Ballard. Larry's place is only two miles off the highway. You won't see his name at the entrance but there's a painted sign says ELDORADO."

"I was at another ELDORADO yesterday. RANCHO ELDORADO."

"Must be lots of people like that name. Larry told me, long ago, it's a Spanish word. Supposed to mean a place where you can find gold. I've always meant to look the word up but never find the time." She moved toward the door, leaving the key on a glass-topped chest of drawers. "You'll want to bring your luggage in and unpack. Your parking space is right here, facing this door."

"That'll be fine."

"I doubt you'll find Larry home."

"No?"

"Yesterday, when I was shopping in Solvang, I heard he wouldn't be arriving until tomorrow. First day of the celebration."

"He'll be here tomorrow?"

"That's why I wasn't surprised when Lars phoned and wanted a room for the weekend. Figured his grandfather was bringing friends and the house would be full." She turned to face him. "Mrs. Svendsen, Larry's housekeeper, may have arrived ahead to get the place ready for guests . . ."

"I've met Mrs. Svendsen."

She hesitated. "You're some kind of policeman, aren't you?"

"What makes you think that?"

"The way you ask questions."

"I'm sorry if I've seemed inquisitive."

"And I noticed you check the mailboxes. Saw there was no mail. Knew my guests hadn't arrived."

"I'm a private detective."

She frowned. "Is something wrong with Larry?"

"That's what I'm here to find out. He's been missing since Tuesday."

"Missing?"

"A friend of his—the actress, Faye Manning—has asked me to find him."

"And Lars? Where is he?"

"I'm sorry, dear lady. I can't answer your questions."

"I understand." She started through the door then turned back and smiled. "Don't forget, Mr. Gahagan. Fresh coffee in my office. Day and night. Just help yourself. I don't sleep too well any more. Read every night. Mostly detective novels." As she stepped outside, she glanced back again and smiled. "You're the first real private eye I've ever met."

Chapter 14

His stomach grumbled tentatively.

"I know, kid. Didn't get our mid-morning snack, did we? We'll take care of that, soon's I check this Eldorado setup."

His body wasn't aching, in spite of sleeping on that balcony last night.

Alamo Pintado Road stretched in a fairly straight line through the green fields of the Santa Ynez Valley. Prosperous looking farms, vineyards and ranches on both sides.

He had a hunch Mrs. Johnson must know Larry Knight well. He'd sensed, as she talked, that she was being cautious. Probably accustomed to shielding the actor from inquisitive strangers. At least she had told him where Knight lived and he would be here tomorrow.

This was beautiful September weather. Fields golden in the sunlight. The air warm but not humid. So fresh he could taste it, feel it in his lungs. He took several deep breaths and savored them.

Slowed the Chevy as he saw the ELDORADO sign on a post, almost hidden in a tall clump of sunflowers.

A wire fence surrounded Knight's property but the gate was open.

He swerved into the lane and drove between cultivated fields toward the distant house. Saw a Mexican in work clothes and a big straw hat stooping between rows of vegetables. He was too far away to answer any questions. His head didn't turn but the eyes under the wide hat-brim would be watching the intruder.

Hopefully, Mrs. Svendsen would be here, around back in the kitchen, and would be able to tell him when Knight would arrive tomorrow . . .

No cars parked near the house.

Mrs. Johnson said Lars stayed at her motel when his grandfather entertained guests. Maybe Knight would be bringing them tomorrow . . .

Lars must've known where his grandfather was yesterday. Where he'd gone after he saw Kerrigan . . .

Slowing, as he reached the house, Zeke saw that it was Victorian but didn't look old. Two stories high and spread out. Three steps led to a broad veranda with comfortable rocking chairs and a cushioned swing. Yellow mums blooming in white pots.

All the windows were shuttered.

This was nothing like Dalby's ranch house yesterday. More American than Mexican . . .

He went up the steps and crossed the veranda to the double entrance doors.

Etched glass windows in both, but he couldn't see through them.

Pressed the button and heard a bell in the depths of the house.

Waiting, looking across the peaceful valley, ears straining for any sound from inside.

He pushed the button again and tried one of the doors.

It was locked.

Walking around the veranda, in the shade, he saw another Mexican weeding a flower bed at the side of the house. Some kind of white flowers he didn't recognize. He stepped to the edge of the veranda. "Where will I find Mr. Knight?"

The Mexican looked up and shrugged.

"Is he here?"

"Don' know, Señor . . ."

"You seen him lately?"

"No see boss. Long time . . ."

"What about his housekeeper? Mrs. Svendsen?"

He shrugged again and resumed his weeding.

Zeke continued on, around the veranda, toward the rear. No rocking chairs here. So nobody sat on this side of the house. Probably because there wasn't much of a view.

All the windows he was passing were shuttered.

Was someone observing him through the cracks? Mrs. Svendsen?

There were three steps, at the rear, down to the drive that circled the house and led to a row of garages with more vegetable gardens beyond.

He went down the steps and started toward the garage doors until he was close enough to see they were padlocked. No point in going any farther. Save his energy.

Turning back, toward the rear of the house, he saw steps leading up to a screened kitchen porch. He reached up and tried the screen door.

It was locked.

Following the drive, around the other side toward the front, all the windows were shuttered on both floors.

As he passed the last windows he had a strong sense, for the first time, of being watched but avoided looking directly at the closed shutters for a flicker of movement between the wooden slats.

Reaching his car, he drove down the long lane to the open entrance gates. Turned right on Alamo Pintado toward the highway.

He would come back tonight, after dark, and check the house again.

Right now he'd better get some food before his gut began to protest in earnest.

Reaching Highway 246 he turned right and headed for Solvang.

Passing the Rancho Sanjo Motel there was no sign of Mrs. Johnson or her maid. Only a flash of sunlight from the surface of the swimming pool.

In less than ten minutes he reached the outskirts of Solvang.

The highway, apparently, became Mission Drive—there was a street sign—and continued straight through the town.

This seemed to be the main drag.

The shops, restaurants and motels had foreign names. Everything neat and, apparently, recently painted.

Then, to his surprise, he was outside the town again.

Solvang was only four or five streets wide!

He pulled into the next drive, leading to a private property, backed out and turned around.

Headed straight down Mission Drive. Turned right on Alisal Road—noticing the name on a street sign—and right again on what appeared to be a business street. Rows of shops on both sides with a few cars parked, at an angle, toward the curb.

Most of the shops were open and he could see customers inside.

He parked the Chevy, facing a bakery, and got out.

Hesitated for a moment, looking for a place to eat. His first stop would be to find food and silence his growling stomach.

He noticed cars parked across the street in front of a small restaurant. Two big men, wearing old Stetsons and dressed like working cowhands, getting into a station wagon.

He'd learned years ago, from Hammett, that whenever you were in an unfamiliar town you should always look for the restaurant that had the most parked cars outside. That would be the one with the best food.

Zeke crossed the street, appetite increasing with each step, opened the door and was engulfed by a delicious smell of cooking.

He glimpsed a plump aproned woman working in a kitchen to his right, behind a long counter with a row of leather stools. Rows of tables in the center and leather booths to the left. Several men eating at the counter, laughing and talking, but most of the booths were empty.

Selecting one toward the back, he stretched his long legs out comfortably. Couldn't do that, seated at a counter.

Two women eating in the booth ahead. Plump and middle-aged, nicely dressed, pleasant faces. Their conversation revealed they owned nearby shops and were old friends. Discussing the business they were anticipating over the Danish Days weekend.

"What'll you have?"

He looked up to see a pretty waitress who looked Polynesian. "What're you serving at this hour?"

"Anything your heart desires, sir. Breakfast, lunch, or dinner."

"I had breakfast hours ago in Los Angeles. I'm on a diet and don't want lunch. Just something light."

"Maybe a nice fresh salad?"

"I like a salad later in the afternoon."

"What about a Danish sausage? Everybody likes them. Any hour of the day."

"Broiled?"

"That's how they're best. What'll you have with that?"

"Buttered whole wheat toast, I think."

She was writing on a pad now. "Fried potatoes?"

"No potatoes."

"I'll bring coffee right away."

"And no coffee. You have apple juice?"

"Large or small?"

"Large."

"Comin right up."

As he watched her go toward the open window behind the counter and give his order to the cook he realized that Mrs. Svendsen had told him her sister had a restaurant in Solvang. Could that woman in the kitchen be Mrs. Svendsen's sister? Not likely. That would be much too easy.

When he left here he would walk through all the streets and get the feel of Solvang. Shouldn't take long. It seemed to be more of a village than a town. He'd thought it would be larger.

Solvang, probably, had no police force. Crime—if any—would be handled by the County Sheriff's office. Traffic problems would be taken care of by the California Highway Patrol . . .

The waitress brought his glass of apple juice.

"Thought you'd be crowded at this hour."

"This is a slow day. Only a few tourists. They'll turn up tomorrow by the thousand for our Danish Days celebration. Every restaurant will have a line waiting outside. Today even some of our regulars are missing. The shop people are getting their shops ready and the hands are staying on the ranches because they'll have tomorrow and Sunday off for the holiday. Will you be here, sir?"

"Oh, yes . . ."

"There's a parade tomorrow afternoon, goes right past here, and a Grand Ball tomorrow night. I won't see much of that 'cause

I'll be working. Make a month's tips, both days. Monday I'll stay in bed. Excuse me, sir. I'll get your sausage."

He sipped the apple juice as he watched the women rising from the next booth. Still chattering.

People seemed relaxed here, much happier than in Los Angeles . . .

Been a long time since he'd seen a really happy face in L.A., far's he could remember.

The departing women had stopped to talk with one of the men eating at the counter. All of them laughing.

His waitress returned with a fat sausage, crisp and brown, and buttered wheat toast. "Are all your sausages that large?"

"Folks complain they're small. You'll eat it, sir. I promise."

"Tell me, Miss . . . Do you know a Mrs. Svendsen who runs a restaurant in Solvang? She's the sister of a Mrs. Svendsen, actually, so her name must be something else."

"No, sir. I don't." She frowned. "Let me ask our cook. She knows every restaurant owner in this town. Enjoy your sausage."

"Thanks." He cut into the sausage which hissed and spurted steam. Sliced off an end and put it into his mouth with anticipation. Chewed slowly, tasting herbs, as he glanced down at his stomach. "Enjoy, kid! You never had it so good."

The waitress returned as he finished eating. "Cook says Mrs. Svendsen's sister owns a restaurant on Mission Drive. It's called the Danish Garden. I've never eaten there, myself, but the food's supposed to be like in the old country. At least that's what Danish people tell me . . ."

"Thanks for the information."

"Coffee now?"

"Just the check."

She whipped out her order pad and added up the total. "Did you enjoy that sausage?"

"Never ate better."

"That's what they all say." Ripping the page from her pad and placing it on the table. "Come in again. We serve dinners, too." She hurried back toward the kitchen.

Zeke picked up his check, glanced at the amount and left a tip.

Paid at the desk and went outside where he paused on the sidewalk and, briefly, checked both sides of the street.

The Chevy was on the other side and there were only half a dozen other vehicles parked in the long block.

He would leave it here for the moment and take a leisurely stroll around Solvang. Check every street carefully. Familiarize himself with the layout and mood of the place.

Turning right, from the position of the sun he was heading east—he kept close to the shop windows.

Saw that the shops were empty except for a few salesladies arranging displays on counters. Neatly dressed, well-fed looking.

This was, obviously, a town where people liked to eat.

One or two older men, most likely owners, also stout. One of them was arranging men's sweaters in his display window. He looked up and saw Zeke staring. Nodded and smiled, as though they were old friends.

That never happened in Los Angeles.

A few customers in the larger shops.

He checked a street sign at the corner and found that he had been walking on Copenhagen Drive.

This cross street, as he already knew, was Alisal Road.

He turned north up Alisal.

First thing he wanted to do was locate the Danish Garden on Mission Road.

He would ask Mrs. Svendsen's sister a few questions.

Chapter 15

Zeke saw the Danish Garden when he turned the corner onto Mission Drive. A low white building with an attractive terrace separated from the sidewalk by a neat privet hedge.

Crossed Mission, taking his time, looking it over.

Red-tiled roof with a carved wooden stork perched on a brick chimney. White tables and chairs on the terrace under bright blue parasols with one tremendous oak tree spreading leafy branches overhead. Would be a fine place to eat on a sunny day like this.

Only three of the tables were occupied. Young couples with small children having an early lunch.

He would do a complete tour of the town before he questioned the owner. Get a feeling for the place. A sense of direction . . .

Several things he hoped to find here. Several people, actually. First of all locate Laurence Knight and his missing housekeeper.

Knight was supposed to show up tomorrow, according to Mrs. Johnson, for the Danish Days celebration, but where was Mrs. Svendsen?

Did she know when Knight would be arriving?

He, also, wanted to learn anything he could about Kara Kolvang.

Was there some connection between Knight's disappearance and the Kolvang murder?

Hopefully he would be able to contact her sister. Inga Jensen . . .

She should be listed in the local directory. Although he didn't know her married name.

He found a public telephone as he walked and checked the directory. Several Jensens but no Inga.

Zeke sauntered on, acting like a visitor, taking his time in the nearly empty streets, pausing at every shop window.

Hadn't done this in years, not since San Francisco.

Hammett and he used to take long walks, Sunday afternoons, before dinner. Especially through Chinatown. Dash said he'd seen a maze of hidden cellars under the sidewalks. Opium dens with long passages stretching in every direction. Hadn't believed him, at the time, but learned, years later, he'd been telling the truth.

Should've known. Hammett was the only man who ever told him the truth. About everything.

Especially about women . . .

Dash had arranged for him to meet the first woman he slept with.

He was shy in those days. Only seventeen. His father had warned him about having sex. Told him the terrible things that could happen if he did. None of which, he discovered later, were true.

His father couldn't have believed the things he said but was only warning him for his own good. Away from home, by himself.

After that first girl he had quickly made up for lost time.

Hammett had helped. He was always a great one for the ladies. Even after he married Josephine Dolan and they lived on Eddy Street. Marriage didn't seem to stop Dash or satisfy his cravings. He had always needed beautiful women.

Zeke smiled.

Here he was, walking down these sunny streets, thinking of Hammett . . .

Dash had warned him, many times, scowling and biting off his words. "You must keep your mind on one thing at a time, kid. That's the person you're hired to find. A good detective has a one-track mind. You must find your track and stay on it. Think of nothing else. Like that time I was looking for a guy who swiped a Ferris wheel. That became an obsession . . ."

Hammett never said whether he found the missing contraption.

Zeke paused outside a bakery window and inspected the trays of rich pastries and frosted cookies. None of which he could eat. The smell of baking bread flowed out through the open door.

He glanced at the endless rows of small china figures in the next window. Mostly children and old people, all with rosy cheeks, smiling and happy-looking. He wished some of them were frowning.

A window with antique clocks and watches fascinated him for several minutes.

As he moved on, shop to shop, he noticed the storks placed on chimneys and thatched rooftops. Most were carved from wood, others seemed to be pottery. They didn't bother the fat sparrows. Some were even perched on their long beaks.

He saw a drugstore on a corner with a display of newspaper stands, including the L. A. *Times*. That would be the same edition he'd seen at his apartment. Remember to pick one up tomorrow. The Saturday edition . . .

A delicatessen window had a printed poster on top of its refrigerated display, saying the annual DANISH DAYS would be celebrated on Saturday as a tribute to the founding of Solvang in 1911. Parade, at 3 p.m., with FAMOUS STAR riding with the Grand Marshal.

Zeke smiled. That famous star would be some actor from a television series. They were better known than most of today's film stars.

He saw more printed posters in other shop windows as he continued along the street.

As he walked he became aware of windmills everywhere. Small windmills and large ones. All had rotating sails which he realized must be turned by machines. Several of them were two or three stories high, with small entrance doors at street level, narrow windows above. All the revolving sails were silent and a few of the smaller ones weren't moving.

His tour of the shops brought him back to the Danish Garden where he saw that the tables on the hedged terrace were no longer occupied.

A waitress in a Danish costume was clearing one of the tables as he walked in from the sidewalk. "Did you want lunch, sir?"

"I'm looking for Mrs. Svendsen."

"There are several Svendsens in Solvang . . ."

"I believe her sister owns this restaurant."

"Oh! That Mrs. Svendsen." She giggled. "Mrs. Nielsen owns the restaurant. She's inside, in the kitchen." Lifting a tray of dishes from the table. "Come in, sir. I'll tell Mrs. Nielsen you want to see her."

"Thanks." He followed her inside. "I suppose you'll be crowded tomorrow."

"Every table. I dread it, each year, but it's fun."

He waited as she carried her tray into the kitchen where a plump gray-haired woman was giving orders to several young girls who were cooking and preparing salads. The woman was, unmistakably, Mrs. Svendsen's sister. Though slightly younger.

The waitress set the tray down and spoke to her employer.

Mrs. Nielsen turned and peered at him as she dried her hands on the apron she was wearing. Smiled as she came toward him. "You wish to see my sister?"

"My name's Gahagan. I'm looking for Mrs. Svendsen . . ."

"That's my sister, all right." Patting at her hair with both hands. "But she's in Los Angeles. Far's I know."

"I just came from Los Angeles where I was told I would find her in Solvang. Probably with you."

"She may be driving up tomorrow with Mr. Knight and his party. My sister works for him, Mr. Laurence Knight, the movie actor. He always brings friends to Solvang for Danish Days."

"I talked to his grandson and he thought they were already here. Both of them."

"Mr. Lars said that? My sister phoned, earlier this week, and told me she would arrive tonight or tomorrow, but she didn't know whether Mr. Knight would be alone this year or have guests. Usually, she comes up ahead of him, in her own car, to put the house in order."

"I paid a visit to his house, this morning, but nobody seems to be there. Only two Mexican gardeners."

"If my dear sister had arrived she would've let me know. Always does, so we can plan to see each other over the weekend."

"When was the last time you saw her?"

"Been several months. She comes up to Solvang every year at Christmas—takes a two-week vacation—and we go off on little trips together. Last Christmas we flew down to Mexico . . ."

"Could you tell me where I could find Inga Jensen? I seem to be looking for people's sisters. Inga Jensen's the sister of that actress—Kara Kolvang—whose name was, actually, Karen Jensen . . ."

"Inga has a different name now. She married Nels Andersen. He's been dead for years, but Inga still owns their shop. It's on Copenhagen Drive. One of the oldest shops in Solvang. The Jensen family opened it years ago. Inga's there every day. With all her money! You'll find her getting ready for the big day tomorrow."

"Where does she live? In case I can't find her there."

"I couldn't tell you that. After all, I don't even know who you are." She smiled again. "You say you know my sister, but I only have your word for that, don't I?"

"I understand."

"Will you be here for our Danish Days?"

"I expect to stay until Monday. I'm at the Rancho Sanja Motel."

"Hildreth Johnson's place . . ."

"You can tell your sister I'm there. If you should hear from her. The name's Gahagan. Say I'd like to see her again."

"I'll do that, Mr. Gahagan."

"Thank you, ma'am." As he left the restaurant he wondered if Mrs. Nielsen would be calling her sister. Warning her, wherever she was, that he was in Solvang.

A scattering of tourists was wandering from shop to shop, aimlessly, but the streets were surprisingly quiet. No traffic moving.

He found Copenhagen Drive again and saw a sign above the entrance to the shop he sought. Realized that he had passed it earlier.

ANDERSEN'S GIFT SHOP
Finest Collectibles

As he went inside he saw that this was one of the larger shops. It was empty, at the moment, except for two women studying a counter display of crystal and a man and woman in a rear room devoted to Scandinavian furniture.

An attractive girl, tall and blonde, watched them from a distance. Standing in front of a glass wall separating the shop from a good-sized office where an enormous fat woman sat at a desk, smoking a cigarette. Impossible to see her face through the haze of tobacco smoke.

Zeke walked toward the blonde girl. "Could I see Mrs. Andersen? For a moment . . ."

She smiled pleasantly. "You a salesman?"

"Nothing like that. This is personal. My name's Gahagan and I'm from Los Angeles. Tell her I'd like to speak to her about her sister."

"Sister? Didn't know the old girl had one. Just a minute. I'll tell her."

He watched her go into the office and, as she talked, saw the fat woman crush out her cigarette in a crystal ashtray. She didn't turn to stare at him through the glass partition but nodded her head as she answered the girl.

He was going to meet Kara Kolvang's sister. He hadn't planned, in advance, what questions he would ask her . . .

The girl returned, still smiling. "Mrs. Andersen will see you."

"Thanks." He passed her and entered the air-conditioned office, closing the door.

"You can leave that door open, Mr. Gahagan. So some of this cold air gets into the shop. Keeps the customers cool."

He opened the door again then crossed the office toward the big woman overflowing her chair. Saw that she was wearing a voluminous blue smock over white slacks. Seated in a massive modern metal armchair which she swiveled slightly to squint at him. Her white hair, cut short, was a mass of curls. Small blue eyes seemed to be embedded in pink flesh. "Your name's Gahagan and you want to speak to me about my late sister who called herself Kara Kolvang . . ." The words poured out in a rush, as though she feared they would catch in her throat. "That right?"

"Yes, ma'am. I'm a private detective."

"Good God! They're not digging up her murder after all these years?" Pulling gold-rimmed spectacles down over her nose from where they had nested among the white curls. Now she stared at his face. "Well?"

"Nothing like that. I'm looking for a friend of your sister's and thought you might be able to help me locate him."

"I haven't been in touch with any of Karen's friends lately."

"This one happens to live outside Solvang and I thought . . ."

"Larry Knight?"

"He seems to have disappeared."

"Sit down, Mr. Gahagan." Motioning toward another large armchair.

He saw, as he sat down, that her fingers sparkled with diamonds. His hips sank into the cushioned seat but he grasped the upholstered arms to pull himself erect and faced this fat woman who had been a plump girl in those clippings he'd looked at last night.

"You comfortable there, sir?"

"Wasn't prepared to go down this far."

"Our furniture was made for us in Denmark. That's my husband's chair. He was a big man—tallest in Solvang—and I'm a big woman. After I stopped trying to be an actress—starving myself, to please the damn studio—I started eating everything I liked and I've never stopped. Karen was the thin one, without ever needing to diet, although the studio made her lose a few pounds in the beginning. I was never jealous of her success, only how she could eat without having to pay for it. When did Larry disappear?"

"Earlier this week. Tuesday, as a matter of fact. A mutual friend, Faye Manning, hired me to find him."

"Faye? What a sweetheart! I knew her, years ago, and liked her. So did Kara. Why would Faye hire you to find Larry?"

"She's worried about him. He told her, Tuesday, that somebody was trying to kill him."

"What?"

"They shot bullet holes in two garages behind his house."

"Where's his grandson, Lars, and their housekeeper?"

"I saw Lars yesterday, but he has no idea what could've happened to his grandfather. And this morning their housekeeper is missing."

"Mrs. Svendsen? Her sister has a restaurant here."

"I've just seen Mrs. Nielsen who told me where to find you. I was hoping she'd know where I could locate her sister, but she hasn't heard from her since earlier this week."

"And why did you wish to see me?"

"I suspect Laurence Knight's disappearance may have something to do with your sister's death."

"How could it? That's years ago! Fifty years last Monday . . ."

"I'm aware of that."

"I'd forgotten about it until . . ." She stopped.

"Until?"

"Larry phoned me Monday evening. Told me about the dinner Paul Victor was giving that night."

"Has he called you since that dinner?"

"No. He hasn't."

"Then you don't know what happened."

"But I do. Lars phoned Tuesday night. Told me everything. What Larry said about Tim Kerrigan. That his grandfather had disappeared."

"Did you know Kerrigan?"

"I guess, in those days, everybody knew Tim. He couldn't pound an ounce off of me. But then I only let him work on me for a couple of months. Didn't like him. Or, for that matter, most of Kara's friends."

"Was he a friend?"

"Well . . ." She shrugged.

"What about Kurt von Zemmering?"

"He was different." The plump diamond-studded fingers moved nervously as she talked, tapping the arms of her chair. "Kurt was a darling. He brought us to America—Karen and me—produced all of Kara's films. Kurt knew I didn't have any talent but he gave me small parts. Until I met Nels Andersen and fell in love. I never worked in movies after Karen died. In case you're wondering, I inherited all of Kara's estate. Still have most of it." She laughed, chins shaking. "In the bank or invested in property. I own several ranches, a prosperous vineyard and, of course, this shop was left to me when my husband died. We had a happy marriage, and I'm a very rich old lady, Mr. Gahagan. All the widowers in Solvang have called on me, but I'll never marry again. Who needs that, at my age?"

"I agree, ma'am. I've had four marriages. Happy ones, to a point. But I'm too tired to try for a fifth."

"Then you know what I mean." She studied his face, squinting through her spectacles. "So you've not come to ask questions about my sister's death?"

"I'm here to find Laurence Knight for his friend Faye Manning."

"Dear Faye! Give her my best. I'd no idea she was in love with Larry."

"Don't believe she is. She's worried for his safety."

"Then she's a true friend. There's nobody would hire a private eye to look for me if I were missing . . ."

"You have any idea where Mr. Knight might go if he wanted to hide for a few days?"

"I can't help you there. Actually, I don't know Larry all that well. Never did. He was Karen's friend. In fact, at one time, I think she had a crush on him. He was so handsome . . . I used to see him at the studio, of course, and more frequently when he and Karen bought properties up here. Larry's wife was alive then. I'm still living in the big house Karen built, north of Solvang. In recent years I've only seen Larry half a dozen times each year. He comes to the house or invites me to a party at his place and he stops in here when he's shopping in the village. My girls always manage to sell him something. Larry still has an eye for a pretty blonde . . ."

"If you hear from him, will you tell him Faye Manning's worried?"

"I'm worried now, myself."

"Tell him I'm staying at the Rancho Sanja Motel and I'd be pleased to hear from him."

"I'll tell him that. Give my best to Hildreth Johnson."

"You know Mrs. Johnson?"

"Everybody knows Hildreth, and loves her. She had a bad time, at first, after Carl Johnson died. He didn't leave her too well fixed because of his long illness—only that property—but she took over. Did a terrific job of modernizing the motel. She's making good money now."

"Tell me, Mrs. Andersen. I know it's been fifty years, but you must remember the night it happened. Who do you think killed your sister?"

"I haven't the slightest idea." She sighed. "Didn't suspect anyone then, and I don't now. There's absolutely nothing to be gained by exposing Kara's murderer at this late date. If he's still alive . . ."

"I agree, ma'am." He pushed himself up from the awkward chair. "Thanks for talking to me."

"I do hope you'll find Larry Knight."

"That's my purpose in coming to Solvang. I suspect he'll show up tomorrow for the Danish Days celebration. Mrs. Johnson thinks he'll be arriving with guests."

"Hildreth may be right. He's done that before. I should be seeing Lars this evening. He said he'll be driving up today."

"Perhaps we'll talk again, while I'm here." He started for the door, avoiding any questions about Lars, noticing through the glass wall that there were no customers in the shop. Only the blonde.

"Mr. Gahagan . . ."

"Yes?" He turned, reluctantly, to look back at the fat woman seated at the desk. There was no resemblance to the young girl in those newspaper photographs with Kara Kolvang.

"Did you ever see an old movie called *The Maltese Falcon* . . . ?"

"Many times. I knew the man who wrote the book."

"I never knew who wrote it. Loved the picture. Always see it on television, whenever they run it again."

"Why do you mention that now?"

"Remember that wonderful scene, near the end, where everybody's there? Bogart, Mary Astor and the others and somebody knocks at the door, or the bell rings and Bogart, I think, opens the door and Walter Huston stumbles in with a parcel . . ."

"I remember."

"I've always hoped some stranger will come to my door one night with an envelope and inside that envelope will be the name of the person who killed my dear sister . . ."

He saw there were tears in her eyes. "I'm afraid, ma'am, that'll never happen."

"I know . . ."

Zeke turned and continued on toward the open door.

There was something coquettish about Mrs. Andersen.

A Hammett word. Coquettish . . .

Hammett would've enjoyed hearing about the stranger Mrs. Andersen saw at her door with the name of her sister's murderer in an envelope.

He wondered if she visualized the stranger as Walter Huston . . .

Chapter 16

Zeke wakened from deep sleep and was, briefly, confused by the unfamiliar bed and strange room.

Puzzled, staring at a curtained window, he remembered where he was.

The Rancho Sanja Motel . . .

Mrs. Johnson. Mrs. Hildreth Johnson . . .

Nice name. Hildreth . . .

He reached out and pushed the curtain back.

Blue shadows across a field, beyond the lighted pool. Stars already visible in the evening sky.

He must've slept several hours.

Never liked to do that during the day. A habit he didn't wish to encourage. He'd never liked people who took naps. Sleep was a form of death, and he resented it. Not for him. Not just yet . . .

He let the curtain drop into place and pushed himself up to sit on the side of the bed.

He'd been dreaming about something—something important—but he couldn't quite recall what it was. Then two pieces of information clicked into focus. They must've been burrowing through his head as he slept.

Laurence Knight was the "famous star" who would be riding in that parade tomorrow. It had to be Knight!

And he was hiding in his house until tomorrow.

He'd felt someone watching him through the shutters as he circled the house.

Laurence Knight was here! Safe at Eldorado . . .

He would go back there tonight. Surprise the actor and have a talk with him . . .

Only then would he call Faye. Report he'd found her friend.

Found him in three days.

Faye had phoned him Wednesday night, and this was Friday . . .

Only two and a half days!

His job would be finished when he talked to Knight.

Wouldn't clear much on this assignment.

Have to return most of that two thousand buck check, after he deducted expenses for this trip to Solvang. Food and gas . . .

No matter.

He would enjoy a good dinner tonight, before he went back to Eldorado. Include that on his itemized bill . . .

He switched on several lamps as he went into the bath and splashed cold water on his eyes. Dried his face with a towel then rubbed a little Knize Ten across his jaw.

Slipped into his jacket and dropped the room key into a hip pocket as he opened the door.

Snapped off the lights and stepped out into the twilight. Closed the door, checking that it had locked.

Stood there a moment, under the arcade, breathing the fresh air into his lungs. No damp fog here.

He saw that several other cars were parked now. Mrs. Johnson had said the motel would be full tonight.

The patio chairs around the pool were empty and no sharks floated in the water. There wouldn't be any sharks here.

Some of the guests must've checked in, then driven into Solvang for dinner.

That's what he would do.

When he reached Solvang he saw that the streets were dimly lighted. The old-fashioned street lamps reminded him of his childhood in Maryland.

Nobody walking and no traffic moving.

The only cars were parked in front of a few restaurants.

He slowed the Chevy and checked them.

The restaurant with the most cars was the Danish Inn, a sprawling, comfortable-looking place with one of the larger windmills at one side. Its sails were not revolving.

The parking spaces in front of the restaurant were filled and the windows of the cars had been left open.

Couldn't do that in L. A., but there would be no crime here.

He parked across the street, leaving his windows down, and walked over to the Inn where he was welcomed by a headwaiter who offered him the choice of a table in a crowded room with an elaborate smorgasbord table or an inner room which seemed less noisy.

He chose the inner room and was led to a table with immaculate white linen, gleaming crystal, and shining silver.

As he slipped into the leather booth he noticed attractive framed paintings on the wall.

"Something to drink before dinner, Monsieur?"

He accepted a menu from the headwaiter. "A glass of Sauvignon blanc."

"Certainly, sir."

Zeke opened the menu. Have to be careful not to order

anything he couldn't eat. He found several items he was permitted.

"Pardon, sir..."

He looked up as a waiter placed a glass of wine in front of him.

"Thank you." He tasted the wine. Cool but not too cold. Set the glass down and continued his study of the menu.

The headwaiter returned. "Has Monsieur made a decision? There's an excellent roast of beef this evening."

"Haven't eaten beef in years. Know exactly what I want."

"Very good, sir." Raising pencil and pad.

"First the onion soup. Not too much cheese. Then the broiled trout. Could I have rice with that?"

"Certainly..."

"Some zucchini and a little of the broccoli. No sauce, just lemon. That should do it."

It was more than an hour before he came out from the restaurant, after the best dinner he'd eaten in months.

The food had reminded him of dining in San Francisco, years ago, with Hammett. That was when he learned about good food. Dash was a finicky eater...

Tonight he hadn't ordered a second glass of wine; and no coffee. He'd drunk his quota of coffee for today.

Zeke paused on the shallow portico, under the low slanting roof, facing the street and checked that the Chevy was where he had left it.

It was pleasant standing here, in the shadow, looking up and down Mission Drive. The sidewalks, under the trees, were dark and empty.

Solvang was like a foreign village at night. Foreign, at least, to him.

There were a few more parked cars.

Must be after nine.

He didn't want to go back to Eldorado before ten. At that hour Knight wouldn't be expecting him to return.

Maybe drive to his motel first and sit beside the pool. Relax for an hour.

Hildreth might be there. Alone . . .

As he made this decision he heard footsteps. Light, secretive steps.

No high heels.

Sounded like a man, thin and short.

Zeke eased back, instinctively, into the shadow.

The steps were barely audible in the silent street. Little more than an echo on the still air.

He turned his head from side to side, seeking their source.

The sound seemed to come from beyond the corner opposite the Inn.

He didn't know the name of that cross street. Hadn't walked down that one today. Or had he? Impossible to remember all the streets he'd covered.

His senses were alert. Eyes and ears straining . . .

The footsteps seemed to be coming closer.

He focused his eyes on the corner.

The slight figure of a man appeared and hesitated, glancing up and down Mission Drive.

Zeke held his breath, the muscles of his body frozen.

Something odd here . . .

The man was, indeed, short. Blond hair. Impossible, from this distance, to see his face.

He was wearing light gray summer slacks and what appeared to be tan suede boots. A curiously patterned sport shirt that could've been designed for camouflage. Large green, brown and gray leaves. He looked more like a visitor than one of the locals.

The man, suddenly, began to move again. More quickly. Crossing the street toward the Inn. Meeting a friend for dinner?

Zeke inched back, careful not to move abruptly and attract attention, into deeper shadow.

The approaching figure walked like a young man, stepping firmly; his torso under the loose shirt appeared to be muscular although his shoulders seemed narrow.

What he could see of his face was unwrinkled. The skin tanned, almost the color of his hair.

Zeke took another cautious step backward but the young man didn't come toward the portico. He hoped the door wouldn't be opened, behind him, by departing diners; he would be revealed standing here.

The blond man was moving with purpose now.

He realized he must be heading for that windmill at the far side of the restaurant.

What possible reason could he have for going there at this hour?

He moved forward, slightly, to get a better view. This was one of the larger windmills.

The young man went straight to the door and opened it.

What could he be after inside?

A beam of light flashed in one of the upper windows and moved on.

This fellow must be a local. Checking the mechanism controlling the sails to make sure they were in working order for tomorrow's celebration.

Still no traffic, in any direction.

The windmill door opened, suddenly, and the young man hurried out.

He held a small flashlight which he thrust under his jacket. Closed the door as he glanced up and down Mission Drive, then continued on his way. Darted across to the opposite sidewalk and disappeared into deep shadow under a row of trees.

Had he slipped between two of the buildings?

Without considering what he was doing, moving automatically, Zeke stepped down from the portico and followed. Kept to the shadow, avoiding the street lamps.

Moved silently on his rubber-soled shoes and stayed close to the dark buildings as he started in pursuit.

Difficult to see the blond young man because there were no lighted shop windows to silhouette his movements.

He glimpsed him again, straight ahead.

Zeke kept following, using every trick he'd learned when he and Hammett were with the Pinkerton office. Avoiding even the faintest light and darting from pool to pool of shadow under each tree.

Could this be a local youth up to some mischief? Or a visitor planning to rob one of the shops?

Why had he checked inside that windmill? What possible reason?

He doubted they had many robberies here. Nothing like a big city, but there would certainly be a few. Mostly pulled by transients.

This man didn't look like a transient.

He lost sight of his quarry for a moment, then saw him as he turned into another street.

Quickened his steps, afraid he'd lost him.

Reaching the corner he realized this was a street he'd checked earlier. Remembered that it led to Alisal Road.

No sign of the young man.

He started to run, aware of a small open park on his left.

Headlights of a slowly moving car beyond the trees on Mission Drive.

Why was he doing this? Following a complete stranger for no logical reason. Except his curiosity.

Zeke smiled.

He was like an old hunting dog his father had owned. Sniffing after anyone who seemed suspicious.

Reaching the corner he squinted down Alisal Road.

The man was standing in the middle of the road, at the far end of the block, staring up at another windmill.

This was, probably, the largest.

He had noticed it several times today. Rising at the end of Copenhagen Drive which was the next cross street.

Almost exactly like that windmill near the Danish Inn, only slightly larger.

The blond young man was moving toward it now. Swallowed up by the deep shadow at the base.

Zeke started to run again, along the row of shops and restaurants edging the sidewalk.

As he ran he checked the time on the lighted clock in a distant tower.

Nine thirty-two.

He'd taken longer than he realized for dinner.

Reaching the corner of Copenhagen he stepped into a recessed doorway and faced the windmill.

The young man must've gone inside.

Another unlocked door . . .

He was reminded of that Hitchcock film—*Foreign Correspondent*—where Joel McCrea checked a field of windmills in Holland. All of their sails were revolving. Only one of them was turning in the wrong direction. Which was a signal to some spies . . .

None of these sails were revolving. That, somehow, made them seem more ominous. Like dead things . . .

The beam of a flashlight was visible, briefly, through the upper windows of the windmill. It swept across what seemed to be a white wall and was gone.

Zeke pulled back into the doorway and saw that it was a small restaurant. A single light in the kitchen revealed rows of tables with chairs resting upon them, legs in air, for the night. The distant bulb was too dim to reveal his presence.

He looked out again and saw the blond young man crossing Alisal Road toward Copenhagen Drive.

Zeke remembered a third large windmill about two blocks down Copenhagen.

That's where he would be going now.

Zeke followed, easing around the corner, recalling the street from this morning. He'd had breakfast in that restaurant in the middle of the block on the other side and he was passing Inga Andersen's gift shop. A dim light in her office, beyond the glass wall, made the crystal objects glitter on counters and shelves.

The young man stopped walking, suddenly, and Zeke ducked into the entrance of a toy shop as the blond head turned and he looked back again.

He was sure he hadn't been seen, although his presence might have been felt.

He'd gotten only a brief glimpse of his quarry's face in a reflection from a shop window.

The face had seemed like a featureless mask.

He moved to the edge of the entrance and squinted down the street.

The young man was gone.

Zeke stepped out again, onto the pavement, and began to run. Keeping close to the storefronts. His rubber soles silent.

The next corner was First Street.

As he ran across it he glanced up and down but there was no sign of the blond young man.

He was heading for that third large windmill.

Zeke kept running, puzzled and curious.

The dark and silent streets seemed threatening.

Continuing, on Copenhagen, he passed a restaurant and several shops he hadn't noticed in daylight.

Then he saw the blond young man again. He was standing looking up at the windmill near the next corner.

He'd been right!

Zeke slowed his steps, moving close to the buildings again.

This windmill looked blue in the light from a distant street lamp.

The blond young man wasn't going inside. Only inspecting the exterior. He turned, abruptly, and looked back down Copenhagen.

Was he looking at that other windmill on Alisal Road?

Zeke glanced back and saw the dark shape of the other windmill at the far end of the street. That was the largest.

When he turned again the young man had gone.

Zeke resumed his pursuit, running to the next corner.

Atterdag Road.

No sign of anyone, in either direction.

The young man would, very likely, head for Mission Drive where he first saw him. His car would be somewhere near there.

Zeke started up Atterdag, moving more slowly, aware that his legs were tiring.

Another poorly lighted street. Small towns wasted no money on electricity.

There was the muffled sound of a motor, the roar of a car taking off.

The blond young man had left his car on one of these dark side streets and now he was gone.

Perhaps his inspection of the windmills had been completely innocent.

Zeke shrugged and, suddenly weary, continued on toward Mission Drive to get his Chevy.

Still puzzled about the blond man who inspected windmills.

Chapter 17

Zeke eased the Chevy into his parking space at the Rancho Sanja Motel.

Stood beside it, briefly, checking the row of closed doors under the arcade. Several lighted windows, cars parked outside. A few curtains had been opened and he could see people watching television.

As he turned toward the pool he noticed the clear night sky trembling with stars that were reflected in the water.

He glanced at the lighted office but Mrs. Johnson was no longer there. She'd been seated at her desk behind the counter as he drove past, and looked up when she heard his car. Now, as he watched, the lights went out. She must've closed the office and retired to her own apartment. Getting to bed early in anticipation of a busy weekend.

There had been a red neon NO VACANCY sign quivering in front when he drove into the motel.

A wire mesh fence surrounded the pool area and it took him a moment to find the entrance.

He opened the gate and went inside, closing it carefully without making a sound.

Nobody occupying the patio chairs or in the pool. He had the place to himself. No one would try to strike up a conversation. Tell him where they were from and how long they'd been driving to reach here.

He selected a padded chaise, turned it away from the lights of the pool to face the dark field he'd seen from his window earlier. Stretched out, eyes on the sky, sinking back against the cushions.

The air felt warm against his forehead. Not a sound, except for some faint rustling noises from the field. Could be horses or it might be rats.

He would relax for half an hour then drive back to Laurence Knight's house. Eldorado . . .

He couldn't hear any voices or music from those television sets in the lighted rooms.

Still preoccupied by that blond young man and his tour of the windmills. Did he do that every night? There must be a dozen or more windmills but he had only checked three. The largest . . .

This trip, so far, had been a waste of his time.

Except he was certain that Laurence Knight was hiding in that shuttered house. Waiting for tomorrow's parade.

He'd been unable to locate the actor's housekeeper. Was she there, in the house, with Knight? Cooking his meals . . .

He had talked with her sister and Kara Kolvang's sister who hoped, one day, Walter Huston would bring her the name of her sister's murderer.

Walter Huston had been dead a long time . . .

He closed his eyes and was aware of his body relaxing.

No arthritis. This dry air was what he had needed. All his aches from that fall had disappeared. Maybe he should stay here a few days . . .

Why not until Monday? Or even Tuesday . . .

The rest would do him good.

Been years since he'd taken three days off.

After he talked with Laurence Knight he would be through with this job.

Maybe put off calling Faye until Monday . . .

No. If he talked to the actor tonight he would phone her first thing tomorrow. Let her know he'd found her friend . . .

He heard a click of metal as a gate was opened.

Somebody, drink in hand, wandering out to the pool for a breath of fresh air?

He wouldn't open his eyes and they would go away.

He was in no mood to talk to strangers.

Footsteps on the cement.

They didn't stop but were coming closer.

He still didn't look around.

"Are you asleep?" Woman's voice, barely a whisper.

Zeke opened his eyes and saw Mrs. Johnson holding a tray with two wineglasses and a bottle. "What's this?" He pushed himself to his feet.

"Bar's open." Resting the plastic tray on a white table under an open parasol. "Saw you come in. Thought you might like a glass of wine."

"That's mighty kind."

"Hope you like your wine white and dry."

"It's the only way." He joined her at the table. "Let me open that for you."

"I've gotten to be rather expert at wine bottles." She picked up a fancy corkscrew and, as they talked, opened the bottle. "Did you have dinner?"

"The Danish Inn. Very good."

"I always go there when I want to give myself a treat." Sniffing at the cork. "Have any luck at Eldorado?"

"The place was locked, shuttered and deserted. No one in

sight, except some Mexican gardeners."

"They drive up from Lompoc." Filling the wineglasses. "Lompoc's a great town for gardeners."

"Lompoc? I used to think that word was invented by W. C. Fields. He used it in a movie."

"Lompoc's surrounded by nurseries. Beautiful in the spring." Setting the bottle down. "Shall we sit here?"

He pulled two white metal chairs away from the table. "How late do you keep your office open?"

"I close shop around eight, most nights." She sank onto a chair. "This weekend we're full and I turned the NO VACANCY sign on before dark. So I wouldn't be bothered."

Zeke sat on the other chair.

"It's heaven when we're full. Otherwise I'm wakened in the middle of the night. Sometimes I put the NO VACANCY sign on even when every room's empty." She picked up both glasses, handing one to him. "Your good health, Mr. Gahagan."

"And yours, dear lady." Raising his glass. "Your very good health."

"And to the success of your visit here. Whatever its purpose."

"I'll certainly drink to that." He touched his glass to hers.

They drank, eyeing each other over the rims of their wineglasses.

"This is a very nice wine," he said.

"From one of our local vineyards."

"Are there many around here?"

"Half a dozen have sprung up in the last few years. People drive up from Los Angeles for our wine tours. You might like to do that while you're here."

"Doubt I'll have time. Were you born here, Mrs. Johnson?"

"I was born in New York, where I tried to be an actress."

"Did you?" That explained her pleasant voice.

"Had several jobs off-Broadway and discovered my only talent seemed to be waiting on tables. I come from strong Celtic stock. Was married in New York and divorced. Came to California. Los Angeles first, which I loathed. Since I was tall and blonde then, a Scandinavian friend said I should come to Solvang. He claimed the men were nicer up here and they were. I worked in most of the restaurants in town. Then I met my future husband and gave up waiting on tables."

"You still think Larry Knight will be here tomorrow?"

"His grandson said he would."

"That's because he's supposed to be riding in the Danish Days parade, isn't it?"

"Found out about that, did you?"

"I saw signs saying there'd be a 'mystery star.' Knew it must be Laurence Knight."

"He's our only local celebrity. Rode in the parade several years ago and they convinced him he should do it again."

"He was here recently?"

"I couldn't say."

Zeke was conscious of her hesitation.

"Larry's frequently here weekends. Usually brings Lars and Mrs. Svendsen. Sometimes three or four friends. That's when Lars stays with me. When there are friends."

"You like Larry Knight, don't you?"

"I adore him! I suppose he was my husband's closest friend. Larry was very kind to me during the bad months after Carl died. They used to ride together all the time. My husband raised horses and died in a stupid accident. His favorite mare threw him. Broke Carl's neck."

"Accidents are always stupid. We're never prepared for sudden death."

"I suppose . . ."

"Accidents and murders. There seem to be some horses in this next field. I heard them earlier."

"That field used to be part of our ranch. I sold it with the horses when Carl died. We'd had a couple running this motel but I let them go and took over myself. I'm a reasonably gregarious person and enjoy meeting people. So, for the moment at least, I'm happy and busy."

"No husband in your future?"

"I keep hoping. Each year it becomes less likely." She set her half empty glass down. "And you, Mr. Gahagan? Are you married?"

"Divorced. Four times. All deceased, but one. She's married again and lives in La Jolla. Talked to her on the phone last night . . ."

"Then you're friendly?"

"Of course. I loved all four of 'em. Unfortunately they got tired of me—of my being away somewhere on a job. Even if I was in Los Angeles, I wouldn't get home until after midnight and off again next morning."

"That would be difficult."

"I loved all of 'em. Still do." He studied her face, briefly, then glanced at the stars again. "Beautiful night. Never see these stars above Los Angeles. Too much smog."

"We rarely have smog here. Maybe a little in Solvang, tomorrow, with thousands of cars arriving for Danish Days but they'll be gone by Monday. Until next year . . ."

"I would like to spend my last days in a peaceful place like this."

"That won't be for several years."

"I'm eighty-one."

"I don't believe it. Well, you're healthy and active. And you keep your weight down."

"I was always on the thin side. Hammett used to call me a scarecrow."

"Hammett?"

"An old friend. Met him in Frisco, when I was a kid. He played a big role in my early life . . ."

"Would you consider living in Solvang? Or nearby . . ."

"I'll certainly do that when the time comes. I give myself two more years as a private eye. In two years I'll be eighty-three. That's long enough."

"Another glass of wine?"

"Haven't finished this one. These days I practice moderation in all things. Eat less and sleep much less . . ."

She picked up her glass and sipped the wine. "Is Larry Knight in some sort of trouble with the police?"

"Not to my knowledge . . ."

"Did that actress really hire you to find him?"

"She did."

"What made her think he was missing?"

"She's not the only one. His grandson hasn't seen him since Tuesday."

"You think something's happened to Larry?"

"People don't disappear without a reason." He couldn't tell her about the bullet holes in those garage doors or the two deaths . . .

"Has Larry been having an affair with Faye Manning?"

"I doubt that. She's been a good friend. Knew his wife. She's worried about him. Wanted me to find him and, if he's in some sort of trouble, protect him . . ." He studied her face for a moment. "You've had an affair with him, haven't you?"

"You do ask questions. He spent many evenings with us—Carl and I—when we had the big house. Like a member of our family. When my husband died Larry comforted me, stayed close. We had a brief affair. Maybe six months. None of the locals suspected. Then, suddenly, we both knew it was finished and Larry didn't drive up from Los Angeles so often. I didn't wish to marry again and refused each time Larry asked. I suspect, now, that I was wrong. It might've been a very happy marriage." She sighed. "I'll never know, will I?" Draining her glass and setting it on the tray. "All that's so long ago. I'll be sixty-five next month . . ."

"You have quite a few years ahead."

"They seem much lonelier now."

"I feel that way, frequently, but then another job drops out of the sky and I'm off chasing clues. I know that can't last forever. There'll come a week when my phone doesn't ring and my answering service has no messages. Two weeks of that and I'll be checking out of Los Angeles. Looking for a quiet spot where I can read, have wonderful food and listen to music . . ."

"When that happens, Mr. Gahagan, I hope you'll glance in this direction."

"My friends call me Zeke. The name's Ezekiel."

"I promise you, Zeke, there'll always be a room for you here."

"Dear lady . . ."

"My name's Hildreth. I told you this morning."

"Dear Hildreth . . ." He placed his glass on the tray beside hers. "No lady ever said kinder words to me. I am touched. Deeply touched. And when the time comes, I'll remember." He realized there were tears in her eyes. "Could be in a couple of months . . ."

She laughed and brushed the tears away. "I know better than that, and so do you." Studying his face again. "There's something I suppose I should tell you . . ."

"Yes?"

"I had two other phone calls this morning. Asking about Lars Lyndon."

Zeke straightened on the chair. "Who were the callers?"

"The first call came an hour after yours. A man. Gave his name, which I've forgotten, said he was a Los Angeles policeman. Wanted to know if I knew Lars. I said I'd known him for three years. He asked when I last saw him. I told him it had been several weeks but Lars had phoned to make a reservation for a room this weekend—told him this was a motel—but Lars hadn't shown up. And hadn't canceled. He asked for the address and thanked me. Hung up before I could question him."

"Did he ask about Laurence Knight?"

"Not a word."

"And the second call?"

"That came just before you arrived here. Man with a foreign accent."

"What sort of accent?"

"Sounded Mexican, but I wasn't certain. Is this important?"

"Very. He asked about Lars Lyndon?"

"Didn't mention him. Wanted to know if I could tell him where he could reach Laurence Knight, the actor. Something about his voice—maybe the accent—made me suspicious. I said I had no idea where Mr. Knight could be reached. And I asked why he'd called me."

"What did he say?"

"He hung up. You won't tell me what's happening, will you . . ."

"I can't. I'm sorry."

"Larry's in some kind of danger, isn't he? That's why Faye Manning has you looking for him. To protect him."

"Something like that. Yes."

She got to her feet. "Don't you move." Picking up the tray with the wine bottle and glasses. "I'll take these to the kitchen. Be right back." She carried the tray around the edge of the pool.

"Can you manage?"

"Been managing for years."

He saw that she had left the gate open. Watched her go toward the office then turned toward the dark field again.

That first phone call was one of the homicide boys from Hollywood Division. He'd found that slip of paper under the phone in Knight's study. Tomorrow or, more likely, the first of next week someone would drive up here to check in person.

The second call was the important one. That had to be Kerrigan's murderer. A man with a foreign accent. Mexican . . .

After he killed Lars and discovered it wasn't his grandfather he had searched every room and found that slip of paper with

Hildreth's phone number. Had left it there. He would already have known that Knight had a home in Santa Ynez. His next move would be to come up here.

The Mexican, if that's what he was, could be a paid killer. Hired by someone to prevent Knight from revealing who murdered Kara Kolvang.

Was he the Latin who strangled Kerrigan?

Zeke got to his feet and walked to the link fence at the far side of the pool area.

He stared into the darkness but was unable to see any horses in the field. No longer any rustling noises. No sound of traffic from the highway.

Only silence.

What would it be like to live here permanently?

The idea was pretty damn attractive.

Being near Hildreth . . .

He hadn't reacted like this—so immediately—to any woman in many years.

Nothing to do with sexual desire. Not any more . . . Or was it?

At eighty-one sex was too much trouble.

Same old physical motions and reactions. Nothing had changed about sex since that first girl he slept with in San Francisco.

Annie Costello . . .

He had been the virgin, not Annie.

He still remembered her name! And her pretty face . . .

He'd moved in with her, into her furnished room, for a month of pleasure with his newly discovered ability.

Hammett had introduced him to Annie.

He'd had enough women in his life, after that, to balance these last empty years.

Zeke turned as he heard footsteps. Saw that Hildreth was

moving with purpose, as though she had something more to tell him.

She smiled as she came closer.

"You look pleased with yourself, dear lady."

"He wants to see you."

"Who?"

"Larry Knight, of course."

"You talked to him?"

"Phoned his house. He answers if you let it ring once, then dial again. That's the signal Lars always uses."

"He's been there—at Eldorado—all along?"

"Since Wednesday evening. He's worried about Lars. That he hasn't called. Larry phoned the house in Los Angeles this morning and there wasn't any answer. Called again, but the line was busy. A third time, and a stranger answered. Larry hung up at once. So he's worried about his grandson. I've told him Faye Manning sent you to find him."

"What did he say?"

"He seemed touched that she cared. Wants you to come back to Eldorado. He'll be watching for you, through the shutters. Drive up the front lane and continue around to the back. Park your car and go to the kitchen door. He'll meet you there."

"I'm very grateful." He leaned down, to his own surprise, and kissed her on the lips.

Her lips pressed against his then pulled away. "I told him your name."

"Good."

"He said you're a famous private eye."

"Only in criminal circles."

"Don't let anything happen to him."

"I'll do my damnedest." He headed for his car, without looking back.

Chapter 18

Zeke slowed the Chevy off Alamo Pintado Road, past the ELDORADO sign—reminded of that other sign in Mandeville Canyon—and started up the private lane.

The air was suddenly chilly, but this was far enough inland to escape most of the coastal fog.

Warm September days, cool nights. Unlike hot and humid Los Angeles.

The fields of vegetables, on either side, were dark but he was aware of delicious scents. Must be herbs planted along the lane.

He saw the black Victorian silhouette of the house looming ahead, against the stars, no glint of light from the shuttered windows.

Circled to the rear and slowed to a stop near the screened kitchen porch. Got out but left the car door open in case he needed to leave here in a hurry for any reason.

Saw that the windows at the back were shuttered, as before.

Went up the steps again and found the screen door unlocked.

As he swung it open and slipped inside he saw another closed screen door, straight ahead, at the entrance to the kitchen.

He moved across the porch silently and turned the handle. The second screen door was latched on the inside.

He bent close to the metal mesh and saw that the wooden kitchen door stood open and he was looking into the dark kitchen. "Anybody here?" He kept his voice low. "Mr. Knight?"

"Your name?" The voice, a trained baritone, came from the darkness.

"Zeke Gahagan."

"Faye Manning sent you?"

"That's right."

"You've got some identification?"

"Certainly." He brought his wallet out and lifted it toward the screen.

A flashlight beam hit his hand.

In the spill from the small bulb he could see a floating face. One he'd seen in dozens of films.

"So you're the 'world's oldest eye' . . ."

"That's what I've been told."

"Wouldn't've guessed, looking at you."

"Faye's been worried."

"Mighty kind of her." A tanned hand, extending from a lean arm, reached out to unlatch the screen door and pushed it open. "Come in, Mr. Gahagan. And welcome."

"Thanks." He stepped into the dark kitchen, aware of a faint trace of recent cooking as the door was closed and locked behind him.

"You weren't tailed here?"

"I promise you I wasn't."

The flashlight aimed down now, revealing a floor of blue and white tiles.

"If you'll follow me. This way . . ."

Zeke went after him, eyes on the moving beam of light, through an open door into a hall. The air was chilly from air conditioning.

The house was silent.

"I'm being careful because someone else was here today. Watched him drive up the lane—I'd heard his car—saw it circle the house. The driver—a man—tried that screen door at the back, as you'd done earlier. I had, also, observed you. Didn't know who either of you were. You rang the front bell, he didn't. Which made me suspicious."

"What did he look like?"

"Short. Black hair and mustache. Latin type, if you were casting a picture."

"Mexican or Italian?"

"Could be either one, I should think."

"What make car was he driving?"

"Black Volkswagen. Didn't get the license number. When he drove up the lane I was busy trying to see his face and when he circled the house to the back he parked where I couldn't see him."

Zeke was startled as Knight swung a door open into a large room where several shaded lamps were lighted.

"This is my study. Don't learn parts any more but I spend most of my evenings in here, if I'm alone, reading and listening to music . . ."

Zeke saw rows of bookshelves, a large television set and an elaborate record player. Heavy curtains covered all the windows.

"Sit down, Mr. Gahagan. We can talk . . ."

They sank into comfortable armchairs near a big carved oak coffee table holding more books with piles of newspapers and magazines.

Zeke observed that Knight was deeply tanned, wearing an expensive short-sleeved sport shirt over tan slacks, rubber-soled white shoes. The actor must be in his late seventies, at least, but he looked more like fifty. His white hair was thick and curly, worn a little long, black eyebrows over brown eyes. Except for the white hair, his appearance hadn't changed much since he'd last seen him in a movie. Probably six feet, three inches. In spite of the age difference, he looked like a healthier version of his grandson. Only this face had more character, the jaw was prominent, the mouth stronger.

"There's a box of cigarettes there. Several brands . . ."

"Don't smoke. Thanks." He was waiting for Knight to start talking.

"Neither do I. Not any more . . . Before Hildreth called, just now, two others had phoned earlier, to say you were looking for me. Kara Kolvang's sister, Mrs. Andersen, and my housekeeper, Mrs. Svendsen."

"I saw Mrs. Andersen, this afternoon, but she said she didn't know where you were."

"People respect privacy in these parts."

"Is your housekeeper in Solvang? I saw her yesterday, at your home in Los Angeles."

"She told me. She's staying with her sister, Mrs. Nielsen. I was afraid she might be in danger if she came here. Didn't tell her that, of course. Anyway, I prefer to be alone at the moment."

"Mrs. Nielsen said she hadn't seen her."

"She would. I'd suggested they both come up here this weekend, Mrs. Svendsen and my grandson. She drove up last evening but I've no idea where Lars has gone. He doesn't like Solvang. Too rural for him. I understand you saw him yesterday . . ."

"And talked to him."

"He'd refused to leave Los Angeles this weekend because he had an appointment today for some stupid television job. He knew I was up here. Didn't think it wise to remain in the city after somebody fired those shots into our garage doors. Maybe he's staying with a friend for the weekend. Must've been packing this morning when I called and it was his friend who answered the phone. I didn't think of that until afterward. Was so startled to hear an unfamiliar voice I hung up. Called back, later, but nobody answered."

"This other man who came here today—this 'Latin type'—did you recognize him? Perhaps from the past?"

"Never saw him before. At the moment, I thought it might be you. I'd just been told you were looking for me."

"Any idea who put those holes in your garage doors?"

"None."

"Couldn't that have been somebody warning you not to say anything more about the Kolvang murder?"

"That's exactly what I suspected. Why I came up here. I'd planned, for some time, to spend the weekend here. You've heard what I said at that dinner Monday night?"

"Paul Victor told me. I paid him a visit, hoping to get a lead as to where you might've gone. Questioned the other three guests, as well as the fourth—the one who didn't show up."

"Clem Dalby? He's an old friend . . . Can't say the same about Paul Victor. Never liked the man."

"None of them could give me any information. Only that you had announced after dinner that a man named Tim Kerrigan had told you, many years ago, he knew who killed Kara Kolvang."

"I'd had too much to drink."

"Only two drinks."

"But I hadn't touched alcohol in years and it hit me. Otherwise, I'd never have said such a thing."

"After you left Faye Manning, Tuesday, you went to see Tim Kerrigan."

Knight looked startled. "How could you know that?"

"Did you talk to him?"

"Only briefly. Explained what I'd done. What I said . . ."

"Was he upset? Angry?"

"He didn't seem to understand what I was telling him. Didn't appear to remember anything from the past. As though he'd never heard of Kara . . ."

"That's interesting."

"I didn't expect him to recognize me but he didn't even remember my name. I finally saw it was useless and left. My only regret is that I didn't give him some money. I was upset, wasn't thinking clearly."

"That's understandable."

"The poor man looked ill. Skin and bones. I feel very guilty that I didn't try to help him . . ."

Zeke was aware, as Knight talked, of his grandson's resemblance to the actor. When Lars came down that dark staircase the killer thought he was Laurence Knight. Shot him but discovered his mistake. Now the killer was here to correct that mistake. Mustn't tell Knight two people were dead. His grandson and Kerrigan. He had to find this man—this 'Latin type'—who had shot Lars Lyndon and strangled Tim Kerrigan. Find him before he killed Laurence Knight . . .

". . . and I don't believe Tim remembered he'd ever told me he knew who killed Kara. He's become senile. I plan to arrange for him to be cared for in some sort of convalescent home. Phone my attorney, next Monday when I return to L.A., and work something out. I can afford to do that for him . . ."

Zeke studied his face, this man who planned to arrange a more comfortable future for a dead man with no future. Knight was a decent guy. Not a crass Hollywood type. No wonder Faye liked him . . .

". . . and that's about all I can tell you, Mr. Gahagan. I'm afraid Tim Kerrigan doesn't remember who killed Kara. The police won't learn anything from him."

"I agree."

"I'm very touched that Faye cared enough to send you looking for me."

"Now that I've found you, I'm sure she would want me to protect you this weekend."

"No need for that. I'm perfectly safe here. Every door and window is locked and I can see any car approaching from the front. I have a large collection of guns. There's a loaded pistol on a table near the front door and a Winchester in the kitchen. I've collected firearms since I began playing cowboys—that's after I stopped working in musicals—and I have a permit for my gun collection. I'm a crack shot. So I don't need protection."

"I saw posters in Solvang saying there would be a mystery star in the Danish Days parade and I suspected that star might be you."

"Agreed to do that months ago. Can't cancel at this late date."

"I would suggest you take no part in the parade. You'll be exposing your person to whoever fired those bullets into your garage doors in Los Angeles."

"I can't believe that. There's no way he could know I'm here!"

"I beg you, Mr. Knight. Don't take part in this parade tomorrow."

"I'm to be honorary Grand Marshal. Can't back out now. Wouldn't want to disappoint my friends in Solvang. Anyway, I'll have two revolvers in hip holsters." He smiled. "They won't be loaded. I don't like carrying loaded guns . . ."

Zeke realized that he wouldn't be able to dissuade Knight. His enthusiasm, as he talked about the parade, meant the actor was looking forward to this public appearance. "All right. I won't try to stop you but I'll be there, in the crowd, looking for trouble. Watching for this 'Latin type' . . ."

"You mustn't say anything to our local police."

"I should inform them that I'm here. Tell them why."

"Solvang has no official police force. It's a peaceful town. The County Sheriff maintains a substation here, I'm told, and the

California Highway Patrol has an office in Buellton. They'll be handling traffic and keeping streets closed for the parade route. I don't want any of them to know you're a private eye sent here for my protection." He chuckled. "That'll only get your name in the paper . . ."

"Very well, Mr. Knight. You may see me in the crowd, but we'll not exchange any signs of recognition. You'll have your revolvers and I'll be unarmed. I rarely carry a gun these days."

"And my unloaded revolvers will remain in their holsters." Knight smiled. "I don't mean to appear rude or ungrateful. Why don't we dine together after the parade and compare notes? Have a little private Danish Days celebration of our own . . ."

"That would be pleasant."

"I'll phone the Danish Inn and reserve a table for seven o'clock. You can bring Hildreth Johnson and I'll pick up Inga Andersen—Kara's sister—to make a foursome. That reminds me!" Pushing himself up from the armchair. "Would you mind watching some television?"

"Television?" He watched Knight stride toward the television set.

"I seldom look at it. Still prefer the big screen in a theater, but they're showing an old film on public television that I made with Kara Kolvang . . ."

"I'd planned to see that myself."

"Was watching it when I heard your car. Switched off the set in a hurry. Thought it might be that other fellow returning." He leaned down to turn the set on and color expanded across the large screen. "It must be half over by now."

The face of a blonde girl singing. Sound was turned low.

He recognized the face from Henri Neri's portrait and the clippings from Paul Victor's file. Now the beautiful face was alive and animated. She was singing a song, alone in a taxi, riding through the night on a broad city avenue where snow was falling. Fifth Avenue? He didn't listen to the words she sang as he studied the face of the dead actress. Saw there were tears in her eyes and on her cheeks.

Knight returned to sit in the other armchair. "This was Kara's last film. Fifty years ago. Isn't that a face?"

"It is, indeed..." His eyes were held by the image.

"And what a voice. Glorious! Pure and sweet. A true lyric soprano. I don't like coloraturas..."

"There was one I used to like. Lily Pons."

"Well... She was exceptional. This is the snow sequence. There was always a snow sequence in every Kara Kolvang feature..."

Zeke stared at the sensitive young face, framed in a white hood of ermine, the same delicious beauty he'd seen in Neri's painting. There was a curious childlike quality that made her face unlike that of any other actress.

"Clem Dalby directed this one. Kara's long dead, and I understand Clem's an invalid."

Now, for some unexplained reason, Kara was dancing surrounded by people in a snow-covered park. She danced alone but the others were dancing around her. Kara was still singing the same song. Beyond the winter-bare trees was a line of tall buildings against a night sky, their lighted windows barely visible through the drifting snow.

"That's supposed to be Central Park," Knight explained, "and those buildings look strange because this was fifty years ago."

"Don't look strange to me. I've only been to New York once. Sixty-four years ago. I was seventeen..."

"We shot all of this on Hollywood sound stages. I'd heard the film was lost but somebody found a print and preserved it. They're showing it because this week's the anniversary of Kara's death."

"That was Monday night. The night of Paul Victor's dinner."

"Monday's an off night for television. They get a large audience on Friday."

Zeke saw that Kara was no longer crying and had finished her dance in the arms of Laurence Knight who was now singing the same song to her. He had a fine voice. At the moment he was wearing a fur-collared coat and opera hat. "Where did you come from? Or did I miss something?"

"It was established, earlier, I've been searching for her. Following her taxi in my chauffeured limousine. Musicals, in those days, didn't make much sense. They were sugar-pastry Technicolor dreams. But they made lots of money. I was never in the dance numbers. I'd done a little dancing on Broadway, but I wasn't much good at it. The male leads in Broadway shows were always singers. Rarely dancers. So, when Kara and I danced together on screen they used a double for me. Of course the camera was always on her. I was only in the close shots . . ."

Zeke continued to study Kara in her reaction shots as she listened to Knight singing. At the end of the song they embraced and walked off, through the snow, as the others applauded.

The next sequence had several familiar character actors—famous ones whose names he didn't remember—playing a dowager and her servants in a fancy ballroom where dress extras were dancing.

Knight laughed during the scene. "They don't have character people like that today. Edna Mae Oliver's playing Kara's grandmother. The servants are Fritz Feld, Franklin Pangborn and Eric Blore. Such great performers . . ."

Doors were flung open and Kara swept in with Laurence Knight. The dress extras stopped dancing and surrounded them as Kara sang another song, moving around the enormous ballroom, still holding Knight's hand.

"This was my third film with Kara. None of us had any idea it would be her last . . ."

"A Kurt von Zemmering production?"

"All of Kara's films were produced by Kurt."

"You liked him—von Zemmering?"

"He had great taste. A rare commodity, even then, in Hollywood. Kara adored him. For good reason! He'd discovered her and made her a star. She had every right to worship him."

"You think he killed her?"

"I could never believe that."

"How can you be positive?"

"Because Kurt was, truly, a sensitive and gentle man. Not the type to kill any one. He was in New York the night she was murdered."

"Who do you suppose did kill her?"

"I can't imagine any one with a motive. Destroying such purity and beauty. She had never, to my knowledge, harmed anybody. Kara was an innocent. Not sexually, of course, but instinctively. Untouched by people. Even her lovers. And they were legion. To Kara, sex was an amusing game. I think that's why she shocked many people. She had the innocence of a child playing with dolls. Male dolls. Men were her toys . . ."

"I'm told you quarreled with her that day, before she died."

"We never quarreled. Kara was furious because I showed up at our final dubbing session after too many drinks at lunch. I'd been celebrating the end of filming with some of our technical crew—it was this picture we're watching—and I returned late from the commissary. Depressed by the thought I might never work with Kara again . . .

"There was much talk that the big musicals were finished. Kurt had announced several projects but none of them seemed to include me. My late return to the dubbing studio messed up the session. I couldn't remember my lines and Kara screamed at me. She was an old hand at dubbing. Never muffed a word or missed a pause. Finally she had them bring me coffee and, eventually, we finished the last scene. Kara began to cry and ran out of the studio as the speakers connecting all the stages and offices were announcing that everyone involved with *Park Avenue Girl* was invited to the largest stage on the lot.

"I managed to stagger there, with some help from Clem Dalby, and had to face several hundred applauding people as I entered. An orchestra was playing music from the picture and people were dancing. There was an elaborate buffet and waiters serving champagne. Kara had arranged this surprise closing party—Kurt, of course, was in New York—for the final day of shooting. Everyone was there but Kara. She never showed up and I never saw her again. She was killed that night."

Zeke saw Knight's face turned toward the television screen. There were tears on his cheek.

"My wife had arranged a little party of our own, that evening, to celebrate the finish of the picture and I really got plastered. Kara was invited to join us but, of course, she didn't. Next day I gave up drinking. When I heard she'd been murdered . . ."

Kara Kolvang, on the screen, was walking down a busy city street. Flowers blooming in front of shops. Must be New York in the spring. She held two white wolfhounds on a leash and a blond young man was hurrying in pursuit. Now they were walking together, side by side, laughing and talking. The wolfhounds pulling her forward as the camera moved back ahead of them.

The dogs reminded Zeke of that sheepdog. He hoped the police had fed him after they found Lars's body. Wondered if they'd placed him in a kennel. Lars had said Rip was "Grandpa's dog" . . .

Would be awkward, at this moment, to tell Knight his grandson had been murdered. As well as Kerrigan. Better wait until tomorrow . . .

On the television screen Kara and Knight were talking quietly in what seemed to be a fancy penthouse. Knight's hair, without a hat, was dark blond and curly. Not like Kara's straight white-blonde hair. Both were wearing evening clothes.

Knight's young face looked even more like Lars. A stronger, more positive version of the same features.

Kara's image was now walking through some kind of gallery or museum, glancing at framed paintings, beside the same blond young man who spoke with a British accent. He wasn't interested in the paintings but was trying to persuade her to spend a weekend on his yacht.

"That's a New York character actor, Sloane Martin," Knight explained. "Clem Dalby brought him out from Broadway to play this part. He became a member of what everyone called the 'Dalby stock company.' Fine actors Clem used over and over in his pictures. He was like John Ford. Only felt comfortable on the set if he was surrounded by friends. There was an unspoken agreement that if you worked for Clem you never worked for Ford." He laughed. "Clem was a dictator, but a benevolent one . . ."

Kara Kolvang and Laurence Knight on a balcony overlooking a night view of the city. Close shots of their faces singing a romantic duet.

"Beautiful voices!" Zeke exclaimed. "Both of you."

"It's a terrific song—'Now or Never'—the big hit of the picture. Erik Wulff wrote very singable music and lyrics. It's been said he's the last of the great Viennese composers. Heir to Franz Lehar. The tragedy is that Hollywood doesn't do musicals any more. Perhaps Paul Victor will make this film about Kara and it will bring a revival of Erik's music. I hope so . . ."

Another scene with Edna Mae Oliver trying to learn from Kara what was happening about her romance with Laurence Knight. They were having tea in an elegant drawing room with another young woman who was Kara's best friend. The butler, Eric Blore, was serving them and interrupting their conversation.

"That pretty girl," Knight explained, "is Kara's sister. You saw her this afternoon."

"Mrs. Andersen?" This smiling plump face had turned into a fat face.

Kara's delicate face was more beautiful.

As he studied her closeups Zeke remembered Henri Neri's

words. "If only she could speak to you. Kara would plead for you to find the person who killed her. She would persuade you . . ."

And now he was hearing her living voice.

Suddenly the face was gone and there was a shot of Knight getting out of an old-fashioned taxi across from a small park.

"That's Gramercy Park," Knight murmured. "Wonderful how Henri Neri reproduced those old New York scenes in the studio. In contrast to the Art Deco shops and night clubs of the early thirties. And his costumes for Kara were incredible . . ."

Knight was taking out his keys to open the front door.

"Had enough of this?"

"I was never one for musicals. Except on the stage."

"Weren't you?" Knight laughed as he pushed himself to his feet and went toward the television set. "Musicals had a big audience in those days. Gone forever, I'm afraid. Even on Broadway."

Knight, on the screen, had opened the door and entered a luxurious hall leading to a curving mahogany staircase.

He leaned down and snapped the control lever.

The image vanished.

"Kara's sister had more scenes in the early part of the film. She was in all of Kara's pictures but, unfortunately, never really wanted to act." He stood in front of the dark screen facing Zeke. "I enjoyed making musicals. Those first years after I came to the Coast. But I enjoyed making westerns even more. Especially for Clem Dalby. Liked working with Barbara Stanwyck and Walter Huston. All those other fine actors. And I didn't have to vocalize for several hours every morning."

"I saw you in many westerns. They were my favorites."

"There's something ridiculous about singing in a film. Never had that feeling on Broadway. But always felt uncomfortable in movie musicals. They seemed wrong. A stage was completely artificial but in a film you would be standing on a busy street and have to start singing. Everyone else paid no attention to you. Kara, on the other hand, would never appear in anything but musicals. I wonder what she would've done when they stopped making them . . ."

"Of course, she must've saved enough money never to work again. I suppose she might've returned to Denmark and bought herself a real castle. Kara the Snow Princess. With a new Prince to warm her, bed and body, every night. There would, eventually, have been one Prince. She would've married him and been happy. At least for a while . . ." He sighed and frowned. "No. That only happens in the movies. In musicals . . ." He chuckled. "I'll be going back to Los Angeles tomorrow night. After we have dinner."

"Tomorrow night?"

"If I'm not too tired, after the parade, to drive. In that case I'll put it off until Sunday. Have to find out what's happened to my grandson and, Sunday night, I want to see one of Clem Dalby's westerns. They're having a Clem Dalby festival at the Nuart in Santa Monica. I'm in this one, and I'd like to see it again."

Zeke got to his feet. "Did you mention to your grandson that you were going to look for Tim Kerrigan?"

"Matter of fact, I did. Told him there was a place, near the Santa Monica pier, called Cantrell's Corner. Always used to leave messages there for Tim. That's how I found him this week. Went to Cantrell's Corner and they told me where he lived."

"You'll be safe here tonight?"

"Of course I'll be safe. Will you be talking to Faye?"

"I'll call her in the morning. Tell her I found you."

"Assure her that I'm all right."

"She tried to reach you here but there was no answer."

"I only answer if it's a signal. Can't understand why my grandson didn't call today. Wants to be an actor, but he has no talent. Can't remember lines. Leaves notes all over the house to remind him to keep appointments."

Zeke remembered the note under the phone.

"Hope he remembered to feed Rip. That's my dog. I've always had dogs . . ."

"You know where I'm staying, if you need me."

"Thanks, Mr. Gahagan." He held out his hand.

Zeke shook it, aware of Knight's strength. "See you at that parade tomorrow."

"Doesn't start until three o'clock." Picking up his flashlight and walking ahead. "I'll guide you back to the kitchen door."

"Thanks."

"After you leave I'll switch the burglar alarm on again. Turned it off when I saw you arriving." He opened the door and went ahead, into the dark hall. "Leave these lights on. Just close the door behind you."

"Right." Zeke shut the door and hesitated in the dark.

Knight snapped his flashlight and the beam hit the polished wood floor. "I'll lead the way . . ."

Zeke followed him through the silent house.

Chapter 19

He was furious with himself.
He'd overslept again.

He hurried through the bright morning sunlight toward the office to have a chat with Hildreth before driving into Solvang.

This morning he had to check every street, follow the parade route.

And he had to call Faye. Report to her he'd found her friend.

Should've done that last night, but he'd been too tired.

Not a cloud in the sky.

The Danes had a fine day for their celebration.

No one in the pool.

Glancing around the sprawling motel complex he saw that the parking spaces in front of each room contained a car. Every size and make of car. Campers, station wagons, battered pickup trucks, one Mercedes and several Volkswagens.

He'd decided, last night, he wouldn't call Faye until after the parade but this morning, in the shower, he'd changed his mind. Phone her this morning from a public booth in town.

Passing the office window he saw a lamp lighted inside. No sign of Hildreth.

There was an enticing aroma of coffee when he opened the door, causing a distant bell to tinkle.

He closed the door and crossed to the counter where a large metal coffee pot sat on an electric warmer beside an inviting platter of pastries. Big framed picture of a sunny field with crows which he recognized as a reproduction of a familiar Van Gogh painting. Leather seat, across the front, under the picture window with magazines handy on a table. He hadn't noticed any of this yesterday. Soft music coming through an open door, beyond the desk, that must lead to Hildreth's apartment.

She appeared through the door as he reached the counter. "I thought it must be you. None of the others will make an appearance before nine."

"I overslept." He saw, as she came from behind the counter, that she was wearing an attractive embroidered linen blouse over tailored white slacks, sandals on her bare feet. "Your beds are too comfortable."

"Heard your car come in last night. Yours was the last. Was curious what happened when you saw Larry, but didn't want to bother you at that hour. Anyway, I was half asleep, myself. Cup of coffee?"

"I could use one, thanks."

"Sugar and cream?" She reached for two blue and white mugs and filled them with coffee.

"Black, no sugar."

"Help yourself to a Danish." Filling the mugs. "They come from my favorite bakery in Solvang."

"I never eat pastries. I'll get some breakfast in town."

She set one mug on the counter in front of him. "Why don't we take these out to the pool? Nobody will bother us."

"That's a fine idea." He picked up his mug and carried it to the door.

She followed with the other mug. "Everybody will get up at the same time. Wanting their coffee and pastries immediately."

Zeke held the door open for her to go ahead.

"They'll be staying until Monday morning. Most of them."

He closed the door and followed her, through the sunlight, toward the pool.

"How'd you get along with Larry?"

"Fine. He's a pleasant guy. Nothing like an actor."

"I've known some pretty nice actors." She laughed. "And several bastards."

"I tried to persuade him not to ride in that parade."

"For what reason?"

"I suspect he could be in danger."

"Are you serious?"

"Damn right I am." Opening the metal gate to the pool area. "He'll be exposed the whole time. Anybody could take a shot at him."

"You think someone might?"

"There's more than a slight possibility. I'll do everything I can to prevent it. Which isn't much. I plan to mingle in the crowd before the parade and look for suspicious faces . . ."

"You really are serious." She set her coffee mug on a white patio table and sat under the parasol.

"During the parade I'll walk along the sidewalk, behind the people lining the curbs." Sitting across from her. "I'll keep abreast of the vehicle with Larry Knight. Watching for anyone to make a sudden move. As though they might be reaching for a gun." He tasted the coffee.

"Will you have a gun?"

"No. But Larry plans to carry two." He needn't tell her they wouldn't be loaded. "You make damn good coffee."

"Everyone will be hurrying into town this morning for breakfast."

"I had breakfast yesterday at a restaurant on Copenhagen Drive. Best sausage I've ever eaten."

"They're a local specialty. You'll get them everywhere today. The young people set up stoves and tables along Copenhagen. They all serve those sausages—they're called medisterpølse—along with aebleskiver . . ."

"What the devil's that?"

"Sort of a round pancake thing, cooked in a special pan and turned over with long metal things like knitting needles. Then it's powdered with sugar. Cooked and served by the prettiest girls in town. I'll be driving in later, myself, for a second breakfast." Her face became serious again. "You really do think someone might try to harm Larry during the parade?"

"Some one was prowling around his property last evening."

"He saw them?"

"Yes. He says it was a stranger. A man with black hair and a mustache. Couldn't see him clearly."

"Thank God you're here."

"You can thank Faye Manning. By the way, he's invited us—you and I—to have dinner with him tonight at the Danish Inn."

"I know. He called me this morning."

"He's going to phone Mrs. Andersen and invite her."

"He told me."

"So there'll be four of us."

"Inga's an old friend. I'll get out the new dress I bought last month but—until this moment—had no occasion to wear. Will you go to dinner from here?"

"I'll take you in my car."

"It worries me to think Larry could be in danger. Riding in the parade . . . You're not exaggerating?"

"I'm a policeman. I learned, long ago, never to exaggerate."

"Had he heard from Lars?"

"No . . ." He studied her face, especially the eyes. "If I tell you something will you keep it to yourself? Absolutely confidential."

"Of course." She put her coffee mug down so suddenly that it splashed onto the white-topped table.

Zeke finished the last of his and set the mug aside. "There is someone who may try to kill Laurence Knight today."

"Surely you're joking." Her eyes belied the doubt in her words. "Aren't you?"

"This is no joke. I can't explain more fully because I don't have any idea who this person is. Something was said at a dinner party, in Los Angeles, Monday night . . ."

"By whom?"

"Larry Knight. As a result of what he said two people have already been killed. At least I believe that's why they died. One of them was Larry Knight's grandson."

"Lars? Good Lord!"

"Shot to death, in their home."

"Does Larry know?"

"No. And I'm not going to tell him. Not yet. He'd panic. Which is the worst thing he could do. He's been trying to reach his grandson on the phone but, of course, there's nobody there. The police have removed the body and, probably, sealed the house. Their housekeeper, Mrs. Svendsen, is in Solvang."

"I know. She's staying with her sister."

"I've reason to suspect the man who killed Lars is a Latin. Like the man Larry saw prowling outside his house."

"And the man who called me yesterday!"

"Yes. I suspect he's in Solvang. Waiting for today's parade. That would be the best time, when the streets are crowded, to shoot him."

"If you told this to Larry he wouldn't appear in the parade."

"That's just it! I'm sure he would. He's obviously a man of great courage. If he knew his grandson had been killed by someone who was now trying to shoot him he'd want to face the man. And kill him."

"Yes . . . I suppose he would. What can you do to protect Larry from this—person?"

"Very little. Unfortunately. I've never seen the man. I can only look for a short man who appears to be Latin. Who has black hair and a mustache."

"You won't find many locals who fit that description. Most of the men are blond and tall or white-haired and tall. A few short ones but they tend to be balding . . . There will be Latin-looking men among the thousands of tourists. Your man could lose himself in the crowd."

"I'm aware of that. However, if he did prowl around Larry Knight's property last night he must've arrived yesterday."

"Then he's staying in one of the hotels or motels. Are you going to check them?"

"There isn't time. I believe this man's smart enough to avoid the local motels. He would, more likely, stay in a nearby town. Perhaps as far away as Ventura or Santa Barbara . . ."

"What can you do?"

"Observe the people as they arrive. Lose myself among them."

"At least he doesn't know you'll be looking for him."

"I can't be sure of that." He hesitated, his eyes on her troubled face. "There's something you can tell me."

"Yes?"

"Is there a young man in Solvang who, every night, goes around checking the windmills?"

"Why would any one do that?"

"Perhaps to make sure the mechanisms operating the sails are working properly."

"I never heard of such a person. I suppose someone might check them before the Danish Days celebration. But that seems unlikely. Somebody would be sure to notice if one of them wasn't working and, being Danish, would fix it himself. Did you see a man checking the windmills?"

"Last night."

"They would be checked by daylight. Not after dark."

"I would think so. I'd come out from the Danish Inn after dinner and paused for a breath of air. Saw this man come around the corner. Walking as though he didn't wish to be seen. Watched him cross the street to peer at that windmill near the restaurant."

"That's one of the largest."

"He didn't notice me in the dark. I waited as he went inside the windmill. Saw his flashlight through a window. After a moment he came out and went on up Mission Drive. I followed, from street to street. He went into one other windmill. Then, suddenly, he slipped around a corner. When I followed there was no sign of him but I heard a car speed away."

"What did he look like?"

"Never got close enough to see his face. Only that he had straight blond hair."

"You say a young man?"

"Moved like one. Fast on his feet. Darted from sidewalk to sidewalk. Avoiding street lamps. Only once did he pause and look back but I couldn't see his face clearly."

"You think he realized you were following him?"

"Not at first but, toward the end, I had a feeling he did. Sensed my presence, rather than saw me, and hurried to his car."

"There are hundreds of young blond men in Solvang. By the way, when you drive into town, leave your car in one of the official parking lots. You'll notice three or four of them. That way you'll find it without any trouble. Park, if possible, under a tree. The radio said it's going to be warm today. Thousands of cars will be arriving this morning. They'll be parked for miles out into the country. Show your identification to the attendant. Tell him you're a friend of Larry's and he'll let your car stay there all day."

"I'll do that."

"You can slip him a five-dollar bill to guarantee it." She looked around the deserted pool. "There come the first customers for coffee."

Zeke's eyes followed a fat, middle-aged couple heading for the office. The man wore a loud flowered shirt over shorts but his wife was wearing a quilted robe. Both wore sunglasses. "They must be from L. A.!"

"They are." She jumped up and called to them across the pool. "Good morning! Be right with you." She snatched up the empty coffee mugs. "If I'm not there they'll gobble two pastries—each of them—and there won't be enough for the others. I give them all the coffee they can drink but only one pastry apiece."

He was on his feet. "Will I see you in town?"

"I'll look for you. After I have breakfast at one of the street tables."

Zeke watched her hurry after the waddling fat couple as he started back, around the pool, to his room.

Were those two men awake yet?

The blond one who checked windmills and the Latin who didn't ring Larry Knight's door bell . . .

Could they be working together?

He would look for both of them this morning.

Chapter 20

He held the Chevy to a crawl, street after street, checking each parking lot, passing rows of tables and portable stoves placed along one sidewalk on Copenhagen Drive where girls in Danish costumes and white aprons were preparing for the day's visitors. Several tables were already occupied by early arrivals, probably locals, eating breakfast.

Left his car under a tree in a parking lot near Fourth Place, between Mission and Copenhagen. Showed his identification to the blond boy in attendance and slipped him five bucks. Told him he would park there all day because he was in charge of security for Laurence Knight. The impressed youth assured him the Chevy wouldn't be moved.

He warned the boy not to tell anyone he was in town because Mr. Knight didn't want people to know he was here to protect him.

The streets were beginning to fill with people as he left the parking lot. Young parents followed by a straggle of small children. Older couples, wearing sunglasses, giggling middle-aged women, probably widows, in groups of four. These must be people who had arrived yesterday and spent the night here. All of them seemed to be laughing. It was a happy crowd.

Zeke walked along Copenhagen, glancing at the restaurant on the other side of the street where he'd eaten yesterday, as he made his way past windows filled with merchandise and souvenirs. Many shops hadn't opened yet.

He followed an open path down the center of the sidewalk between a row of small tables placed in front of shop windows and portable stoves lining the curb where young girls, most of them blonde, were preparing the food. They held the long metal sticks Hildreth had described with which they were turning puffy looking pastries. Other girls surrounded an immense coffee urn from which steam was spurting. And fat brown sausages sizzled on hot plates.

He found an empty table and paused beside the nearest girl turning pastries. "I'll take one of those goodies, young lady."

She looked up, flashing a smile. "They're called aebleskive, sir."

"I'll never be able to say that."

"Would you like one aebleskive or two aebleskiver? That's the plural. Aebleskiver . . ."

"One please. And I'd like a sausage."

"That'll be two dollars and fifty cents. Coffee's included. You get that at the machine. This aebleskive looks ready." She lifted the pastry with her hooked needle onto a paper plate and set a sausage beside it. Sprinkled powdered sugar over the pastry and handed the plate to him. "The sausage is called medisterpølse."

"So I've been told." He gave her the money. "No knife and fork?"

"You only need your fingers. Hold them in a paper napkin. You'll find plenty of napkins on the tables."

Zeke carried his plate to the empty table where he saw a neat stack of napkins. Set his plate down then went to get coffee.

Another pretty girl filled a paper cup with steaming coffee.

The metal urn was a converted water heater that some ingenious Dane had turned into a monster coffee pot.

He carried the coffee back to his table. Sat down and prepared to enjoy breakfast, the pastry and sausage with their impossible names which that girl had pronounced so sweetly. Took two paper napkins and using one to hold each, discovered it wasn't difficult to manage.

The sausage was exactly like the one he'd eaten yesterday and the pastry—Hildreth had called it a pancake but it wasn't like any pancake he'd ever eaten—was crusty on the surface and soft inside. There was a jar of what appeared to be homemade jam but he didn't try any. The pastry was delicious, without anything.

And the coffee, to his surprise, was first-rate. Strong and fragrant. Could rarely find coffee this good in Los Angeles. Unless, of course, he made it himself.

As he ate he kept studying nearby faces.

Many of them he quickly realized, from their conversation, belonged to people from the shops, having breakfast before they opened for the day. Some of the older women must be owners. Several of the others seemed to be visitors who had attended earlier Danish Days, because they knew the girls serving food and were greeted by the shop people. Most of the outsiders wore sunglasses. The locals did not.

He was looking for two faces.

That Latin type and the windmill man . . .

He noticed several young men on the opposite side of the street with blond hair but none of them were anything like the windmill man.

No swarthy men in sight. Any Latin would stand out among these Nordic people.

As he finished the last morsel of sausage he watched an

elaborately decorated brewery truck, pulled by a team of sturdy gray and white percherons, rolling past with a costumed band playing a jaunty tune.

The people eating breakfast, including the locals, applauded and waved.

Zeke studied their faces.

Could there be a murderer among them? A man who had, already, killed twice and, unless he was prevented, would kill again.

He swallowed the last of his coffee reluctantly and got to his feet. No more coffee today. He'd drunk more than he was allowed.

Made his way to the curb, between two of the small stoves, and realized that no cars were parked on either side of Copenhagen.

Walking close to the curb lined with portable stoves, moving slowly and casually—in case anyone noticed him—glancing at every face, he reached Alisal Road and turned left toward Mission. No parking here.

The side streets were filling. Some people would have to park on Highway 246—which became Mission Drive as it sliced through the center of Solvang—and every other road leading into town.

A bus filled with squealing people was hunting for a place to park.

He saw that an empty bus was already parked beyond the Post Office.

As he walked, Zeke became aware of the sweet smell of baking bread. There were several bakeries—he'd noticed at least three yesterday—and they must be making extra bread and pastries this morning. Bakers always did their work early. So this must be a second baking to provide for today's extra customers.

He noticed each stork perched on the rooftops and checked every windmill.

Today their slowly revolving sails looked peaceful against the blue sky. Last night, standing still, they had seemed ominous.

Everyone he passed was smiling. If they had any problems they were forgotten or left behind.

He paused with a group of people in a circle around some costumed dancers. Boys and girls—most of them blond—dancing and clapping their hands as a trio of older people sang what must be a Danish folk song. At least he couldn't understand the words.

The sound of the band on that distant brewery truck was in counterpoint to the singers who were not disturbed.

Zeke moved on, checking everything.

The sky was a pure clear blue. Still midsummer blue in late September. Not a cloud.

People walking in the center of the road now.

Turning down Mission, he glimpsed the Danish Inn, in the distance, on the other side. Be dining there tonight with Larry Knight, along with the ladies. That should be pleasant.

After dinner he would drive back to Los Angeles. Even though he'd have to pay for another night at the motel. He would include that in his list of expenses.

He wondered if this was called Mission Drive back when Kara and her friends came to Solvang for weekends . . .

More costumed singers, marching along the road, arms linked as they sang. Their young voices floating sweet and clear.

Another bus slowing to a stop, doors opening for a load of visitors to pour out. A sign on the bus said they'd come from Los Angeles. They were fanning out in every direction. Children scampering ahead.

A Highway Patrol officer at the far corner directing traffic.

Walking on, he checked the big windmill near the Danish Inn and saw that the door at ground level was closed. He wondered what was inside. Probably some sort of machine to revolve those overhead sails and nothing else. Later, when people crowded the streets, he would be less likely to be noticed slipping inside to check what was there. The small windmills weren't large enough for a man to enter.

Reaching First Street, he heard the band playing more distinctly and turned to see the percherons pulling the brewery truck along Copenhagen again. The sound of the brass instruments and thumping drums faded as he started down First.

Not so many people here. They kept to the main streets where the parade would pass.

He must find the exact route the parade would take.

There was a drugstore on the far corner of First and Copenhagen. Should be a public phone there.

Pausing on the corner, he glanced down Copenhagen and saw that the brewery truck was turning up Alisal again. All the sidewalk tables were crowded, the blonde girls busy with their gleaming needles. Several young men, strolling in groups, wearing Stetsons and western outfits. Must be cowhands, from nearby ranches, in town for the celebration.

As he started across the street toward the drugstore he saw a sign saying it was the Solvang Pharmacy. He'd made a mental note, yesterday, of the newspaper vending machines on the sidewalk outside.

Dropped coins into one and pulled out an L. A. *Times*. Checked the date to be sure it was today's edition. It was but, of course, would've been printed last night to be shipped up here by truck.

He stood on the sidewalk, outside the pharmacy, and checked the crime news. Didn't expect to find anything on the front page, and there wasn't. Turned to the second page, ran his eyes over the Region section. The usual rapes and robberies, none of which concerned him.

Nothing about the two murders. Lars Lyndon or Tim Kerrigan.

Maybe the story of an old man strangled in a Santa Monica rooming house wasn't important enough to make the paper. Too many crimes in the city to report most of them.

He had expected to find something on Lars Lyndon.

Hollywood Division must be sitting on the story until they located his grandfather. If they tried to reach him here they wouldn't have any luck. Knight wasn't answering his phone.

There would be no policeman on guard at the house on Curson but the doors would be sealed.

Unless there was a listing in Knight's address book—if they found one in the Curson house—there would be nothing to connect him with Solvang. People didn't usually keep their own address in such a book.

If there'd been anything about Lars on television, Faye would've heard it and would tell him.

He folded the newspaper and dropped it into a trash receptacle, then went inside and found a public phone. Brought out the torn sheet from his desk pad on which, before leaving the apartment, he'd typed several phone numbers he thought might be needed while he was in Solvang.

Dialed Faye's number. Listened to her phone ring three times, as he slipped the list back into his pocket. Heard the phone picked up and hoped it wouldn't be one of the servants.

"Yes?" Woman's voice, sounding tentative.

"That you, Faye? Zeke Gahagan."

"Thank God! When you didn't call last night I was really worried."

"I've found him. He's in Solvang. I drove up here yesterday but didn't see him until late last night."

"Well, thank heavens . . . He's all right? You've talked to him? How long has he been in Solvang?"

"He drove up Tuesday, soon after he saw you. Been locked in his house ever since. Not answering the phone."

"Are the others with him? Lars and the housekeeper . . ."

"Mrs. Svendsen's here, but staying with her sister. I haven't contacted her. No sign of the grandson . . ." So she didn't know about Lars.

"I've called the house on Curson, several times, but there's never any answer."

"Larry thinks his grandson must've gone to stay with friends when Mrs. Svendsen left."

"When's Larry coming back to Los Angeles?"

"Not until tomorrow. He's appearing in a parade here this afternoon."

"Parade! What parade?"

"This is the annual Danish Days weekend in Solvang. Lasts two days and they always have a parade on Saturday. There's a big crowd. Been arriving all morning. Larry's been in the parade before. Several years ago."

"I never heard such nonsense! Once an actor, always an actor . . ."

"They have posters all over the place saying a mystery star will be riding with the Grand Marshal."

"You mean he's riding on a float or something?"

"Wearing a cowboy outfit. Guns in holsters."

"Isn't that dangerous? Appearing before a crowd of strangers! There could be somebody else with a gun. Whoever shot holes in those garage doors. Or some other kook . . ."

"I tried to persuade him not to make this public appearance but he has many friends in Solvang and won't let them down."

"That's our Larry. Everybody's friend!"

"I told him you'd hired me to find him."

"Was he furious?"

"I think he was touched that you were worried about him. Pleased you did it."

"I'm glad I did it." She hesitated. "Listen to me, love. You've found him for me. And I'm grateful. Now I want you to stay right there and protect him. Let nothing happen to him. In that damn parade or anywhere else."

"I'll try but I can't guarantee a thing. He's a very stubborn guy. Won't listen to reason."

"I know that, but you watch out for him, Zeke. That's an order. Stay with him until he comes back to Los Angeles. Larry's the only man I ever loved—except for my three husbands—the only one I didn't marry. I'll never marry him now, but I don't want him killed by some crazy because of what he said at Paul Victor's stupid dinner party. I heard from Paul this morning."

"What did he want?"

"To find out if I had any news of Larry. I didn't tell him you were looking for him. I never tell Paul anything. Five minutes after you hang up he's calling somebody and repeating everything you said. He's worse than Lolly and Hedda together. At least they got paid for their gossiping. Paul has no excuse. I detest him. I'm much relieved, now you've found Larry. When are you driving back to Los Angeles?"

He hesitated, considering his answer. "Probably not until tomorrow. I'll start back when he's leaving."

"That's a good idea. Call me when you get home. Maybe drive up and tell me everything that's happened."

"Right."

"I'll be anxious until I know Larry's okay. And take care of yourself, love. Wouldn't want anything to happen to you, either."

The phone went dead.

Chapter 21

Zeke was smiling as he returned the receiver to its plastic cradle.

Faye was one terrific dame. Still worrying about her friend.

As he headed for the street he noticed a pile of small magazines on a counter. Saw that it was a visitors guide to Solvang and took one, paying the girl at the cash register.

Looking through the pages as he left the drugstore he found a small map giving the route for today's parade. He would check the streets it would follow and then he would get a bite of lunch.

As he walked he would look for those same two faces. The windmill man and a Latin type. Would be a miracle if he found either of them.

He was still smiling, he realized, like everyone else in sight.

This place, Solvang, must make you smile.

He frowned, immediately, and glared at the smiling people.

There may be a killer among you, folks! Maybe he will kill again . . .

Nobody even glanced at him as he started down Copenhagen.

No food being served on this side of the street, except for the small restaurants, but the sidewalk was crowded with visitors. Most of the tourists moved close to each shop window and studied the articles on display. Many would linger, after the parade, to buy things they had noticed earlier.

"Having a good time, sir?"

Zeke looked around and saw the Polynesian waitress who had served his first meal in Solvang. "Yes, I am, young lady. Aren't you working?"

"Had to do an errand." Holding up a small parcel. "Have a nice day."

"And you." He watched her hurry on, pushing through the crowd and into the restaurant where she worked.

Zeke continued on, slowly, glancing at faces as he moved along the street. The crowd was getting thicker near the shop windows so he began to edge toward the curb as he walked.

He checked the magazine again, quickly, and saw that the parade would move down Copenhagen. For the next half hour he would follow the route, street by street.

Folding the small magazine, he stuffed it into an inside pocket as he continued on his way.

His attention was caught by an American Indian standing alone at the curb, unaware of the people moving behind him, staring across the street.

Zeke slowed his steps, as he passed the lone figure, wondering if the man was a visitor. He took up a position behind him, against a windowless section of wall between two shops, and watched the motionless Indian.

Nobody else was paying attention to him. Maybe he would be riding in the parade.

Zeke realized that the Indian's attention was focused on the people eating across the street. Was he too timid to go over there and buy a plate of food? Or didn't he have enough money?

He looked out of place here. Shiny black hair, neatly parted into braids that hung down over his ears to rest on the shoulders of his fringed leather jacket. Impossible to see the man's eyes but his skin was dark brown. Lean cheeks, without a wrinkle. Appeared to be in his thirties, though you could never judge the age of an Indian. This one could be younger or older. He looked down and saw he was wearing faded dungarees tucked into worn leather boots. Medium height with muscular shoulders, slim hips. Looked as though he could ride a horse. Maybe worked as a hand on some nearby ranch . . .

Zeke moved on, toward the corner, and when he glanced back saw that the Indian hadn't changed his position. He was engrossed, watching those people eating on the opposite side of the street.

Started up Alisal again, toward Mission, and saw that the crowd was getting larger. People walking into town on Highway 246, where they must've left their cars, and coming down Alisal.

He passed a group of ranch hands wearing old Stetsons and fancy tooled boots. Younger than the ones he'd noticed earlier.

Checked the time in a window of The Clock Shop and saw it was past eleven. Later than he thought.

Turning down Mission again, he wondered what had happened to Hildreth.

He walked all the way to Fourth and followed that to Copenhagen. Not many people here. A car in every parking space but everyone had headed for the center of town.

Noticed a park area shaded by tall trees and turned up Second to discover its purpose.

There was a large sign saying SOLVANG THEATERFEST and OPEN AIR SOLVANG FESTIVAL THEATER. Tonight they would be showing *Hamlet*. At least he was a Danish prince.

Zeke went inside, past the empty box office, and saw people

seated on rows of seats, shaded by trees, watching dancers on the stage. A sign to one side said DANISH FAMILY DANCERS. Pairs of young people in embroidered costumes. Girls in long skirts, but the boys had short trousers. The musicians were seated behind them. He'd been hearing their music for several minutes but thought it came from that band on the brewery truck.

He left the theater and continued on to the next street which turned out to be Oak. Followed that to First and turned left up Copenhagen again. He always came back to Copenhagen.

This crowd was getting larger, milling in the center of the street but not out of control as a gathering of this size would be in Los Angeles. No sign of police except for that Highway Patrol officer guiding traffic earlier.

The brewery truck hadn't rolled past in several minutes and he didn't hear the band. They must've pulled into a side street to water their horses and give the musicians a rest.

That Indian had disappeared. Must've gotten bored watching people eat and gone to get some food for himself.

More activities now.

A troupe of young gymnasts performing acrobatic tricks at the entrance to another crowded parking lot. Handsome blond kids, well trained. A circle of admiring visitors applauding.

His attention was drawn to a young man who had passed behind him, walking briskly and, after only a brief glance at the gymnasts, moving on.

Straight blond hair, neatly combed.

It was the young man he'd followed last night. The one who checked those windmills.

Zeke, automatically, went after him. Was he inspecting windmills again?

The young man wore a neat sport shirt over white slacks instead of a suit and hadn't noticed he was being followed.

People rarely sensed when they were.

He would ask him about last night. What his interest was in

those three windmills? There had to be a simple and logical reason for his tour of inspection at night.

Zeke glanced at an enormous fat blonde—she reminded him of Kara Kolvang's sister—dancing with a tall man in the middle of the street. People cheering. The guy, who must be her husband, was laughing.

When he looked back the blond young man had disappeared into the crowd.

Zeke hurried on and, after a moment, glimpsed him again. He was standing beside a low clipped hedge, separating a cafe terrace from the sidewalk. People were eating at tables shaded by large parasols.

The blond young man was talking to a young couple seated at a table inside the hedge. A pretty blonde girl and another blond young man. The girl was laughing as she looked up at the young man outside the hedge.

Now Zeke could see his face.

It wasn't anything like that face he had glimpsed last night. This one was much younger. Same straight blond hair but this face was thinner.

He hadn't really seen that other face. Only a vague shape.

These people must be locals having early lunch before the visitors occupied every table.

The air was getting warmer and he felt thirsty.

"Mr. Gahagan!" Woman's voice.

Who the hell could know him here? Somebody from Los Angeles?

He turned, seeking the voice among the women seated in shadow under the parasols.

"Zeke! Over here . . ."

It was Hildreth!

He walked back to the end of the hedge and made his way across the sunny terrace where she sat at a table drinking something in a tall glass. "Been looking for you."

"Please . . ." She gestured toward a white metal chair.

He pulled it out from the table and sat down. "Been up and down every street. Checking the parade route."

"I couldn't leave earlier. Two of my guests slept late. I knew they'd want their free coffee and Danish when they got up. And they did. So I was late driving into town. Parked the car and strolled for half an hour, but didn't see you. Decided to have breakfast. Hoping you would turn up . . ."

"This is pleasant."

"One of my favorite spots. I'm having fresh orange juice. You like waffles?"

"Certainly do. Haven't eaten one in years."

"I've ordered one with strawberries. See?"

He looked up as a costumed waitress set a plate in front of Hildreth. Saw a crisp looking waffle with a pale globe of melting butter on top of it alongside fat strawberries nested in a cloud of whipped cream. "I'll have the same, miss. But no strawberries or whipped cream. Could I have some other fruit?"

"Fresh pineapple?"

"That would be fine. And no coffee."

"Shall I take your waffle back to the kitchen, Mrs. Johnson?"

"No, Betsy. I'll eat it and help my friend work up an appetite."

As the waitress went inside the small restaurant, Zeke saw a sign above the entrance.

THE BELGIAN CAFE
Fresh Baked Belgian Waffles

He turned to Hildreth. "Something special about Belgian waffles?"

"They seem crisper than others I've eaten." She picked up her knife and spread the butter across her waffle.

"I had one of those other things, earlier, with a sausage."

"The Aebleskiver Breakfast! You enjoyed it?"

"Could've had seconds. If I wasn't watching my diet. Did have too much coffee. No more today."

Hildreth was eating the first bite of waffle, her eyes on Zeke. "I was going to do that but there wasn't a free table. Larry Knight phoned this morning. Soon after you left. Wanted to tell me how much he liked you. And trusts you . . ."

"Always a big help."

"He's glad you're going to be here for the parade. How was your morning?"

"Saw a lot of people—cast of thousands—but no one like the two men I'm looking for."

"I was hoping you'd find them."

"Nobody looked Latin. Mostly Scandinavian types but not my windmill man."

"Maybe they aren't here . . ."

"I'll be looking for them—both of them—until the parade starts. Then I'll be busy watching only one person. Larry Knight."

"Your waffle, sir . . ."

Chapter 22

Zeke put his fork down and sighed. "Best damn waffle I ever ate."

Hildreth laughed.

"And the fresh pineapple quenched my thirst. Walking always makes me thirsty."

The waitress returned to remove their empty plates. "Something more, Mrs. Johnson?"

"Just coffee."

She took their plates away as Hildreth found a pack of cigarettes.

He saw there were no matches on the table. "Sorry I don't have a lighter. Haven't owned one since I gave up smoking."

"And when was that?" Producing a lighter after returning the pack to her handbag.

"Thirty years ago. Gave them up the day some doctors, at a

medical convention, announced cigarettes could give you cancer. Read it in the paper and never smoked again."

"Such will power!" Snapping the lighter and holding the flame to her cigarette. "Smoking relaxes me."

"I would never tell anyone else what to do. About cigarettes or anything else. All four of my ex-wives smoked. Three of them are dead, but not from cancer."

The waitress brought a coffeepot to refill Hildreth's cup.

Zeke smiled as she dropped two lumps of sugar and a generous splash of cream into her coffee.

"You're on a diet?" she asked.

"One I've worked out, over the years, for myself. I can have the waffle and the pineapple, but I wouldn't have ordered pineapple if it wasn't fresh."

"Why not?"

"Never eat anything canned or frozen, not if I know it."

"What'll you be doing this afternoon, until the parade?"

"Covering every street. Walking and checking faces. Following any short man who appears to be Latin."

"We don't have many streets here."

"Which makes it easier. I've walked all of them this morning. Several times. And you? What'll you be doing?"

"When I leave here I'll drop past Andersen's Gift Shop to see Inga. Find out what she plans to wear this evening. So we don't clash. Inga likes pale colors and I like strong ones. She called and told me Larry's picking her up, this evening, as he drives into town. You'll be coming back to the motel after the parade?"

"No reason to hang around Solvang. Once the parade's over and Larry goes home my job's finished. After all this walking, I'll need a nap and shower before dinner. I look forward to seeing Mrs. Andersen again."

"Inga's a love. One of the first friends I made when I arrived here. She introduced me to my husband. Now she's the last real friend I have left. Most have moved away or—passed on. As you grow older, friends leave you . . ."

"You found a place to park, with this crowd?"

"Near Inga's shop. Visitors don't know there are parking spaces behind some of the larger shops. Used for delivery, mostly. Outsiders never find them."

"I noticed one person in the crowd, this morning, who surprised me. An American Indian. The genuine article. Hair braided. Not in fancy costume, but an old leather jacket and dungarees."

"Must be one of our local Indians. They come into town to see the parade."

"You have Indians here?"

"Not so many as when I first came to Solvang. A tribe called the Sanja Cota settled here, I'm told, more than a hundred years ago. They got that name because they lived along Sanja Cota Creek. Cota was the name of an early family. They owned Rancho Santa Rosa and Joaquin Cota built a big ditch to connect the creek with the first grist mill in California. The ditch came to be known as Sanja de Cota. That's Dutch, so some Dutch people must've lived here in those days. The Sanja Cota tribe, what's left of it, still farms the land. Their reservation's east of Mission Santa Ynez which you pass as you drive out to the motel. That's why my husband named it Rancho Sanja Motel. You should visit the old mission. I do, at least once a week—although I'm no longer Catholic—to sit in the silent church."

"I'll try and do that before I drive back to Los Angeles. Will you be seeing the parade this afternoon?"

"I may, if Inga invites me upstairs. She has a little parlor over her shop. We can sit there with a cold drink and watch everything from the windows."

Zeke brought out his wallet as he glanced at their check.

"Thanks for lunch."

"My pleasure, dear lady." He left three five dollar bills.

Hildreth closed her handbag. "You have almost two hours before the parade. Can't be later than one o'clock. I never wear a watch."

"Nor do I." He got up, careful not to bump his head against the open parasol.

"In two hours, you can walk around this town many times." She rose, slipping the leather strap of her handbag over one shoulder.

Zeke realized, for the first time, that she was wearing a white summer dress dotted with circles of yellow. White and yellow slippers and, as they talked, she had pulled on short white gloves.

He liked to see women wear gloves.

Hildreth touched his sleeve with white-gloved fingers. "Watch out for Larry. Like a good cop. See that nothing happens to him. Do that for me?"

"I'll do my damnedest."

"I know you will." She lifted herself onto her toes and touched his cheek with her lips. "See you at the motel."

He walked with her to the sidewalk and stood there, watching her cross the street. Aware of her shapely ankles. Waited until she went down a narrow passage, between two shops, he hadn't noticed before.

Resuming his tour, he headed back to Copenhagen and bought a local newspaper from the same corner pharmacy. The Santa Ynez Valley *News*. Folded it into his left hand as he walked east on Copenhagen again. Would sit in the Chevy and have a look at the paper. Small town newspapers always interested him. Told you a great deal about its citizens.

The street was overflowing with people. Hundreds promenading down the center. New faces at all the tables on the other side, eating pastries and sausages. Those young girls were really working. Their long needles flashing in the sunlight above the stoves.

A glaring sun overhead flooded the streets. No breeze from any direction.

He walked on, eyes darting, looking from face to face quickly, in order not to draw attention to himself.

No Latin face with a black mustache.

More young men with blond hair. Straight blond hair and curly blond hair. Some escorting blonde girls who looked like sisters from one family.

He checked the clock in the distant tower and saw its hands were at nine past one. Hildreth had been close.

Turning north, on Alisal, he saw more people hurrying into town from the highway.

Among them were two Indians, walking slowly and with dignity, paying no attention to the stares of curious strangers. Heavyset men with stolid faces. Straight gray hair hanging down from under their old felt hats. These must be members of the local tribe Hildreth had mentioned.

He wondered if that other Indian had come from some other tribe . . .

Mission Drive was even more crowded than Copenhagen.

He discovered the reason, as he made his way forward between the friendly people. They were pressing toward the streets running north from Mission where the parade seemed to be forming. He glimpsed groups of youngsters in costume with older people who seemed to be their leaders. A large group was rehearsing a song. Their voices clear and sweet, the melody as simple as a Jerome Kern tune.

Moving on, street to street, he glimpsed decorated floats as well as the familiar brewery truck. Members of the band were walking up and down to stretch their legs and the Percherons were eating from leather feed bags hung around their necks. A row of antique cars was parked in the shade under some tall trees. Costumed men and women, relaxing in the back seats, laughing and talking.

No sign of Laurence Knight.

He was the star and would arrive at the last minute.

This should be a good time to have a look inside those two

largest windmills. One on Alisal Road, the other at Second and Copenhagen.

Both streets were thronged with visitors who paid no attention when he slipped inside the windmills.

People, as usual, were unobservant. Every policeman knew that. Question five witnesses to a crime and no two descriptions would match.

The doors to both structures were unlocked.

He closed them silently and looked around the airless interiors which vibrated with the rattling and clanking of the revolving sail.

In both windmills the ground floor was bare. Unpainted two-by-fours and plaster walls. Small open windows through which he saw closed shutters on the outside. A flight of wooden steps led to the upper floors.

Zeke realized, as he went upstairs, that it was hot inside and he was perspiring.

Climbing the steps, the sound of the rotating mechanisms grew louder. The complicated machinery filled the second floors with barely enough space to walk around them.

There were several windows at this level with smaller ones on the third floors under the domed ceilings. All were open but there was little air to breathe.

He moved close to a window in each and looked down at the people jamming the two streets, before the slowly revolving sails cut off his view for a moment as the turning vanes swept past.

The two windmills were almost identical, except the one on Alisal was slightly larger and had a window facing straight down the center of Copenhagen Drive where the parade would come. While the window of the other windmill faced across Copenhagen and would have a view of the parade from the side as it passed.

In both structures he touched the wooden steps with his fingertips and found no trace of dust. They must be cleaned regularly.

As Zeke left the second windmill and stepped out into the crowd waiting for the parade on Alisal, he brought out his handkerchief and mopped the perspiration from his forehead.

And suddenly, because of the heat and the walking, he felt very tired. His back, bruised from that fall, was paining him again.

Happened more and more frequently these days, whenever he overexerted himself. Recently, after that Mornleigh investigation —when it took so many weeks to find the missing body—he'd stayed in his apartment for a week. Slept and ate and read detective novels. Told Nettie, at his answering service, he was spending the week with friends in La Jolla. She knew that wasn't true but, as usual, didn't disturb him or put any calls through. And he hadn't answered his phone all week. Too many people, complete strangers, managed to get his number these days.

La Jolla reminded him that he hadn't phoned Emma. His ex-wife had sounded troubled when she called. Seemed weeks ago . . .

Must remember to phone her when he returned to the apartment. He hoped she wasn't having any kind of trouble with her husband at this late date. Not likely. Aldo was a fine human being. Gentle and considerate . . .

He would take them—Emma and Aldo—out to dinner next week. Maybe Tuesday night. Most of the good spots were closed Mondays . . .

He realized, without thinking, that he was heading back to his car. Rest for half an hour and read the local paper.

Maybe he should take another week off when he got back to Los Angeles tomorrow. Sleep, eat and rest. Renew his energy.

No! He would leave here tonight. After dinner with Hildreth and the others, he would drive home to his own comfortable bed.

Right after the parade he would tell Knight about his grandson and Tim Kerrigan.

Let the L.A.P.D. find out who killed them . . .

What about Kara Kolvang?

Her murder had remained unsolved for fifty years.

As far as he, Zeke Gahagan, was concerned it could stay unsolved.

He didn't give a damn who killed Kara Kolvang. And neither did the L. A. police.

They had their own problems at the moment. Santa Monica Division with an aged man strangled in a rooming house and Hollywood Division with the grandson of an old-time movie star murdered. They would be having a busy weekend.

Wasn't going to involve himself with either of those jobs. Not if he could avoid it.

Would have to tell them what he knew about both murders. Knew or suspected. Do that Monday . . .

He wondered, briefly, what had happened to Knight's dog. The sheepdog that spooked. Did all sheepdogs do that?

Approaching the parking lot on Fourth Place, checking that his car hadn't been moved, he saw the blond youth lounging near the entrance.

"You're back, sir?"

"Got a mite tired walking. No vacant benches anywhere. Thought I'd sit in my car for a while and ease my legs before the parade."

The youth checked an expensive wristwatch. "Won't start for another hour."

"Let me know if it takes off early."

"No chance of that, sir. No way!"

Zeke saw, as he collapsed into the Chevy, that every space in the parking lot was occupied. Two cars parked between his and the street, hiding him in case anyone looked in. He'd left his windows open and the roof was shaded by that tree, so the interior was comfortable.

He settled down and unfolded the newspaper. Glanced, from habit, at each headline. Nothing about the Near East, Washington or Russia. Every story was concerned with today's celebration.

Photograph of a pretty blonde who was the official Danish Days Maid. Another showed that windmill on Alisal Road. Said it was the largest of Solvang's many windmills.

Crowds of people hurrying through the suddenly darkened streets.

Must be clouds moving in overhead.

He saw that the street lamps had been lighted.

Impossible to see faces in this dim light.

Too many men with blond hair. All walking alone. Kept glancing back to see if they were being followed . . .

No sign of a short man who looked Latin.

Had a feeling he was lost. Must've come down the wrong street. No matter. Could always reach Copenhagen if he kept walking . . .

Must find his way back or he would be late for dinner with Hildreth and her friends. Larry Knight and Kara Kolvang's sister . . .

Who killed Kara Kolvang?

Nobody was going to harm Larry Knight but somebody, fifty years ago, had murdered that actress and gotten away with it all these years . . .

He would like to find her killer.

Except nobody had hired him to do that . . .

"Sir!"

Zeke felt something hard pulling at his arm.

"Wake up, sir! Wake up!"

He opened his eyes and saw the young attendant.

"Parade's starting."

"Starting early?"

"It's ten after three. They're late, as usual."

"So am I!" He pushed himself up, aware of the newspaper sliding to the floor as he left the Chevy. "Thanks, kid. See you after the parade."

"Won't be here. I'm taking off on my bike before the crowd starts leaving. There's a traffic jam every year . . ."

Zeke was already heading for the sound of the crowd in the distance.

He fingered his hair, as he hurried, smoothing it down.

Fourth Place was empty but he could see people lining the curbs on both sides of the next street which, as usual, was Copenhagen Drive.

He crossed to the far side and hurried down Copenhagen toward the area where the crowd was thickest. Kept going until he passed the pharmacy at the corner of First Street then slowed his steps and, finally, came to a stop in the middle of the block. Froze there, only his eyes and head moving.

The first thing he noticed was that the tables and stoves had been removed from across the street. Replaced by people—hundreds of people—talking and laughing. They formed a solid wall, three deep, along the curbs on both sides, stretching to each end of the block.

He ran his eyes along the signs above the shops until he found the Andersen Gift Shop. Squinted up toward a row of open windows on the second floor and glimpsed faces inside. Hildreth and Kara Kolvang's sister?

They had seen him and were leaning forward into the sunlight.

Hildreth was waving.

He raised his arm and waved back.

Mrs. Andersen fluttered a small handkerchief.

People were crowding the windows above all the shops.

Somewhere, far away, the band struck up what sounded like a march.

Faces turned, as though the crowd had a single head, looking toward the western end of the street. For a moment the laughter was silenced and talking stopped but, almost at once, was resumed.

Zeke glanced, again, toward the two women but they had pulled back out of sight.

The music continued, although it didn't seem to be coming any closer.

Larry Knight would be riding with the Grand Marshal. Probably on the last float. The "mystery guest" would be the big surprise at the end.

He wondered how many of these people remembered Laurence Knight? The older ones certainly. Maybe the kids would've seen his western movies on television.

Zeke's eyes darted. Searching for that Latin face with the black mustache. Larry Knight had seen him, yesterday, and Tim Kerrigan's landlady saw him earlier this week. A short man who looked Mexican.

Would be impossible for this Latin type to fire a shot at the actor as the parade passed. Someone would notice him pull the gun from under his jacket.

Today, in this peaceful Danish village, there were no police visible in any direction from where he stood. He was the only one here to protect Laurence Knight.

Zeke, unexpectedly, felt alone and vulnerable.

There wasn't much he'd be able to do if that man who shot Larry Knight's grandson was in this crowd. Gun in pocket or, more likely, in a holster under his left arm.

All he could do was wait.

He felt a quiver of panic.

For the first time in years he wished he had brought a revolver.

His guns were resting, peacefully, in a safe-deposit box on Sunset Boulevard. He hoped they were asleep.

He was wide awake now, alert, still perspiring slightly.

The sun was hot, but no longer overhead and there was a slight breeze from the west.

He glanced up at those windows again but was unable to see Hildreth or her friend.

A loud burst of music from the band.

Zeke looked around and saw the gray and white Percherons pulling the brewery wagon down Copenhagen toward him.

The crowd lining the curbs, both sides, pushed forward to get a better view. Several people stumbled out, or were pushed, into the street. Voices getting louder as the parade came closer.

It appeared to be moving forward like a procession of gigantic toys propelled by invisible mechanisms.

In addition to the band he could hear distant singing.

He glanced at the faces around him.

All eyes were on the Percherons pulling the brewery wagon with its bright-colored decorations and the seated musicians in their fancy uniforms.

There was no face in this crowd that looked Latin.

All the sounds increased as the Percherons passed, their hooves clomping, bridles jangling, wheels creaking and the band blaring.

Next a group of costumed dancers. They looked like the ones he'd seen earlier dancing on that stage. Now they were swaying and whirling to the music of the band.

After them were several motorized floats. One displayed a sign—TRIBUTE TO HANS CHRISTIAN ANDERSEN—with a seated man surrounded by small children, all in costume, as he mimed reading to them from a large prop book.

Another float displayed a lettered banner—THE VIKING SQUARES—with an older group doing a vigorous square dance as a trio of musicians played.

These were followed by the old cars he'd seen earlier. A sign said they were from the Los Angeles Antique Car Club. The drivers wore visored caps, goggles, gloves, and linen dusters. Their attractive female companions had feathered hats and lace dresses with long white gloves.

Zeke was distracted by the ancient cars, many of which he remembered from his own past. Although he'd never owned a car in those days.

Then a marching band with another group of dancers and more elaborate floats. One held a number of seated people, posed under a banner proclaiming them to be descendents of the original Danes who founded Solvang—Sunny Field—seventy-three years ago.

This float brought cheers from every side.

He was surprised to see that most of the people on the float were not blond, although many had white hair which could've been blond in their youth.

The next float was marked SANTA YNEZ VALLEY LIONS CLUB and held a group of young gymnasts in white tights performing acrobatic tricks.

Finally a horse drawn stagecoach in which a smiling man was seated beside the driver. A sign said this was the Grand Marshal. He was bowing and waving toward the crowd.

Larry Knight wasn't riding with him!

Last of all was a black convertible with a uniformed chauffeur at the wheel. A sign draped across its side proclaimed:

MYSTERY GUEST!
our own
LAURENCE KNIGHT!
FAMOUS HOLLYWOOD STAR!

Zeke's eyes were held by the handsome figure in an elaborate white cowboy outfit and white Stetson, standing alone, behind the chauffeur. Both arms extended toward the crowd.

Laurence Knight was smiling as he acknowledged the shouts and the applause. It was the professional smile of an actor.

The convertible appeared to be moving more slowly than the rest of the parade. Giving his public a chance to see the star.

Zeke looked at the faces again. Saw that every eye was focused on Knight. Some people were calling his name.

He noticed two young ranch hands waving their Stetsons and whooping.

The music faded as the last band turned around the distant corner up Alisal Road.

He saw that Knight had swept off his Stetson and dropped it into the back of the convertible. His deeply tanned face against the curly white hair made him look even younger than he'd seemed last night. This was the famous star of a dozen westerns.

He was wearing a fancy gun belt with shiny pistols in each holster.

Knight had, apparently, recognized people in the crowd because he was pointing at them and nodding. Must be locals, old acquaintances or shopkeepers.

Zeke walked along the sidewalk, slowly, keeping pace with the black convertible. Avoiding the rows of people lining the curb.

The actor was laughing, waving his arms.

Zeke wondered if Knight had noticed him. Not likely.

In another half hour the parade would be over.

Laurence Knight would be home and unharmed.

After dinner tonight he would say goodbye to Knight, pack his bag and drive back to Los Angeles.

Or, maybe, spend one more night at the Rancho Sanja Motel?

Pick up a nice bottle of wine from the local supermarket and drink that beside the pool with Hildreth. Have coffee with her tomorrow morning before he took off.

Hildreth was the most interesting woman he'd met in many a year . . .

There was the sharp but unmistakable crack of a rifle shot.

Zeke whirled to look at the actor.

Knight was reaching for the gun on his left hip. His hand never got that far but, instead, clutched at his chest. Pressing the white silk shirt against his heart.

The shocked crowd was silenced.

Zeke didn't move as, far in the distance, he heard the brass band still playing.

Bright red blood was pumping from between Knight's fingers, staining his white shirt, as he swayed and began to collapse.

The chauffeur had stopped the convertible and was turning to stare at the actor. "Somebody get a doctor!" he shouted. "A doctor!"

Now there was a tremendous reaction. The sound coming from hundreds of nearby throats. Like a monstrous wave roaring in from a distant storm.

Zeke still hadn't moved a muscle. Only his eyes. They swept the street in every direction until, unexpectedly, they came to the large windmill at the end of Copenhagen.

The sail was revolving but he couldn't see the base of the structure because of the crowd, unaware of what was happening here, watching the last float turn up Alisal Road.

And he knew where the man with a rifle had stood to aim over all these heads.

He started to run, without realizing what he was doing, pushing people out of his way, running as he'd never expected to run again. Muscles functioning. Without pain or complaint.

He dashed across Alisal and pushed through the crowd of people waiting to see the mystery star.

They didn't know what had happened. That they would never see him.

He noticed a television crew on a truck pointing their cameras up Alisal toward the parade that had passed.

The door was wide open.

Someone had been inside!

He went in, without touching the door, and hesitated at the steps.

There was no dust to reveal prints.

He was aware, at the same time of the mechanical sounds coming from the machine overhead, revolving the sail.

He bounded up the steps, two at a time, surprised by his agility.

Nobody on the second floor but, as he reached the landing, he smelled a reek of cordite.

He went to the open window facing the street and saw the clot of people around the distant convertible. Like maggots swarming over a dead body.

The revolving sail sliced through the image.

Whoever fired that shot was an expert. Had to time it to the revolving sail. Aim precisely at his target and shoot between the fins.

Only a professional could do that.

Zeke peered down at the floor. Nothing to show that somebody had been standing here.

He turned toward the steps and went down, as he'd come up, two steps at a time.

Left the entrance door open, as he'd found it.

Pushed through the crowd more slowly. No reason to hurry now.

These people hadn't been aware of the rifle shot because that last band must've been passing and covered the sound. He could still hear music as the parade moved along Mission Drive.

Laurence Knight was dead. Or dying . . .

He'd failed to protect him.

How would he explain this to Faye?

There was no way he could've saved his life. None . . .

As he made his way down Copenhagen, toward the convertible, he didn't bother to check the puzzled faces staring toward the people crowding around the car.

The gunman would be far away by now. His car must've been waiting in one of the public parking lots. Maybe the one where his Chevy was parked.

The blond young man who checked that windmill last night!

He should've realized what he was doing . . .

So it wasn't that Latin type.

Or had the blond young man checked the windmill for the Mexican?

As he reached the convertible he saw a young Highway Patrol officer waving people away.

The curious were pressing close, trying to see the body.

An old man, obviously a doctor from the crowd, was standing in the car and peering down at the body.

The chauffeur was slumped behind the wheel, his face blank.

Zeke went straight to the officer. "You in charge here?"

He shrugged. "Until somebody shows up."

"Mr. Knight's dead?"

"Yes, sir. 'Fraid he is."

"The killer used a rifle. Aimed from a window of that windmill at the end of the street."

The officer turned, wide-eyed, to stare at the distant windmill. "How the hell could you know that?"

"I just went up there. The place stinks of cordite."

"Who are you, sir?"

"I was hired, by a private party in Los Angeles, to protect Mr. Knight. Couldn't do it in this mob." Producing his identification and holding it up. "I'm a private detective."

"Thank God you're here, sir."

"The name's Gahagan. Zeke Gahagan."

"Yes, sir."

He realized the officer had never heard of him.

Book Four

Finale: Presto

Chapter 23

Zeke headed east, out of Solvang, through the deepening twilight.

There was no traffic on Highway 246.

All the shops had been closed as he drove through the streets where the parade had passed and the visitors were gone.

None of the sails on the windmills were turning.

Laurence Knight's body had been taken in an ambulance to the County morgue for the present.

He noticed a church, to the right of the highway, he hadn't seen before. Tonight it was silhouetted against the clear evening sky. Must be that old mission Hildreth had mentioned.

He wondered if she'd gone somewhere to have dinner with Inga Andersen. There'd been no sign of them in the confusion following the murder.

Couldn't see any houses as he drove. Only peaceful fields and distant trees.

He turned off the highway into the entrance drive of the Rancho Sanja Motel and, as he passed the lighted office, glimpsed Hildreth rising from her desk behind the counter.

No cars in the parking area.

Zeke slowed to a stop and, as he got out, saw Hildreth coming from the office.

"Who did it? Who killed him?"

"I don't know."

"You've no idea?"

"Nobody knows." He walked toward the door to his room and she followed.

"I've been worried. About you."

"I'm fine." He unlocked the door, opened it and stepped into a blast of chilly air from the air conditioner.

"Didn't know where to call you, to find out what was happening. Wouldn't have called if I did."

"I've had a long session with the local police—County Sheriff's Department—telling them everything I knew. Wasn't much." He snapped a wall switch and the lamps came alive. "Talked with L.A.—Hollywood Division—and they're sending a friend of mine up from homicide to help here. Talked to him. Explained the little I could about the grandson's murder. Told him I believed the same person killed Laurence Knight." He picked up his overnight bag from the floor and rested it on the bed.

"Where are you going?"

"Heading back to L.A. in a hurry. Nothing more I can do here." He opened his bag and began to pack as he talked. "Monday I have a meeting with the Chief of Homicide at Parker Center. Another old friend. I'll give 'em every fact I've turned up. Tell 'em what I know and suspect about both murders—Knight and his grandson—as well as an old man who was strangled in Santa Monica. All of 'em, I'm convinced, killed by the same person."

"I won't ask any questions."

He looked at her and smiled. "Wouldn't be able to answer 'em."

"Will I ever see you again?"

Zeke saw that her eyes were troubled. "First of next week."

"You're not just saying that?"

"I'll very likely be back here Monday. So keep this room for me."

"You really have to go to Los Angeles tonight?"

"For two reasons." He continued packing, aware that he was weary and only wanted to stretch out on this comfortable bed and sleep for several hours. "I have to tell Faye Manning that Knight's dead."

"I understand."

"Don't want to break the news on the phone. Hope to get there before she hears it on television. It happened around four, so they shouldn't have the story until eleven and the papers won't print it before the early Sunday editions. If I can get there before ten, Faye won't have heard anything. Much easier for me to tell her—less shock—than if she heard it cold on some news program."

"You are a kind man, Zeke. But I knew that . . ." She sat on the side of the bed to watch him pack.

"The other reason I have to get back to L. A. is I think the murderer came from there and, probably, drove back this afternoon. To whoever hired him to kill Laurence Knight."

"Then you think he was hired?"

"That's the most logical explanation. I suspect it's that man—the Latin type—who was sniffing around Knight's house yesterday. I've told the local police about him. A man with black hair and a mustache. They're checking the motels in Solvang and Buellton. Starting with them and spreading out to other nearby towns next week."

"Haven't come here."

"They will."

"Something I must tell you . . ."

"What's that?" He folded his pajamas and laid them in the overnight bag.

"I talked to Larry Knight this morning . . ."

"You didn't mention that at the waffle shop."

"I was feeling very guilty. Afraid I'd done something wrong."

"Oh?"

She raised her head, facing him. "I told him his grandson had been murdered."

"Did you . . ." Zeke hesitated, beside the open bag.

"Shouldn't I have done that? You didn't say not to tell him."

"I'm glad you did. It's only right he should've known. Yes, I'm very glad you did. Also it would've put him on his guard. Aware of his own danger."

"There's something else . . ."

"Yes?"

"He said he was going to be ready for whatever might happen during the parade. He would load his guns with real bullets."

"I discovered they were loaded. He tried to reach for them, as he was shot, but never made it. I was watching when the bullet hit him. That's how I knew where the killer was standing."

"You knew! Where?"

"Inside that big windmill on Alisal Road. He stood at a second floor window and aimed his rifle. I went there at once, but he'd cleared out. I could smell cordite inside the windmill. Proving I was right."

"You think it was that 'Latin' fired the shot?"

"Until your local police turn up a better candidate."

"I wish you could stay until morning . . ."

"Impossible." He went to get his toilet articles from the bath.

"I understand."

"What happened to you and Mrs. Andersen? I looked up but couldn't see you at the windows."

"Inga fainted. When she recovered there was a mob around the car and I heard people saying Larry was dead. We went down to the office and Inga brought out a bottle of brandy. Stayed there until we heard the ambulance, then went out back to get our cars. I followed Inga home to be sure she was all right. Then came back here and found the whole place in an uproar. Everybody leaving."

"Leaving their bills unpaid?"

"They'd paid in advance. Most of them had planned to stay until tomorrow but they seemed to panic. I suppose the second day of the celebration will be canceled."

Zeke tucked his leather shaving kit into the bag. "That does it, I think . . ." Closing the bag. "Did you and Mrs. Andersen get dinner?"

"Haven't heard from Inga since I followed her home. She had a cook, so she'll be taken care of."

"And you?"

"I couldn't eat a thing. Can I fix something for you?"

"I'll get a bite after I reach Los Angeles. I'm going straight to see Faye. Then home to my apartment and, hopefully, a good night's sleep."

The phone buzzed on the table between the two beds.

Zeke frowned. "Who the hell could that be?"

"I connected the incoming line to your phone before I came in here. In case there were any calls." She got to her feet and circled the foot of the bed to pick up the phone. "Rancho Sanja Motel. Mrs. Johnson . . ." Her eyes were on Zeke. "Oh, yes! He's right here." She held the phone to him. "One of the Sheriff's men . . ."

Zeke took the phone from her hands and lifted it to his ear. "Gahagan speaking."

"Officer Swenson, sir. Hoped to reach you before you left for Los Angeles . . ."

"Something's happened?"

"We think so, sir. One of the local ladies, Mrs. Rasmussen, may have seen the man who fired that rifle."

"Where?"

"She noticed him hurrying through the crowd, a rifle resting against his shoulder."

"The best way to hide anything is to carry it out in the open."

"That's the way it was with Mrs. Rasmussen. She thought it was a man who'd been on one of the floats. Wasn't until later, when she told her husband about him, they realized there hadn't been any Indians in the parade."

"She saw an Indian?"

"Mrs. Rasmussen only saw him for a second but she was able to describe him. His black hair was in braids hanging down onto his shoulders and he was wearing what looked like a fringed leather jacket. She claims he didn't look anything like our local Indians. They don't wear their hair in braids, and this guy was thin."

"Mrs. Rasmussen's description is on the nose."

"What, sir?"

"I saw that same Indian this morning."

"Where?"

"Standing on Copenhagen Drive, near the spot where Laurence Knight died later. He was watching people eating at those tables across the street. Looks like he's your killer."

"We think so, sir."

"He may have done the job for that 'Latin type' I told you was prowling around Laurence Knight's property yesterday."

"You mean he'd been hired to do it?"

"I suggest you add this Indian to your list. Check every motel. For him and that Latin type. You're looking for two people now. Which is better than one. That's what I'll be doing in Los Angeles."

"When will you be leaving, sir?"

"I was packing when the phone rang. You have my L.A. private number and my answering service."

"I'll call, sir. Soon's we have any news."

"And I'll do the same. See you next week. Probably Monday."

"Yes, sir."

Zeke set the phone down.

"You really are coming back."

"You didn't believe me?"

"You and Mrs. Rasmussen saw an Indian?"

"I didn't connect him with the murder but she saw him carrying a rifle. He must've been coming from that windmill. Returning to his car. Now we'll be looking for an Indian, as well as a Latin . . ."

"I hope to God you find them!"

"I've a feeling they're back in L. A.—both of them—where they came from." He took his summer jacket from the row of hangers and slipped it on as he talked. "I always like it when there are two suspects. Catch one and he'll lead you to the other." Lifting his bag from the bed. "Dear lady . . . I didn't expect to find you here, when I came to Solvang."

"Guess I'd been waiting for you, Zeke. A long time . . ."

He moved close to her as she talked.

"I'm glad it turned out to be you." She whispered the words.

"So am I. Been years since I've given any thought to marriage . . ."

"Who said anything about marriage?"

"I just did." He leaned down and kissed her gently on the lips. "Was surprised to hear myself saying the word . . ." He saw tears in her eyes. "We'll talk about it next week. And I'll probably call you tomorrow." He went out, without looking back, and carried his bag toward the Chevy.

He was returning to L. A. with not one goddamn clue to the murderer of Laurence Knight.

Or Lars Lyndon, or Tim Kerrigan . . .

Or Kara Kolvang!

All he had was three suspects.

A Latin type, a blond windmill watcher and, now, an Indian . . .

Chapter 24

Zeke aimed the Chevy through heavy fog, between the open wrought-iron gates and down the sloping drive toward the glow of light.

A gray shadow moved, like a ghost, across the fog.

Faye was waiting in the open doorway.

He'd called her from a public phone on Sunset, told her he'd be here in fifteen minutes.

He parked facing the light and got out.

"That you, Zeke? What's happened? Is Larry all right?"

So she hadn't heard.

He could see her, as he went toward the light, arms outstretched again. "Got a lot to tell you."

"Dear Zeke . . ." She raised her face, in that same familiar gesture and he kissed her on the cheek. "Thought you'd call this afternoon." Walking beside him into the house. "Was worried when you didn't."

"Had a rough day." Closing the door and following her across the hall. "I need a drink."

"Opened a bottle of wine when I heard your car. White wine."

"That's fine. I could use a glass." He saw the open bottle in the silver cooler as she went ahead, across the familiar living room to the same sofa. Saw that all the curtains were closed against the fog. "Good to see this room again." He sat beside her. "Nothing changed."

"You sound tired." She lifted the bottle from the cooler and filled a glass. "Here you are, love." Handing it to him.

"None for you?"

"Not until I've heard your news. Then I'll celebrate."

He took a swallow of the wine and let it flow down his throat. Studied her lovely face, briefly, wondering how she would react to what he must tell her. "Came here before I went home. Wanted to give you the first-hand report . . ."

"Larry's all right?"

He took another swallow of wine and set the glass down. "Well . . . He rode in the parade. There was no way I could protect him in that crowd. A hundred armed men couldn't have saved him."

"He's dead." Her voice was a whisper.

"Shot."

"My God!"

"I was standing within twenty feet of him when it happened. Watching him. Thousands of people crowding the sidewalks . . ."

"Who shot him?"

"Someone fired a rifle from a window in one of the big windmills they have in Solvang."

"I've seen them."

"I think it was the same man who killed Lars."

"Lars is dead?"

"Found his body, yesterday morning, in the house on Curson. That's what sent me up to Solvang. Lars had left a phone number on a pad. I called the number and it was a motel in Santa Ynez where he'd made a reservation for the weekend. Through the owner I learned that Larry was holed up in his house there. That's where I saw him. Last night. Watched an old Kara Kolvang picture with him."

"Did you? I was watching it too . . ."

Mustn't tell her about that Latin type who'd been looking for Knight yesterday. The Indian with the rifle or the windmill man.

"You must find him, Zeke. This person who killed them. Larry and his grandson."

"I plan to continue the investigation."

"Do it for me. Find their murderer—it must be one person—and see they pay for what they've done."

"I'm working with the police. The Santa Ynez Sheriff's department and Hollywood Division. An old friend, from here, is on his way up to Solvang tonight. And Monday I'm meeting the head of Homicide downtown to tell him what I know and suspect. You didn't hear anything on the news or read about Lars's death in the L. A. *Times?*"

"I didn't turn the radio or television on all day. Or open the morning paper. Guess I didn't want to hear anything, unless it came from you. The truth . . ."

"And the truth isn't pleasant."

"I think I knew it wouldn't be . . . You're not drinking your wine."

"Had enough. Have to drive down Outpost in this fog."

"Larry looked so young in that old picture, last night, with Kara. Both of them did. Was he pleased with it? Seeing himself . . ."

"Seemed to be. Talked about making the picture. Tried to appear relaxed but I could tell he was worried about the parade. Riding in an open car. Surrounded by thousands of strangers . . ."

"Why did he do it? Why?"

"Actor's ego, I suppose. You do what you've promised to do. No matter what happens."

"That's true. I always did . . . And Larry had an ego. Even when we were young—on Broadway—nothing could stop him."

"He planned to drive back to L. A. tonight or early tomorrow. Wanted to see a film showing at the Nuart tomorrow night. The first of a series of Clement Dalby features. Kind of a tribute, I guess, because he's ill."

"They always do this when an actor or director is about to die. Hitchcock, Bergman, John Ford. So many others! Had retrospectives of their films. I would get worried if anyone wanted to honor me like that. Little chance . . ."

"I think Knight wanted to see this picture tomorrow night because he's one of the stars."

"Which film is it?"

"*Rancho Eldorado.*"

"Saw it, last year, on cable television, and it still holds up. Like *Shane* and *Stagecoach* . . ."

"I plan to see it again tomorrow night. Care to come along?"

"I couldn't take it. Seeing Larry. They may not show it when they learn he's been killed."

"You kidding! That'll only sell more tickets in this town."

"I suppose . . ."

"Could even attract the murderer."

"You think so?"

"Stranger things have happened. I'll take a good look at the audience, before the lights go out."

"Have you had dinner?"

"Stopped off, driving down from Solvang, and ordered a sandwich but couldn't eat it."

"My cook stays up late Saturday nights, watching television. I'll have her fix something."

"Don't want a thing. Much too tired."

"Will you sleep?"

"Hopefully. How 'bout you?"

"I doubt it. Too upset . . . I certainly won't watch the late news. Don't want to hear about Larry—and Lars—from strangers. There's something obscene about hearing of a friend's death from one of those cold fish who do the news. They always seem to be smiling, showing their beautiful caps, when they tell you something tragic. After you leave, I'll put some old Broadway show recordings on and stretch out on the sofa. That always brings back happy memories. Ella singing Rodgers and Hart or Cole Porter. Eventually I'll drift off . . ." She straightened. "You really don't have any idea who killed them?"

"I don't. That's the God's truth."

"I believe you, when you say it like that." She hesitated, studying his face. "Not even a suspicion?"

"Several suspicions."

"Amazing Larry would die like that. Playing a death scene in front of an audience. That's how I'd like to die. With a friendly audience. Any actor would. Rather than turning my face to the wall in some hospital surrounded by strangers. I often think about that. How it'll be when I die. I'll be alone."

"We are all alone when we die. Don't you know that?"

"I suppose . . ."

"Death is a private moment. No matter where it happens."

"I know."

"And I must get home." Zeke got to his feet. "I'm going to take tomorrow off and go back to work Monday morning."

"Zeke . . ." Fay rose from the sofa and followed him toward the hall. "I want you to find whoever killed them—Larry and his grandson. I want them found and punished."

"I intend to do that. Find them and let the law convict them."

"Whatever it costs, I'll pay for it."

"That's not necessary."

"You're still working for me. Understand?"
"I understand."
"No matter how much it costs. Send me your bill."
"No. There won't be any further charge."
She opened the door and faced him. "What do you mean?"
"This one's on me." He walked past her, into the gray fog.

Chapter 25

He heard birds singing.
Santa Ynez?
Hildreth would have coffee waiting . . .
The up and down shriek of a squad car?
On Sunset!
He was in Hollywood.
That was one lousy bird singing . . .
Opening his eyes he saw the photograph of Hammett beyond the foot of his brass bed. The two of them, like shadows, fading into that San Francisco doorway.
He had slept without dream or nightmare.
This was Sunday! He was taking the day off.
Moving his body, cautiously, there was no protest from any muscle.
He'd silenced both phones last night. Pulled out the plugs, after

checking with Nettie. She had no important messages and he'd told her not to call him before Monday.

Turning toward the windows he saw a reflection of sunlight through the closed blinds. Another nice day. Indian summer?

Which reminded him of that Indian with a rifle . . .

Too early for Indian summer. That was in October.

Remember to phone Emma today . . .

And he would call Hildreth. Late in the afternoon or this evening.

Hildreth . . .

He smiled.

Checking the bedside clock, he saw—to his surprise—the hands were at seven past ten.

His stomach growled immediately. "Okay, kid. Breakfast . . ."

Shoving the covers back, he heaved himself out of bed.

Slipped into his old summer robe as he went into the living room. Unlocked the hall door, picked up the *Times* and locked the door again.

Carried the heavy Sunday paper out to the balcony and dropped it on the floor beside the chaise. Glanced at the opposite balconies but there was no sign of his neighbors and nobody in the pool. Hollywood slept late on Sunday. Even the sharks.

After a fast shower he fixed breakfast, arranged it on a tray which he carried outside. Placed it on the low glass-topped table and sank onto the chaise. Ate breakfast as he checked his potted roses. Better water them today. Hadn't done that in—was it two or three days? The damp air had kept them from drying out.

He ate with relish. Two baked sausages and a toasted granola muffin with apricot jam. Half a cup of black coffee. That out of the way, he dropped the paper napkin onto his plate and snatched up the newspaper.

Nothing on the front page about Laurence Knight.

A photograph of the actor—taken many years ago—was on

the third page with a two column story continued on the last page of the first section. The heading above the story said:

> Laurence Knight Killed By
> Sniper In Solvang Parade

There was only a brief paragraph about the murder. Giving basic facts, nothing more. The rest of the article was devoted to Laurence Knight's long and successful career on the New York stage and in motion pictures. Near the end it said that, by curious coincidence, a film starring him—*Rancho Eldorado*—would be shown tonight at the Nuart in Santa Monica as the opening film in a series being given to honor the famous director, Clement Dalby, who would be unable to attend the performance because of illness.

A note below the story said there was an additional article in the Metro section on the murder of Laurence Knight's grandson.

Zeke dropped the front section onto the floor and picked up the Metro section. Saw the story immediately.

> Famous Star's Grandson
> Murdered In L. A. Home

The second story was even shorter but contained more facts. Lars Lyndon, grandson of Laurence Knight, was found shot to death in his grandfather's Los Angeles residence. No address given, as usual. The murder weapon, according to homicide police, had not been found. Young Lyndon was alone in the house with a sheepdog which neighbors said belonged to his grandfather. The investigation was being handled by Hollywood Division of the L.A.P.D., where reporters were told there was no clue to the identity of the killer and no motive for murder. Mr. Lyndon was born in New York but had been living in London for many years with his parents. His mother, the only child of Laurence Knight, had been born in Los Angeles.

There was no photograph of Lars Lyndon.

Zeke tossed the second section on top of the first.

The story about the grandson had been written and in print before the paper knew about Knight's murder. It implied that Lars had been killed by a prowler. Nothing was said about those bullet holes in the garage doors.

There should be a more complete coverage tomorrow, when the two investigations would be joined.

And when he told them, downtown, about Tim Kerrigan, that investigation would be combined with the others.

Three murders . . .

He would see that showing of *Rancho Eldorado* tonight. Been years since he watched it on television and he would enjoy seeing it again.

Also, somehow, he had a hunch he ought to be there tonight. There was a reason for him to see it but he didn't know what it was . . .

He'd had many such hunches in the past, and always followed them. Most times they paid off.

At the moment he needed more than a hunch.

Three dead men.

And three other men who might or might not be connected with their deaths. The Indian, the windmill man and that 'Latin type' . . ."

He wasn't going to think about any of this until he went downtown tomorrow morning for a meeting with the homicide officers in charge of the two cases—Laurence Knight and Lars Lyndon—who wouldn't connect them to the strangling in Santa Monica until he told them about Tim Kerrigan and his apparent knowledge of who had murdered Kara Kolvang.

That's when the story would hit the front pages.

Kara Kolvang . . .

Zeke got to his feet and went inside to put on sandals and fill the metal watering pot.

For the next hour he went back and forth, watering his plants.

While he was doing this he put more Glenn Gould on the record player, turning it low, and began to relax as he listened to Bach.

The sound of water splashing into the pots seemed to flow from the music.

He tried not to think about the murders but that was impossible.

Better find out what time they were showing *Rancho Eldorado* tonight.

He would have an early dinner. Maybe at the Tick Tock. Hadn't eaten there in some time. They always served good food. Almost like home cooking.

Too bad Dalby wasn't well enough to attend the showing of his picture.

He'd been to several of these retrospectives and the actor or director who was being honored was always introduced after the film. When he stepped out onto the stage the audience would give him a standing ovation and he would make a speech. Some of their remarks had been pretty damn funny.

Tonight Dalby would be sitting in his Mandeville Canyon ranch house thinking about what was happening. Wishing he was there . . .

Terrible thing for a man with all that talent to be an invalid.

Thank God his own health was pretty damn good. Better than most men his age.

Dalby, of course, was two years older.

Eighty-three . . .

Zeke finished watering the plants. Carried the *Times* into the living room and stacked it on the floor near his desk. Went into the bath and took his vitamins. He'd forgotten to do that after breakfast.

Washed his breakfast dishes and left the kitchen in order.

Made the bed carefully. He had his own way of making a bed, which he could do in a matter of seconds.

Laid out his good summer suit with clean linen, fresh white shirt and a favorite tie.

He would shave and have another shower before he went out.

For the next hour he made out checks to pay the bills that had arrived during the week. Straightened some books on the shelves that he had mixed up several weeks ago. His Mexican maid, who came once a week, never touched his books because he liked them in alphabetical order on the shelves and she couldn't read English.

He heard people laughing outside and splashing in the pool. Some ate their breakfasts down there. By midafternoon there would be twenty or thirty around the pool. Mostly young couples who seemed to know each other. The place would get noisy until the sun moved away. Then the pool would empty and within an hour the entire terrace would be deserted.

Zeke, finally, checked the time and discovered it was after one.

He'd accomplished a lot. Straightened his apartment and, as he did so, put all problems out of his mind.

He plugged both phones back into use and, still wearing his old robe, sank onto the living room sofa and dialed La Jolla. Heard the phone ring twice.

"The Accaro residence . . ."

"Aldo?"

"That you, Zeke? Was hoping you might call."

"Been thinking about Emma. Ever since she phoned . . ."

"Then she told you!"

"Told me what?"

"Said she wasn't going to, but I suspected she would. I was asleep when she talked to you. And she didn't mention anything next day, in all the excitement . . ."

"What the hell are you talking about? I had a feeling, when we talked, that something was worrying her. But she didn't say what it was. I just had a feeling . . ."

"Emma went into the hospital next morning."

"Hospital? What the hell's wrong with her?"

"They did a heart bypass yesterday."

"My God! No . . ."

"Heart's been bothering her for several years now. Remember last summer? She wasn't feeling well . . ."

"Dammit! She never told me it was her heart."

"You know our dear wife never talks about illness. She didn't want you to know about this but I thought, perhaps while she was talking to you, she might've said something . . ."

"So how is she? She gonna pull through?"

"They don't know. She's in intensive care. Will be for several days. They won't let me into her room."

"I'll send some roses. She loves yellow roses . . ."

"Don't send any flowers, Zeke. They won't allow them in her room. Friends, here in our building, sent some yesterday. I had the nurse give them to the children's ward. Wait 'til we know she's going to live, my friend."

Zeke hesitated. "You okay?"

"I'm doing fine. Miss her, but at least I know she's still there and everything's being done to save her."

"These bypass operations are like having your tonsils out in the old days."

"They let me see her, this morning, through a little window. It was like looking at a stranger. I'll call you when I know anything . . ."

"I'd be very grateful, my friend."

"Tried to reach you, yesterday and this morning. Used the signal, but got no answer."

"Been out of town on a job. Got back last night and turned the phone off. Until just now. I'll leave it plugged in. If I don't answer you'll know I had to go out. Leave a message with my service and I'll get back to you."

"I'll do that, Zeke."

"Take care of yourself. For Emma . . ."

"I'm trying . . ."

Zeke put the phone down and stared at the bright sunlight on the opposite balconies.

Impossible to think of Emma dying . . .

That could wreck Aldo. He had two loves. Emma and his music . . .

Dear God! Let her live.

He rose from the sofa and went into the kitchen. Took an unfinished bottle of wine from the refrigerator and poured himself half a glass.

A California Chardonnay—one of his favorites—but much too cold. No matter. He needed a drink.

Tilting the wineglass, he drank it down and rinsed the glass.

Returning to the living room he decided he'd better eat dinner around six-fifteen. Which should give him plenty of time to drive down to the Nuart in Santa Monica.

Better check when they'd be showing Dalby's film.

He got the phone number from their ad in the paper and dialed.

A tape answered. There would be only one showing of *Rancho Eldorado* tonight. Seven-thirty.

That was because it was a long film.

Zeke set the phone down.

He would finish dinner at the Tick Tock before seven and could easily make it to the theater in twenty minutes.

For the next hour he paced his apartment.

His mind on Hildreth and Emma. As well as three murdered men and a trio of possible murderers.

The Latin type, the windmill watcher and that Indian . . .

What was it that connected them?

The need to prevent the revelation of Kara Kolvang's murderer? Had they been hired by the murderer to prevent his exposure?

Zeke went into his bedroom to get the slip of paper with the phone numbers he'd written down yesterday.

Carried it into the living room and sat on the sofa again. Reached for the phone, dialed, and heard the phone in Santa Ynez ring once.

"Zeke?"

"How'd you know?"

"Been waiting all morning for you to call. Knew, if you didn't, I would never hear from you again."

"Told you I'd probably call today."

"I didn't like that one word. Probably . . ."

"I'll be seeing you tomorrow afternoon. Have a meeting with the L.A.P.D. brass in the morning. Should get away before noon. Then I'll be on my way. First stop Santa Ynez and the Rancho Sanja Motel."

"Your room will be waiting."

"Having a busy day?"

"No business at all. I was up before dawn. Couldn't sleep. So much to think about. Drove into Solvang and picked up the Sunday paper. Not a soul on the streets and every shop closed. They've canceled the rest of the Danish Days celebration. I suppose a few of the larger restaurants may open for dinner but Inga Andersen says she doubts it. Everything's closed to honor Larry."

"You've seen Mrs. Andersen?"

"Talked to her on the phone. She's called twice. Inga's a great talker."

"I found that out."

"They had a Mass for Larry, this morning, at the old mission. I had no idea he was Catholic. Inga said it was crowded. She went, but I didn't."

"Does she know what the police are doing?"

"Nobody's heard anything. They're working out of the Highway Patrol office in Buellton. This is their first major crime in years. They need your help."

"A good man from Hollywood Division is already there. Old friend of mine. He's been working on Lars Lyndon's murder."

"Do they know who did that?"

"They don't have a clue. I'm certain it's the same person who shot his grandfather."

"Wish you were here, Zeke. This place has never been so quiet. Seemed so empty. May get a couple of customers tonight. Salesmen on their way somewhere. I've been lost since you left. Haven't felt like this since my husband died . . ."

"I'll see you tomorrow. That's a promise."

"That'll only be for a few days. Or hours . . ."

"We'll have to talk about that. Do you suppose I could commute from Solvang to Los Angeles every day?"

"You're not serious. And I know it."

"We'll discuss a number of things when I see you."

She hesitated. "I love you, Zeke . . ."

"That goes both ways."

"Never thought I'd tell that to another man. Ever again . . . Larry Knight said yesterday, on the phone, you were the finest human being he'd met in years. I agreed."

"I'd better hang up while I'm way ahead."

"Take care of yourself. Please . . ."

"I always do."

"This murderer has already killed twice. Larry and his grandson . . ."

"At least twice."

"I'll be thinking about you. And worrying . . ."

"I've been taking care of myself for a long time. Better part of a century."

"See you tomorrow, for sure?"

"Middle of the afternoon."

"I'll be waiting."

"All my love . . ." He whispered the words, surprising himself.

"And mine . . ."

He put the phone down and got to his feet. Walked to the open window and leaned across his balcony but saw nothing. None of the opposite balconies or the people now swimming below.

Only Hildreth's face. That beautiful face . . .

He turned abruptly and went into the bath, shaved then showered again. Dried himself and stretched out on his bed for a nap, before he dressed.

His thoughts continued to be about Hildreth. And Emma . . .

Two wonderful dames.

He still cared about Emma. Hoped she would be spared to have a long and happy life with Aldo . . .

Would Hildreth put up with his absences when he was on a job? Emma never could . . .

Hildreth had a motel to run. That should occupy her.

Emma was more mature now than when they were married. Happier with Aldo than she'd ever been with him. She taught him to enjoy music but Aldo was a professional musician. They had much in common.

A private eye—even the world's oldest—would never really know and understand classical music.

He remembered a concert—the L. A. Philharmonic—seated beside Emma. Whispering to her. Asking questions, as usual. She had, finally, turned. "Will you be quiet? I can't hear the music."

He smiled.

She had clutched his hand but he didn't ask another question. He wondered if Hildreth enjoyed classical music . . .

Wouldn't matter if she didn't . . .

Glenn Gould, he realized, had stopped playing Bach . . .

Driving the Chevy through Solvang again.

The dark streets empty. No traffic.

All the sails revolving on every windmill. Turning slowly and silently.

Shop windows dark but the street lamps had been lighted.

He was following the same route, street after street, the parade had taken.

His headlights picked up the dark figure of a man.

That blond young man who toured the windmills?

This man's hair was black and, as he turned to face the headlights, Zeke saw that he had a mustache.

It was the Latin!

Still in Solvang . . .

There was a rifle in his hand.

Not the Indian but the Latin . . .

Now he was lifting the rifle with both hands.

Impossible to see his features. Only the black hair and mustache. No eyes, nose or mouth . . .

The man was aiming the rifle, precisely, pointing the barrel toward his head.

He swerved the Chevy to the right. Realized he was going to jump the curb and crash into a shop window filled with crystal and porcelain.

In the distance he could hear the brass band.

The parade was returning . . .

Zeke opened his eyes slowly and saw Hammett watching him from beyond the foot of the brass bed.

He sighed with relief.

Hadn't had a dream like that in many a year.

Did it mean anything?

Was the Latin type the murderer?

Balderdash! This kind of dream had no meaning but was a direct result of fatigue and what had happened in Solvang.

Checking the clock beside his bed he saw it was five-forty.

He lunged from the bed and went into the bath to towel his perspiring body.

The phone rang as he dressed. Once . . .

Aldo again? More news about Emma.

He sat on the side of the bed and snatched it up to his ear. "Yes, Aldo? What've you heard? She's all right?"

"Detective Gahagan?" Man's voice, young and cautious.

Zeke smiled. "Officer Swenson?"

"Yes, sir. Calling from our substation in Solvang."

"What's happened?"

"We've been checking all motels and hotels within twenty miles."

"Yes . . ."

"Found a man who answers your description. Black hair, mustache. Speaks with an accent. Checked into Anderson's hotel in Buellton. Largest in the area. Almost a hundred rooms."

"Big place is always the best place to hide. You won't be noticed among so many people."

"He checked in last Friday. Early afternoon. Gave a Mexican name and a phony address in San Diego. We contacted the police down there. They never heard of the street."

"Probably came from Los Angeles."

"And here's the big news. An American Indian was seen going into this man's room Saturday afternoon. After Mr. Knight was shot. His description matched that Indian you noticed in the crowd. The one Mrs. Rasmussen saw carrying the rifle."

"Has the hotel room been checked for prints?"

"The place was wiped clean."

"Sounds as though you've traced the killer."

"One more thing. Another man was seen going into this person's room. Friday night. The same maid saw both of 'em."

"You got a description of this other man?"

"Not too much, unfortunately. Light wasn't bright enough.

This was after dark. She noticed this man was young and he had blond hair."

Zeke leaned close to the phone. "So there are three of them . . ."

"Yes, sir. But the room was taken by the first man. The Mexican."

"Better send out descriptions on all three."

"We've done that, sir."

"Did the desk clerk get the Mexican's license number? See the make of his car?"

"We've checked the license. Another fake. And you can't see visitors' cars from the registration desk. Nobody noticed which car he drove."

"Anything else happening?"

"Nobody's working today. I'm the only one here at the substation. The others are over in Buellton with your friend from Hollywood Division."

"I'll be back tomorrow. Got a meeting downtown, in the morning, with the L. A. police brass. Should get up to Solvang mid-afternoon. Unless something develops here."

"I'll tell the Captain. He ordered me to call you and report what we'd learned."

"Thanks." He set the phone down and rose from the bed. Considering what he had learned as he finished dressing.

They were working together. Those three. The Mexican, that blond young man and the Indian.

Somebody had hired them to prevent the truth from being revealed about Kara Kolvang's murder.

Was it possible, after fifty years, the murderer was alive and had arranged to have three people killed to prevent anyone, including the police, from learning his identity?

Twenty minutes later, Zeke was seated in a booth at the Tick Tock studying a menu and discussing what to order with a waitress he'd known for years.

"... and the rabbit's always good." Pencil poised above her order pad. "Haven't read about you in the paper lately."

"Been avoiding publicity. After a small salad, I'll try the roast turkey. A little white meat, sliced thin, with mashed potatoes."

"And no gravy."

"No gravy, no parsley, no string beans."

"Kidney stones kickin up again?"

"Not lately. I'm still being damn careful."

"Broccoli's fresh . . ."

"Broccoli's fine, but no Hollandaise."

"Coffee with that?"

"No coffee, no dessert. Glass of white wine with the turkey."

"You betcha." She disappeared toward the kitchen.

Zeke glanced around the spacious restaurant, its walls covered with every size and shape of clock, as he put the menu aside. They reminded him of Solvang. The window of that clock shop and the big clock in the tower on Alisal Road.

He noticed the usual number of aged character actors, many of them European, eating their Sunday dinners. Waving to friends, moving from table to table, chatting and gossiping.

He'd been coming to the Tick Tock since it first opened—this had been one of Emma's favorites because of the musicians she met here—and it still amused him to recognize familiar faces from old films.

He kept his eyes on the nearest wall clock and didn't dawdle over dinner.

But it took longer than he'd anticipated, in the Sunday evening traffic, to reach Santa Monica and several minutes to find a place to park near the theater.

As he bought a ticket and went into the Nuart lobby there were half a dozen people ahead of him, going into the auditorium.

Two of them were Erik Wulff and Madame Krauss.

They didn't notice him as he handed his ticket to the attendant and followed them inside.

Found a vacant seat on the aisle, in an empty side row, at the rear.

Saw that the front and center seats were filled. No sign of Erik Wulff and his plump mistress.

His seat was perfect because he was farsighted and needed an aisle seat to accommodate his long legs.

He made a quick check of nearby faces but didn't recognize any of them.

The house lights dimmed as stragglers hurried down the aisles and a circle of pink light came up on the curtains covering the screen.

Nobody tried to push past him for a seat.

The place was, maybe, three-quarters full.

A man wearing a sport jacket stepped into the glow of the spotlight with a handmike. "Ladies and gentlemen . . ."

The other voices quieted down.

"I want to welcome you to the opening film—*Rancho Eldorado*—in our six-week Sunday-night retrospective devoted to those great western classics of the late thirties directed by Clement Dalby. Mr. Dalby's health doesn't permit him to join us tonight, unfortunately, and we have been saddened to learn that one of the stars of this film—Laurence Knight—died, tragically, yesterday afternoon . . ."

Zeke heard gasps of surprise. Some in the audience hadn't heard about Knight's murder.

"We wish, also, to pay tribute to him tonight. Larry told me, recently, that this film was one of his favorites. And, as you know, he made dozens of fine pictures. So, while we enjoy tonight's film, let's remember the pleasure Laurence Knight has given us over the years. Pay tribute to his memory and to that great director—Clement Dalby. Let's salute both of them as we watch *Rancho Eldorado!*"

Zeke applauded with the others as the spotlight dimmed and the curtains parted.

There was a crash of music—a big orchestra—as the title spread across the screen. Enormous letters in brilliant colors.

Zeke remembered this opening. How thrilling it had been, years ago, when he saw it for the first time.

Behind the title was a tremendous expanse of western countryside stretching toward rolling foothills with distant mountains against a seemingly endless blue sky.

This shot was one of the first ever made from a moving helicopter.

The entire picture had been shot on location.

As the main title faded the names of the actors, in golden letters, rose from the bottom of the screen. Listed alphabetically because there were so many stars, but even the supporting players were famous.

This film was said to have the most big names ever used in a feature up to that time.

The audience applauded as remembered names—some no longer alive—moved up the screen.

Zeke smiled. Many of these actors were his favorites.

Behind the names the camera continued to sweep across the open countryside as the music soared.

Following the cast came production credits which silenced the applause.

When they finished the peaceful landscape remained for a moment.

Then an enormous final credit filled the screen.

PRODUCED AND DIRECTED
BY
CLEMENT DALBY

Tremendous applause.

The credit faded as the camera moved down toward the ground and discovered the tiny figure of a man riding a white horse.

The music changed to a simple folk melody that Zeke recognized as the major theme of the film.

A close shot of the figure on the horse. Laurence Knight, looking very young, wearing an old Stetson and a shabby cowboy outfit.

More enthusiastic applause.

Then the remembered opening dialogue.

Knight spoke first. "Gittin tired?" As though he was talking to his horse.

Some reactions from those in the audience who knew what was coming.

"Gittin hungry?"

"I am always hungry, Señor . . ."

It was as though the gentle female voice came from the horse.

"Shoulda stayed back there in Nogales. There'll be trouble here . . ."

"I am with you, Señor. We have seen trouble before."

Knight smiled and glanced over his shoulder.

The camera panned to see a beautiful Mexican girl seated behind him.

Zeke sighed. It was Dolores Del Rio. One of his early favorites.

"Almost there." Knight's voice. "You can see it . . ."

The girl pulled herself higher, grasping his shoulders with both hands, to peer into the distance. "This is your home?"

"My home. Rancho Eldorado!" He urged the horse on with his knees.

Zeke also leaned forward.

The cowboy and the girl on the white horse galloping toward the big ranch house in the center of a vast spread of green land.

It was a larger version of the house in Mandeville Canyon where Dalby would, no doubt, be sitting tonight, thinking about this showing of his film.

The homecoming of the prodigal son.

Familiar faces in every scene. Walter Huston playing Knight's father and a skinny Richard Widmark his younger brother who, immediately, was attracted by Dolores Del Rio. Barbara Stanwyck, who had inherited the next ranch and was the girl Knight left behind when he rode off to seek his fortune. Fay Bainter as his mother and Beulah Bondi as Stanwyck's aunt. Complicated plot developments. City men buying land to dig oil wells. Stanwyck had already sold part of her property but Huston was refusing. Indians stealing horses. Wagonloads of Chinese on their way to lay tracks for the new railroad. Claire Trevor running a fancy dance-hall in the nearest town. Charles Butterworth, Gladys George and Zazu Pitts in comedy scenes. A pretty dancer whose face Zeke couldn't place. Jane Withers as a snoopy little girl and deep-voiced Edward Arnold the rich banker. James Gleason, Harry Davenport, Henry Travers. The familiar faces continued.

Knight returning home in time to help Walter Huston defeat the oil men, marauding Indians and Edward Arnold who was after both ranches.

Widmark falling for Dolores Del Rio and Knight realizing his old love for Stanwyck was stronger than ever.

Scenes with the Chinese laborers laying tracks across wild land. Indians rounding up Huston's horses which were saved by Knight leading a posse of cowhands.

The young Indian on a black horse leading the others looked familiar but Zeke couldn't remember his name. Some actor in very good Indian makeup with a braided wig. Like that Indian in Solvang. In those days the studios didn't use real Indians. That had been changed, in recent years.

He realized that he was enjoying the film as much as when he first saw it. Much more than watching it on a small television screen.

The people seated around him were reacting to every scene. Much of the script was corny but Dalby knew how to hold an audience. His direction made you a part of each scene. They were shot so tight you were always in the middle of what was happening.

Every performance was a gem. Huston at his best and Laurence Knight was excellent.

A scene with Knight warning the young Indian to leave the Mexican girl alone. The Indian threatening to kill him and riding away on his black horse. A tender scene with Knight and Del Rio in which she realized, for the first time, he had transferred his love to Stanwyck.

Strong scene with Huston and Knight in which the father bluntly questioned him about his intentions toward Stanwyck and the Mexican girl. Telling him to make up his mind. Never tease a woman or she'll make you pay for it.

Big rodeo scene with young Widmark outdoing his brother in every event and Knight realizing he's not a youngster any more . . .

The dark streets of Solvang.

He was following that windmill man again. Both of them on foot. Watching as he slipped through the unlocked door of each one.

Bright sunlight as the parade rolled past. Laurence Knight bowing and waving.

The crack of a rifle shot.

Knight didn't collapse but pulled out his pistol and fired several times toward the distant windmill.

The door of the windmill opening. That Indian, rifle in hand, escaping down the street into the crowd.

Zeke was running after him. Impossible to get close . . .

He opened his eyes and saw Laurence Knight on the screen, with Stanwyck, sitting on the porch of her ranch house. They were in a swing, swaying back and forth, in the darkness. She was trying to learn his plans for the future and he told her that once he'd settled everything to save Rancho Eldorado for his family he would be on his way again . . .

Dammit!

He'd been asleep and missed part of the picture. Some of the most important scenes.

Dreaming about that parade in Solvang.

Still tired, in spite of sleeping late this morning. One day soon he was going to have to take things easier.

The young Indian, on the screen, was watching something from a grove of trees.

He looked like that Indian in his dream. The one in Solvang! Was it possible?

The Indian was watching Knight and Del Rio.

Knight had said Dalby used the same actors over and over. Would this actor look the same, so many years later?

He certainly could with makeup.

Knight was telling Del Rio he would send her back to Mexico. They argued then he jumped onto his horse and rode away.

The Indian watching her.

Del Rio's face as she realized Knight still loved Stanwyck.

The Indian kidnapping her, snatching her up onto his black horse.

A sequence with Knight and Widmark searching for Del Rio.

They find her dying. The Indian had, obviously, raped her and left her for dead. Tender scene with both brothers grieving as she dies, then carrying her back to the ranch.

Funeral scene then the brothers going after the Indian. Knight finding him and killing him.

A long sequence leading to the end of the film with Knight and Huston working together to save the ranch. Widmark eloping with Claire Trevor. Edward Arnold putting a bullet into his head at the bank. Elaborate barbecue to celebrate Trevor's marriage to Widmark with a tender farewell when Knight takes Stanwyck home in a bright red surrey. A family scene, next morning, with Walter Huston and Faye Bainter watching their son ride away on his white stallion.

The audience started to applaud as they realized it was the end. Knight riding across sunny open country again. Another helicopter shot. Camera pulling back, higher and higher, until horse and rider are no longer visible. Wiping to the ranch house. Rancho Eldorado. Then continuing on until, far in the distance, can be seen a white column of smoke from a train coming along the tracks the Chinese laid earlier. The train getting larger and larger until it filled the entire screen.

Cast credits rising again.

People were already leaving the theater.

Why couldn't they stay in their seats until the lights came on?

Zeke got to his feet and peered over the moving heads at the names of the actors.

Impossible to tell who played that Indian.

Erik Wulff should know who the actor was. He would look for him in the lobby. Hopefully he could escape without answering questions about Laurence Knight's murder.

The lights came on in the auditorium before he reached the exit.

He heard two names repeated over and over. Clement Dalby and Laurence Knight.

The film, from what they were saying, had been a great success again.

Bright lights in the small lobby dazzled his eyes as he checked the faces of people who had stopped to chat with friends.

He saw Erik Wulff and Madame Krauss talking to a man. Unable to see his face until he got closer.

Paul Victor! Hands gesturing as he talked.

Victor would know the name of the actor who played that Indian.

Pray God he wouldn't say the guy had died years ago.

"Good evening, folks . . ." He was amused to see their surprise as they turned and recognized him. "Madame Krauss, Mr. Wulff—Mr. Victor!"

Victor was the first to speak. "Who killed him? Larry Knight?

". . . And his grandson! The 'world's oldest eye' surely knows."

"Sorry, Mr. Victor. I know nothing."

"Ach!" Madame Krauss exclaimed. "It is all so terrible. Murdering people . . ."

"We are shocked." Wulff's face was troubled. "So tragic for Larry to die like this."

"Is there no clue to the sniper's identity?" Victor asked.

"Not, as yet, Mr. Victor. Can you tell me the name of that actor who played the Indian in tonight's film?"

"The Indian?" Victor frowned. "He's an actor who's in nearly every Clem Dalby film. I noticed him, Friday night, in *Park Avenue Girl* . . ."

"What part did he have in that?"

"A smarmy young Englishman."

"Oh, yes . . ." Zeke remembered immediately.

"I don't recall his name. A New York actor. Dalby brought him out here in the early thirties. Don't know what's happened to him . . ."

Zeke turned to Wulff. "Do you remember this actor?"

The composer shrugged. "I never remember actors' names. Only musicians."

"Where would I be able to get his name?" Turning back to Victor. "Would they have a cast list here?"

"They never have them. Call the Motion Picture Academy tomorrow. Ask for their library."

"Of course!"

"They have complete casts on every film that's made. Of course, you could phone Clem Dalby, although it's a bit late. He'd be able to tell you."

Zeke turned and pushed through the departing crowd toward the exit.

"Just a moment, Mr. Gahagan!" Victor's voice again. "I want to ask you . . ."

He didn't look back but left the theater and hurried around the corner to his car.

Chapter 26

Zeke turned the Chevy off Mandeville Canyon, past the mailbox—his headlights wiping across RANCHO ELDORADO—up the long drive toward the invisible ranch house.

He hoped to God the director would know where he could reach that actor.

Once he had his name he could trace him through the Screen Actors Guild.

The actor would be fifty years older than he was when Kara Kolvang was murdered.

What was his connection with the actress? Had he worked in all four of those pictures she made with Dalby? Was he, like all the other men, in love with her?

Zeke glimpsed the eucalyptus trees, dark against the serene star-drenched sky, as the Chevy followed the remembered curve toward the ranch house.

Past the white picket fence and slowed to a stop at the open gate.

Left his headlights on and hurried up the gravel path toward the columned veranda.

The ranch house looked very different at night. Smaller, less imposing.

He crossed the veranda and heard the deep tone of the bell as he yanked the metal pull.

Waited, facing the heavy wooden door, wondering if Dalby was asleep. There must be a staff of servants, in addition to that houseman Dalby had called Godfrey . . .

The door was eventually opened by the sleepy houseman. Looking startled as he recognized the visitor. "Mr.—Gahagan—isn't it?"

"Have to see Mr. Dalby again."

"Afraid he's asleep."

"It's important."

"Very well, sir. Come in."

Zeke followed him through the same long corridor which was filled with deep shadows. Saw, as the houseman switched on more lights, that he was wearing a light robe over tan pajamas. Bare feet in sandals. His cropped gray hair looked coarse and unbrushed. "You knew my name, this time."

"Mr. Dalby told me. After you left, the other morning."

"Sorry to disturb you."

"That's quite all right, sir. Part of my job."

Zeke was aware of the British accent again.

The houseman opened a door and snapped wall switches.

He saw it was Dalby's study again.

"Make yourself comfortable, sir. There's a bar. If you care for a drink."

"Not at this hour. Thanks."

"I'll wake Mr. Dalby." He bowed slightly and hurried away.

As Zeke crossed the Indian rugs toward the desk he was aware of the massive primitive heads on their tall pedestals. Tonight they were lighted from overhead. They circled the room, spaced at precise intervals, and their blank stone eyes appeared to be watching him. The light came from spots above their heads and a large shaded lamp on the desk as well as that other spot focused, as before, on Dalby's black leather armchair.

The rest of the room was in shadow.

Zeke circled the pedestals. Studying the carved faces. Realized that all of them were larger than life and decidedly male. Hooded lids, beaked noses, cruel mouths. Their invisible eyes seemed to follow him as he walked.

He counted them. Five on each side of the room. They gave him the feeling he was standing in some ancient forum with ten hawk-faced judges peering down at him.

The bookshelves behind them were barely visible except, as he walked, gilded bindings caught slivers of light which were also reflected in the glass cases holding Dalby's gun collection.

He was conscious of the silence.

The air was chilly, but the air conditioning wasn't humming.

He heard voices from the hall and faced the open door as Dalby appeared, hunched down in a metal wheelchair, pushed by his houseman.

"So the 'world's oldest eye' gets people out of bed at this ungodly hour!"

"Sorry about that."

"I heard, on the evening news, Larry Knight was killed. Nasty business." He motioned the houseman away. "I'll handle this, Godfrey. Go to bed."

"Yes, sir."

"Mr. Gahagan can let himself out."

The houseman nodded as he turned to leave.

"And close that door!"

Dalby clicked a lever under the arm of his wheelchair and, as it rolled forward, guided it around the desk. Snapped off the motor and heaved himself to his feet. Walking carefully, taking obviously painful steps, to the desk and lowering himself into his black leather armchair.

Zeke looked away, briefly, and saw that the houseman had closed the door as he departed. When he turned back to Dalby, seated at the desk, he noticed the coarse textured white robe he wore over his pajamas. Was aware, again, of his piercing blue eyes under the black eyebrows.

Dalby stared at him with anticipation.

He noticed the director's hands once more, the ropy arthritic fingers, his black-rimmed spectacles resting on the desk near the small magnifying glass.

One hand gestured toward the armchair facing the desk. "Sit down. Tell me what's happened."

Zeke recognized the tone of authority in the director's voice. "Shouldn't take long." He moved close to the back of the chair but remained standing. "Couple more questions I need to ask."

"Afraid I still have no answers for you." Dalby smiled. "As I told you, I hoped you would find Larry Knight."

"And I did."

"Not in time, it seems."

"Impossible to save his life. Not in that crowd of people."

Dalby appeared to be surprised. "You were in Solvang when he was killed?"

"Drove up there Friday afternoon. Saw Mr. Knight that evening."

"Talked to him?"

"For several hours. We watched that Kara Kolvang film on television. One you directed."

"Larry saw that? The night before he died? Amazing . . . I was sound asleep. I've seen that damn film so many times I never want to see it again. If I did, which is unlikely, I can run it here in my projection room. I've got prints of every film I directed." He sighed. "Don't enjoy looking at them any more. Too many memories. Good and bad . . ."

"I've seen another of your films tonight—*Rancho Eldorado*—the first in a series at the Nuart."

Dalby's eyes brightened. "Was there a full house? How'd they like it?"

"They cheered and applauded." No point in upsetting him by telling him the theater wasn't packed.

"Larry was damn good in that one. Losing his old Broadway musical tricks. That picture changed his career. He never sang in any of his films after that and, in my opinion, became a much finer actor. Poor bastard! I suppose you've no idea who shot him?"

"This may surprise you, sir, but I do."

"Indeed?"

"At least I'm on the trail of the man who fired that rifle. I suspect he murdered Kara Kolvang."

Dalby straightened in his armchair. "You know his identity?"

"I believe he also strangled Tim Kerrigan."

"Tim—strangled! When?"

"And murdered Lars Lyndon . . ."

"Read about that in the paper."

". . . mistaking him for his grandfather."

"I didn't know Larry had a grandson or, if I ever did, I'd forgotten. That's three murders for you to solve."

"Four. Counting Kara Kolvang."

The shrewd eyes narrowed. "And who do you suspect, sir, is the murderer?"

"Several things point to one person. An actor."

"Which actor?"

"One you, apparently, used in several films."

"What's his name?"

"Larry Knight told me his name as we watched that Kara Kolvang film. He played a supporting part in it. I never heard of him and promptly forgot the name because, at that moment, it didn't seem important."

"How can you be certain that an actor you saw, briefly, in a film . . ."

"I saw him again, in person. This was in Solvang, yesterday afternoon. He stood out from the crowd because he was disguised as an Indian. I saw him before the parade. And one of the locals, a woman, saw him carrying a rifle—possibly the murder weapon—after Knight was shot. She thought it was somebody from the parade—which, of course, was his intention—but she realized, later, there were no Indians on any of the floats. I saw him again, tonight, playing an Indian in *Rancho Eldorado*. The Indian who killed Dolores Del Rio . . ."

"You're certain of this?"

"I am. Can you tell me his name?"

"I remember that actor, vaguely, remember his face. But I don't recall his name. My memory isn't what it was, when it comes to names." He shrugged. "You must have the same problem, my friend . . ."

"Not yet, I don't. I'd hoped you could help me tonight. Instead of having to wait until tomorrow morning."

"Tomorrow?"

"The Academy library has cast lists for every film."

"They don't always have complete casts, not that far back. Not fifty years. I don't remember that actor's name because I haven't heard of him in years. Never kept in personal touch with most of the actors who worked for me. Casting always found them, if I needed them again. You're certain this actor—whoever he is—shot Larry?"

"He fired the shot but, I suspect, he wasn't alone."

"There were others?"

"I believe at least two others were involved. A blond young man and a man who appears to be Latin. Possibly Mexican. They were observed going in and out of a motel in Buellton. That's a town near Solvang."

"I know the place."

"The motel room was paid for by this Mexican who gave a phony name when he registered. The other two were seen visiting him."

"So three men are involved?"

"Larry Knight saw the Mexican yesterday. He came to the ranch and tried to find out if Larry was there. The place was locked and shuttered but Larry watched him through the shutters. Described him to me. And it was this man with a Mexican accent—the landlady talked to him—who, probably, strangled Tim Kerrigan."

"And the blond man?"

"I noticed him the night before Knight was killed—Friday night—prowling the empty streets of Solvang. Realized he was checking inside each of those big windmills they have up there."

"Windmills?"

"One of them was the windmill the Indian used next day. Stood at an upper window to fire his rifle as the parade came down the street. Fired a single shot."

Zeke felt a breath of air pass across the back of his neck.

Somebody had opened that door behind him.

He resisted the urge to turn.

"I'm afraid there's nothing I can tell you, Mr. Gahagan." Dalby smiled again. "Unfortunately . . ."

"In that case, I needn't keep you any longer." Zeke turned, abruptly, and faced the door.

It was wide open.

The houseman, Godfrey, stood there, wearing a sport shirt over slacks. Holding a .32 caliber pistol. "He knows, Clem."

"Don't say a word," Dalby ordered. "Not a damn word."

"Knows everything." Taking a few steps toward them. "I've been listening."

Zeke saw that the gun wasn't aimed but pointed toward the floor. "And who are you?" he asked quietly. "Now that you no longer have a British accent."

"I'm an actor. Goddamn fine actor."

"Be quiet, Marty." Dalby's tone was persuasive now. "We all know you're a great actor. Just keep your damn mouth shut."

Zeke heard Larry Knight's voice saying the actor's name. He whispered it now. "You're Sloane Martin, aren't you?"

"How could you know that?"

"Laurence Knight told me about you. You're from New York." Glancing toward Dalby. "Worked in many of your pictures. A member of what Larry called your stock company." Turning back to Martin. "We were watching Kara Kolvang's last picture. Larry Knight and I. You played the role of a blond Englishman in that one." He suddenly realized several more things. "It was you, Friday night, checking those windmills."

"You were following me! I sensed somebody, but couldn't see you."

"Damn it, you fool!" Dalby shouted. "Keep quiet."

"You were the Latin type," Zeke continued, "who strangled Kerrigan and, probably, shot Lars Lyndon. And you were that Indian who killed his grandfather. The same Indian I saw tonight in *Rancho Eldorado*. Saw you kill Dolores Del Rio. How many others have you killed? In films and in real life? Is it hard to keep them apart? The blanks from the bullets?"

"All actors have that problem." Dalby chuckled. "I've told Marty, many times, he's always slipping toward the edge."

"Now, Clem!" Martin's voice was almost plaintive. "Please . . ."

"I've arranged for him to have periods of rest at a pleasant estate above Santa Barbara."

"Cut it out, Clem."

Zeke realized that Dalby was in charge of the situation again, had taken control from the actor and was directing the scene.

"Now, it seems, you've slipped over the edge again. I hadn't realized."

"Clem, I'm warning you."

Zeke's eyes moved down to the gun in Martin's hand. It was still aimed toward the floor.

"He's threatening me," Dalby said. "You heard what he said, Mr. Gahagan. Heard him threaten me . . ."

Martin's hand came up with the pistol but before he could aim there was a shot.

Zeke turned to see a gun in Dalby's hand.

"Sorry, Godfrey." Dalby was smiling. "You forced me to do that. Had to protect myself." He laid his gun on the desk.

Zeke turned as the actor sank to the floor, blood spreading across his flowered shirt, the gun resting on an Indian rug.

"You heard him, Mr. Gahagan," Dalby continued. "Saw that pistol in his hand."

"I'd better call a doctor . . ."

"We should talk first. You and I."

Zeke crossed the room to the wounded man. Checked the wound in his chest. "He's alive, but not for long." He straightened and faced Dalby across the desk. "You think he killed three people to cover up the murder of Kara Kolvang?"

"I know for a fact he killed her."

"Do you?"

"Happened in my house. The beach house I used to have in Malibu. Marty had phoned and I'd invited him to drop by for a drink. Then, while we were drinking, Kara showed up. She did that all the time, without an invitation. Not that I minded, although it could be inconvenient . . .

"She liked Marty. So we had a pleasant evening. I opened a bottle of champagne. No servants at the beach house. My wife and I used it weekends, to be alone, when I was shooting a picture. Malibu wasn't so popular those days. Small houses, mostly, except for the Marian Davies complex up at Santa Monica . . . Am I boring you?"

"I'd like, very much, to hear the truth about the Kolvang murder."

"Wasn't murder. It was an accident."

"That so?"

"The three of us were relaxed and happy, late in the evening, when I went to the kitchen for a third bottle of champagne. Kara adored champagne. It was an unusually warm night for mid-September. I walked from the kitchen out onto the patio. Stood there, looking at the moon—it was almost a full moon—enjoying a breeze from the ocean.

"Listening to their voices from inside. Kara and Marty. Thought they were laughing but then I heard her scream. Didn't go in right away. Wanted them to have their fun . . .

"Marty, finally, came out and joined me. He was wild-eyed. Told me Kara was dead. I went in with him. Saw her on the divan. Her neck seemed to be twisted . . .

"Marty was in shock. Told me he'd tried to lay her and she'd fought him. He'd torn her clothes off. That's when I heard her scream. He'd raped her.

"Marty was always a muscular little guy, but Kara was tiny. Without meaning to, he'd choked her. Broken her neck. I swear he didn't mean to kill her."

"And you've helped him conceal this for fifty years?"

Dalby shrugged. "They were my friends. Both of them. There would've been a nasty scandal if the public found out an actor had killed a famous female star in my beach house! Careers would've been damaged. Lives ruined. Remember the Arbuckle case?

"Without even thinking, I gave Marty a shot of brandy. Had one myself. Helped him wrap the body in a blanket and put it into Kara's car. Marty drove ahead, up the Coast Highway. I followed in Marty's old car. Didn't dare use one of mine.

"Pulled off the Highway onto a road leading down to the ocean. We carried her body to the beach and laid it on the sand behind some boulders. Left Kara's car where somebody would find it. She hadn't bled much but I burned the blanket and her clothes when we got back to the beach house.

"When the police questioned us—they talked to everybody who knew Kara—we gave each other an alibi for the whole evening. Said we'd been together until after one o'clock. Nobody suspected the truth. Very few people knew I had the beach house. That was my hideaway . . ."

"You covered up Kara Kolvang's murder—which you say was an accident—and now you've shot the man who killed her."

"He's still alive. He'll tell you he did it. Can't we say this was an accident here tonight? Marty was looking at a gun from my collection and fired it accidentally. I'll phone my own doctor and he'll take care of Marty. Look here, Gahagan, you're not a cop any more. You're a private eye. You can twist the facts a little. Bend the law any way you want . . ."

"That's true. Only, I never have . . . Why did you give Martin this job as your houseman? Was it a payoff?"

"Certainly not! When Marty stepped getting jobs in the fifties—when television nearly closed down the majors—I told him he could work for me. The rest of his life. Couldn't let him starve! He has his own apartment here. Good salary, nothing much to do. What do you say, Gahagan? Can't we work out a deal? I'm a wealthy man. I pay well—in return for a favor . . ."

"What is it, Mr. Dalby? Thought I heard a shot . . ."

They turned, startled, toward the door.

Zeke saw a plump white-haired woman, a robe over her nightdress.

She was staring at the figure on the floor. "What happened to Mr. Martin?"

"Marty's had an unfortunate accident," Dalby replied quickly.

"Dear God!"

Zeke stepped toward her. "I'm a policeman, ma'am. Dial 911 and give this address. Tell 'em there's been an accident. Say a man's been shot. They should hurry."

"Yes, sir." She scurried away. "Poor Mr. Martin . . ."

Zeke faced Dalby again and walked toward the desk. "Three people are dead because Larry Knight said he knew someone who could name Kara Kolvang's murderer. Was it you or Mr. Martin who told Kerrigan you knew who killed her? The irony is that Tim Kerrigan could no longer remember anything."

"What're you saying?"

"Larry Knight saw Kerrigan and talked to him. The old man didn't even recognize him. Couldn't recall anyone named Kara Kolvang. I suspect the autopsy will show Tim Kerrigan had Alzheimer's disease."

"Alzheimer's . . ."

"He remembered nothing from the past. He would never have been able to tell anyone that this actor—Sloane Martin—killed Kara Kolvang."

"I did not kill her. That's a lie . . ."

Zeke looked around to see Martin struggling to his knees, the pistol in his hand again.

"It was Clem who killed her. Not I. Exactly the way he said it happened. Only it was Clem who raped her. I helped him take her body up the coast. Don't do that, Clem! No!"

Zeke turned to see Dalby picking up his pistol.

There was another shot.

Dalby slumped forward onto the desk.

Zeke whirled to see Martin still aiming his pistol at Dalby but, as he watched, it dropped from his hand and Martin pitched forward onto the floor.

Zeke turned back and strode toward the desk. "Mr. Dalby! What's the truth? Was it you killed Kara Kolvang?"

The director slowly pushed himself erect in the leather armchair. "Made a mess of this scene. Didn't I? Like the—

shoot-out—from *High Noon*. Badly directed. This time . . ." He frowned, gasping for breath as blood seeped out through the front of his robe. "Truth is . . . Yes. I killed her. Not Godfrey. I was—passionate man. Always wanted—have my way. Kara refused to let me—touch her. Long as I'd known her. That night—tricked her into coming—the beach house. Told her—several people—would be there. Didn't mean—kill her. Swear I didn't! So easy—break a woman's neck. When I realized—what had happened—phoned Marty. He drove down—helped me dispose of the . . ." He collapsed onto his desk again.

Zeke moved away from the desk and glanced toward Martin's body.

He walked, slowly, to the center of the study and looked up at the impassive circle of stone heads.

Judges staring down at opponents in an ancient arena. Only, in this battle, there was no winner.

When Dalby arranged to have those stone heads installed on their tall pedestals—probably at the suggestion of some Beverly Hills decorator—he had no idea that, one night, they would witness this scene.

Zeke took out his handkerchief and wiped the perspiration from his face.

He was the only winner here.

He'd found the murderer of Laurence Knight, his grandson and Tim Kerrigan. An actor named Sloane Martin . . .

And the man who, fifty years ago, killed Kara Kolvang. Dalby . . .

And he, Zeke Gahagan, would have to spend most of the night explaining everything to the police.

Chapter 27

The world's oldest eye was gone.
 Happened every few months. Somebody would swipe his card.

Zeke smiled as he opened the door.

He was always amused when a card was stolen. Even if it was only one of the neighbors' kids. Pleased they would want it.

He would insert a new card behind the Plexiglas in the morning.

Closing the door he snapped all the locks.

His apartment felt comfortably cool and he walked across the dim living room.

How long had he been gone? Only since late this afternoon? Seemed more like a week.

He glanced at the clock on his desk.

Just past two-thirty.

Quite a night!

He didn't switch any lights on until he reached the kitchen.

Took a wineglass from the cupboard and a bottle of wine from the refrigerator. A bottle he hadn't finished. Filled the glass and returned the bottle to the refrigerator, still unfinished.

Tasted the too-cold wine as he returned to the living room.

Paused to switch on the record player, then continued out onto the balcony.

He'd left another Glenn Gould record on the machine and began to relax as the Bach, very low, followed him outside. Bass notes relentlessly pursuing treble notes.

The apartments on the opposite side of the complex were dark and no sharks were in the pool.

He stood there, aware of the silence, sipping his wine.

It had taken several hours in Dalby's study to tell his story, over and over, to the homicide officers—he knew most of them—from Hollywood and Santa Monica Divisions.

After the wounded had been removed to a hospital.

He'd finally driven to Hollywood Division where a police stenotypist took down his story once more.

Fortunately there were several more old friends there.

He'd requested that his name be kept out of all publicity as much as possible. They would have to mention his participation but he wanted no headlines. They could have all the credit.

Word had come from the hospital that Sloane Martin was dead.

Dalby wasn't expected to live. The director was a tough bird and might fool the doctors. Anyway there was a man from Santa Monica Homicide beside his bed who had a tape ready in case he talked.

Tomorrow he would have to attend that meeting downtown and explain everything all over again to the brass.

He'd phoned Faye Manning from his car as he drove home. Told her, briefly, about Dalby and Martin. Promised to see her early in the week, after everything was cleaned up.

Must call Nettie tomorrow. Tell her another job was finished.

He carried his empty wineglass into the living room and left it on the coffee table.

There was only one call he still had to make.

He sat on the sofa and switched the shaded lamp on.

Picked up the phone and, after a second, remembered the number.

Dialed and heard the phone ring once before it was picked up.

"Zeke?"

"This is getting to be a habit."

"Are you all right?"

"Preening my feathers. I caught the murderers."

"Murderers?"

"Two of 'em. One killed Kara Kolvang and the other killed Larry Knight, his grandson and an old man I didn't tell you about."

"Never mind about them. I'm only interested in you."

"I miss you, Hildreth." He hesitated. "You've made me feel young again."

"World's youngest private eye?" She laughed. "I need you, Zeke. But don't talk. You must be tired. Get to bed . . ."

"I'm about to head in that direction."

"I love you . . ."

"I love you, Hildreth. Didn't think I'd ever feel this way again."

"Good night, my darling . . ."

He heard the connection broken and set the phone down.

Snapped off the shaded lamp and headed into his bedroom, followed by the faint but crystal-clear notes of the piano.

Took off his jacket and draped it over the back of a chair.

As he started toward the bath he paused in front of the framed photograph.

Two skinny young men in gray suits standing in a forgotten doorway.

Hammett's eyes must be twinkling under that hat brim.

"Remember that Kara Kolvang murder, Dash? You said the police wouldn't catch the murderer. You were right, pal. They didn't. I did. Took me fifty years. Abyssinia . . ."